happily NEVER after
AS IT IS WRITTEN

T.L. JONES

Happily Never After: As it is Written, is a work of fiction and is the product of the author's imagination. All persons, events and/or businesses depicted in this book are either a product of the author's imagination or are used fictitiously.

Copyright © 2015 TL Jones

All Rights Reserved

ISBN-13: 978-0692446126
ISBN-10: 0692446125

No part of this book may be reproduced by any means, electronic or mechanical including photocopying, recording or by any information storage or retrieval system without the written permission of the author and publisher.

First Edition 2015

Cover Design and Formatting by
Wicked Book Covers
www.wickedbookcovers.com

Published and printed in the United States of America

Published by Cedar Loft Productions

Cedar Loft PRODUCTIONS

www.cedarloftproductions.com
Cedar Loft Productions
J & P Enterprises, LLC

happily NEVER after
AS IT IS WRITTEN

CHAPTER ONE
Romance and Roses — Ellie 1

CHAPTER TWO
I Put a Spell on You — Daniel 19

CHAPTER THREE
As It Is Spoken — Anastasia 31

CHAPTER FOUR
Am I My Sister's Keeper? — Anastasia 55

CHAPTER FIVE
Do You Know the Muffin Man? — Anastasia 81

CHAPTER SIX
Kiss of Doom — Ellie 107

CHAPTER SEVEN
And Then Comes a Baby Carriage — Ellie 121

CHAPTER EIGHT
Wandering Eyes — Daniel 141

CHAPTER NINE
Downhill from Here — Anastasia 153

CHAPTER TEN
And He Shall be Called King — Ellie 173

CHAPTER ELEVEN
There Can be Only One — Muffin Man 187

CHAPTER TWELVE
Three's a Crowd — Prince James 225

CHAPTER THIRTEEN
The First Noelle — Noelle 235

CHAPTER FOURTEEN
Light at the End of the Tunnel — Anastasia 243

ABOUT THE AUTHOR 252

ACKNOWLEDGEMENTS 253

SYMON SAYS — CHAPTER ONE
Once Upon a Time — Jaylin 255

This book is dedicated to Joan Kreutzer;

She was one of the many people to keep pushing me to write the book even when I wanted to quit. I will miss your smile and your grace.

You are amongst angels now, including my grandmother and little sister.

R.I.P

CHAPTER ONE
Romance and Roses
Ellie

"Well, welcome home, Mrs. Charming."

"Thank you, Mr. Charming," I say as a slight giggle escapes my lips.

Here I am, Ellie Charming being carried over the threshold by my one and only true love, Prince Charming. I never thought this day would happen and now, here I am, cradled in the arms of my love. I grab onto his neck just a little bit tighter as he takes me to the oversized kitchen and places me on the counter.

"I just need to make a pit stop, Mrs. Charming, is that ok with you?" he asks as he opens the refrigerator and pulls out chocolate covered strawberries and chilled champagne. He then goes to the cabinet and retrieves two champagne flutes.

"To us!" he says as he pops the cork and fills both glasses, putting chocolate covered strawberries in each glass.

"I thought you had a maid or someone to prepare stuff

like this. Where are they?" I ask as I take a sip of the champagne. It's very smooth with a fruity flavor that tickles my nose as I slowly sip.

"I gave them the night off, since they wouldn't get a lot of sleep anyway due to the noise we'll be making," he says as he winks at me and takes a big gulp of champagne.

I blush. I've never been intimate with a man. I never thought I was beautiful enough. I got a lot of compliments from some of the townspeople but they were always refuted when I got home with my stepmother and two sisters. They would always remind me of how ugly I was or how unattractive I had become. They would also take that time to tell me of what the townspeople really thought about me and what they said behind my back. I never thought I would be married and look at me now. I try to shake these feelings off and enjoy this moment alone with my husband.

"What's wrong?" he asks as he places his empty flute in the sink.

I look at my husband holding that strawberry and looking sexy. I immediately get upset.

"Of all the women in this kingdom, this nation, this world, and you chose me. Why?"

"It's simple, Mrs. Charming, you're the fairest of them all," he says as he feeds me the strawberry.

It's so sweet, just like his comment. I want to believe this sweetness will last forever, but I know eventually I'll have to swallow and only be left with memories of how good it used to be.

"Now, Mrs. Charming, don't think too hard about it. We are meant to be. Wipe that frown off your face and let's start this new chapter off right!" he says as he swoops me into his arms and heads towards the master bedroom.

"What about my glass!" I squeal.

"Leave it, you won't need that," he growls.

I blush again. Will this man ever learn how to be candid?

I shake my head as a smile crosses my lips. No, he won't and I am perfectly content with that thought.

I hold on tighter as my husband ascends the stairs taking two and three steps at a time. As he gets closer and closer to the bedroom door I feel a deep sinking sensation in my stomach. What if I'm not good? What if I can't please him? Will he get rid of me because I can't fulfill his needs?

This is supposed to be the happiest day of my life and all I can do is focus on my insecurities. I take a deep breath and let it go as it makes some of the butterflies subside.

Although he's flying up these steps like a madman, he's completely calm, not appearing to be out of breath even a little bit. He stares into my eyes and all of a sudden the rest of the butterflies disappear. I realize why I married him. It's not because he's beautiful. It's not because he has money and power. It's because he loves me even when I don't love myself. He loves me when I feel as if I'm nothing or have anything. He loved me mentally as well as spiritually and now he wants to show me he loves me physically. I couldn't wish for anything better. Well, maybe I could but I am pretty sure my Fairy Godmother wouldn't approve. Why did she have to be on vacation? He kisses me, breaking me from my train of thought. It's deep, passionate, and has so much meaning. I love this man, more than either he or I can fathom and now I can show him because we have finally come to the room.

"Are you ready, Mrs. Charming?"

"As ready as I'll ever be, Mr. Charming," I say, breathless with desire.

"Welcome to happily ever after," he says as he kisses me deeply, placing me on the bed and closing the door.

"How do you like your eggs?" I ask, as I search the enormous kitchen for a pan.

"We have people to do that," he replies with a smile.

"I know, but I just want to thank you for…" I can't even finish the sentence before I begin to blush. Last night was amazing. Honestly, I never knew pain and pleasure could go hand in hand in such a wondrous manner. Mr. Charming definitely gave me a good crash course lesson.

"I didn't spend all those years in a hot kitchen for nothing," I say as I locate the pans and pull out a couple. He then gets up and comes around the island and stands right in front of me.

"That was your old life; you don't have to remember that anymore," he says as he tucks a piece of hair behind my ear.

"I'm here to protect you, please you, and love you. So, if you want to cook me breakfast I would like an omelet, not out of obligation. What I did to you last night was not out of obligation but out of love. No need for repayment," he says as he gives me a kiss and then goes back to sit down.

"You have a lot to compete with because Ms. Hannon knows how to make a mean omelet."

"Who is she?" I ask, my words laced with jealousy.

"She's the cook," he replies as he gives me his boyish grin, grabs his paper, and begins to read.

I roll my eyes. I'm not going to lie, hearing another woman's name come out of my husband's mouth makes me a tad bit jealous, but why? I have the ring, I have the house, and I have the man. None of these women can take away what I have.

I go to the refrigerator and grab all the necessary ingredients to make one of the best omelets he has ever tasted. I begin chopping ingredients for the omelets, when in walks the most beautiful man I have ever seen. He is very tall, has dark chocolate skin, smooth cut, light eyes, big lips, and very white teeth. As soon as he walks in I'm assaulted with the most pleasant aroma I have ever smelled. I don't even think my husband smells this good. I start to blush. Why am I thinking about him in this manner? I continue to cut the mushrooms, trying to take my mind off this gorgeous man in front of me.

"Daniel, I didn't expect to see you until next week!"

I can tell my husband is excited just by the way he addresses this man.

"I didn't expect to see you either," says Daniel as he gives my husband the biggest smile. "I just stopped by to see how my best friend and new bride are doing. There's nothing bad to report, scouts honor," he says as he looks at me and pauses.

I look up at him and just stare. He is so mesmerizing that it's hard to take my eyes off him. It feels like an eternity, but it couldn't have lasted longer than 5 seconds, before he breaks eye contact. I blush deeper. My God, why is he affecting me like this?

"How are you doing Mrs. Charming?"

"I'm fine, thank you for asking."

I turn away from him, heating the skillet.

"Daniel, we were about to have omelets, would you like one?"

"If Mrs. Charming is cooking one then, of course, I'll have one. I need to check out her cooking to make sure it's good enough for the future King!"

Suddenly, I feel bold. For the first time in my life I feel as if I need to defend myself.

"What if it isn't?" I challenge Daniel, looking right into his beautiful hazel colored eyes.

"Then there are always lessons," he says as he takes an apple from the bowl on the bar. He takes a bite while looking directly at me.

"Who are you?" I ask, slightly mesmerized by how he slowly chews the apple.

"I'm Daniel the…"

"Royal advisor and my best friend," the prince interrupts

as he quickly rounds the island and hugs me around my waist, calming me down.

"He's a bit crass at times so please forgive him. He doesn't have the slightest idea on how to behave himself around women," he says as he throws a sly look at Daniel.

"I have a lot of experience with the ladies. Some would say that I'm an expert."

Once again, he takes a bite of that apple and stares at me with those tantalizing eyes.

I turn back to the stove blushing. Why does he affect me like this? He gives me this fever that I just can't shake; but at the same time I can already tell that I cannot stand him. I wonder what he's doing here. I know it is not just to sample my cooking.

I begin breaking the eggs. With every egg I break, I get more and more agitated. It's my honeymoon for goodness sake! He's a rude individual to interrupt me and my husband's alone time! I already have to go through rigorous training in order to get myself prepared to take on the role of future queen and I'm not sure I'm ready. Right now, I don't need any added pressure but at the same time I feel the need to impress him. Why do I feel the need to impress him?

I add the butter to the pan and add the seasonings to the egg mixture. I then add the spinach, cheese, mushrooms, ham, chives, and bacon. Every time I add an ingredient I think of how all these new elements will be incorporated into my life. Royalty, money, power, marital bliss, children…

"Are the omelets done, honey?" My husband interrupts my thoughts causing me to snap to attention.

"Yes, almost done. I promise this will be the best you've ever had," I say turning around and giving my husband a wink.

"You've already proven that to me, Mrs. Charming."

I blush as I turn back to the skillet. I feel Daniel's eyes burning into the back of my head. I can't face him. I know that if I look at him I will all but die from the intensity of his stare. I must get it together. I have a husband and a nice house. I have everything a girl could want, everything, but Daniel. I gasp at the sudden thought. This is wrong. I flip the omelets. There's one down, one more to go. Why do I feel the need to choose? I finish cooking the other omelet and place it on the second plate.

"Bon appetite!"

My husband takes a bite and rolls his eyes giving a sound of satisfaction.

"This is the best omelet I've ever had! You must share this recipe with Ms. Hannon at once," says the prince.

"I've had better," Daniel says as he looks at me with a coldness that wasn't there before. I don't know why but I'm crushed by his lack of approval. I can't remain in this room. I must get out. I must breathe.

"If you'll excuse me, I'm going to freshen up."

I turn to leave the room; careful to not let anyone see the tears welling up in my eyes. Damn you, Fairy Godmother, why do you have to be on vacation? As I leave, all I hear are the two men sharing a good laugh. If they only they knew what I was thinking. I don't think they would be laughing.

As I ascend the stairs to go to the bedroom I realize that I am very lost. Last night I didn't have to walk much of anywhere. I try to imagine my husband carrying me up these stairs two at a time. It's difficult to do simply because these are quite easily the biggest, longest, and most extravagant stairs I've ever seen in my life and I'm out of breath. How did he carry me up these stairs last night without even breaking a sweat? I'm not even halfway up the stairs and I'm already dying. I really need to start working out. I'm glad the two men are still in the kitchen because I can't see myself making a dramatic exit using these stairs until I go through some conditioning.

Finally, I make it up the stairs. Even though I've made it up the stairs I still have no idea where I'm going. I try to think back to last night, but I was so distracted by desire that I can't remember anything else besides what happened in the bedroom. I blush. If I keep this up my face is going to be permanently red.

I decide to go exploring. This is my house, too, so I need to know every nook and cranny. I turn left and start looking into random rooms. The first door I come to has a lock that I can't open. Of course, this only makes me more curious. I'll be sure to mention this to James later on in the day. There will be no locked doors here! I walk a little bit down the hall and I'm suddenly surrounded by big, picturesque windows overlooking the kingdom. It's such a beautiful sight. I can't believe this lowly house maid is now a soon to be co-ruler of this beautiful place. I could look out these windows for days. There are so many beautiful colors and buildings.

This Kingdom and surrounding village almost looks like they were frozen in an earlier time. We enjoy many modern conveniences; but prefer a much slower pace. We have no cars, cell phones, or computers. Living without all those devices prevents us from disconnecting from our families and community. We have always enjoyed our simple way of living.

From up here, all the people look like ants. They keep working, playing, and socializing as if there is not a care in the world, oblivious to the fact that they are being watched. I feel a sense of power as I watch the people swarm in front of me, their future queen. I snap out of it. There are many undiscovered rooms and I can't waste my time here any longer. If I'm to find out about this huge castle I live in I have to keep moving.

Just a little bit down the hall there are three rooms; each with a painted door. There are two blue doors and one pink door. I open all of them and each has the same type of furniture inside. A baby crib, a rocking chair, stuffed toys, a dresser full of baby clothes, and a whole changing station. Was this done before I got here? It looks like none of this stuff was ever used. Does the Prince expect two sons and a daughter? What if I can't give him that? I only just experienced a man and now I am expected to have a child?

I softly caress the baby clothes and I'm reminded of Mother and her beautiful face, or at least what I remember. I remember that she had the kindest eyes and the warmest skin. I also remember that she was very beautiful but no major details of her face. That's what happens when your mother dies while you're young. Then, my mind flashes to the time when my father let me ride on his shoulders. Things were a lot simpler then. I smile but the smile quickly fades. How am I supposed to be a good, no, a great mother if I don't have a good example? By both my parents dying while I was young it did not leave me with a lot of positive influences. When they died, I died inside and so did my importance to my step mother. I don't think I could ever forgive that woman for what she did to me.

Tears start to fall down my face as I remember the nights when I was cold, hungry, afraid, and alone. All I wanted was someone to play with or talk to, but I was considered an outcast. There were times I wished I could join my mother and father wherever they were. I knew if I could join them I would be loved, but that wasn't possible. I tried a couple of times but my plans always went awry and I ended up in even more trouble and wishing I was dead after the punishment was over. I couldn't take it anymore so I became meek and quiet. I became the good house-slave my step mother wanted me to be. I made friends with the mice and the creatures that frequented my room. It was them that kept me alive. It was that friendship that got me to where I am today. I miss them terribly. Hopefully, they will visit me soon.

I need to leave this room. I feel smothered and I'm slowly suffocating under my predetermined duties. It's only day two of my marriage and I am already drooling over another man and dreading raising children. Not a great start. Maybe I'm not ready for this. Maybe I should go back to being the lowly housemaid. I know Prince Charming will not go for this, but maybe it's for the best. At least when I was a housemaid my life was not complicated as long as I kept my sisters and step-mother happy. Who knew love could ever be this complicated? No wonder my step-mother kept me from it.

Leaving the room I see that there is nothing at the end of this hall but a big steel door. I try the handle, it opens, and there are more steep stairs waiting for me. I wonder where these stairs lead. I've regained my energy since climbing the first set of stairs so these should be a breeze. These stairs don't look challenging at all. They are not as big and grand as the other steps but I'm still curious. I slowly start to ascend the staircase. It seems like I'm climbing forever. The staircase is winding around and around. Just when I think the staircase is about to end I go around the corner and there are even more steps waiting for me. Finally, I reach the top and come face to face with a fence. That is not at all what I expected. I open the fence and am not prepared for what I see next.

I can't believe my eyes. There is so much beauty that my eyes can't focus. Having this much beauty in one place should be criminal. Who knew when I opened that fence I would walk into one of the most beautiful rooftop gardens I've ever seen in my life.

"I wonder who put this together," I ask myself aloud.

"That would be me."

I don't have to turn around to know who it is. Daniel.

"Why are you here?" I ask him; still admiring the deep blue roses.

"I came to find you," he replies huskily.

"Why? You're obviously married; you have a ring on your

finger," I inquire still trying my best not to look this beautiful man in his face.

"You noticed my ring?" He asked me with a slight smirk on his face.

"Yes, only because it is such a beautiful ring," I answer. My face turns deep red.

His smirk deepens as he realizes that he caught me in a lie and he has me where he wants me. He looks deep into my eyes.

I stare straight back into his. I can't concentrate. I have to look away before I say or do something I might regret later. I break the eye contact and make my way towards the door.

"I came to apologize. I was really rude at breakfast. I made a horrible first impression. That really was the best omelet I have ever had but I couldn't say it too loudly, especially since my mom is the cook."

His apology and the little bit of information stops me in my tracks. What he says piques my interest.

"Your mom is the cook?"

"Yes ma'am," he starts to explain, "My mom has been cooking here since I was little. That's how the Prince and I became really good friends. When my father died I was only 16 years old. I was too old for games but too young for a job. So instead of having two incomes we only had one. At that time, my mother and I couldn't support ourselves so the Prince took my mother under his wing, promoted her to head cook, and then appointed me as his advisor. I have my own room on the other side of the hall and this place became mine. When I started, it was nothing but concrete and despair. I turned it into an oasis. Every time I had my heart broken I planted another type of flower."

He paused, waiting for a response.

I had none.

"Like the blue roses you're looking at while trying to avoid looking at me. They are my most prized possession. They are very rare indeed. It took me a while to find out where to even obtain the seeds to plant them. I was determined to find them. Her name was Yanci. She was my true love. I never loved another before or after her. It's her ring that I wear on my finger. Her favorite color was blue; and just like the rose she always smelled so sweet."

He paused, trying his best not to cry.

He clears his throat and continues, "She died giving birth to my son, his name was Symon."

He stops a minute to regain his composure.

"The love we shared was rare and so is that rose."

I turn toward him. I'm speechless. This beautiful man crying in front of me is almost too much for me to bear. I want to comfort him. I want to kiss away those tears to let him know that everything will be alright and that he can love again, but I can't move. I'm stuck.

I break the silence with a question.

"Where's your son?"

"My mother told me the baby died during childbirth due to complications. My mother was the one who helped deliver the child and told me of his death."

There is a moment of silence.

"What is your favorite color?"

"Pink," I respond barely above a whisper.

"What's your favorite flower?"

"Roses."

He inches closer to me as he whispers, "Don't deny it. I know you feel it too.

I step back.

"I don't feel anything. I don't know what you're talking about," I say.

"I've not felt anything like this since Yanci," he says as he still inches closer to me.

"You feel nothing but the satisfaction of a good meal."

"I feel the intensity too."

I felt the air leave my lungs.

"I think you are beautiful inside and out. I hear the Prince talk about you and I get jealous because you remind me so much of Yanci. It was love at first sight and you can't deny it."

He closes the gap and kisses me.

I see fireworks and the air leaves my lungs. I'm hot and cold at the same time. I feel electricity flowing through my body. I've never felt this with another man, not even my husband. I push him away with tears in my eyes.

"Don't you ever come near me again," I say as I run out of the beautiful oasis.

"You can't escape me, I'll always be here," he calls after me as I run down the stairs faster knowing that he's right.

I run down the stairs, through the steel door, and run down the hallway with all of its mysterious doors. I have no idea where I'm running, but I don't care, I just need to get away from Daniel.

I keep going straight toward the right side of the castle.

The first door I come to is the master bedroom. The covers are still crumpled and the pungent smell of love making assaults my nose. I cry harder. I go into the room and look for a place to freshen up. Surely the Prince cannot see me so disheveled.

I open random doors in the room finding closets of clothes, shoes, and some weird objects I've never seen before. Maybe the Prince can explain those to me later.

Finally, the last door I open is the bathroom. It's gorgeous. It has a big, spacious shower, deep porcelain tub, and beautiful golden fixtures. A girl can get used to this. I close the door and lock it as I gravitate toward the tub. A good soaking is what I need to take away this stress, worry, and doubt. I need to relax.

I start to run the bath water as I go to find bath salts. I find an array of them under the cabinet. Everything from peach to something called cashmere. The cashmere sounds expensive and right now, I just want to feel luxury. I smell it. It's a very pleasant smell. I add it into the scalding hot water and the room fills with the most wonderful scent. I must remind the Prince to get me more of this particular bath salt.

Finally, the tub is filled. I take off my clothes and slowly ease into the steamy water. This is wonderful. I don't move for quite some time. Gradually, the water gets cold and I have to wash up really fast and exit the tub.

I look in the rest of the cabinets in the bathroom and I find towels, beauty and hygienic products, lotions, baby powder, and many other things. Everything a girl needs in order to pamper herself and feel good. I get some lotion and rub it all over my body before I sprinkle powder on myself. I wrap a towel around my body and then it hits me. I have nothing to wear!

I think back to the closets with all the clothes. I didn't really look and see who the clothes belonged to. I decide to go look anyway. Worst case scenario is I have to put on one of the Prince's oversized shirts until something can be arranged.

I go back to the first closet and open it again. Once again I see a lot of clothes. More clothes than I've ever seen in my lifetime. I turn on the light and walk in to a closet the size of my old room, filled with the most beautiful gowns I've ever seen in my life. There are so many beautiful clothes that I don't even know where to begin. Then I see it. A teal dress that has gold embellishments. It's like this dress was made for me. I take it off the hanger, expecting it to be heavy but it's surprisingly lightweight. I try it on and it fits like a glove. I twirl around looking at the floor length mirror. I look beautiful in this dress, but my hair needs to be done and so does my makeup. I go back to the bathroom, look into the cabinets and I find makeup that fits my shade exactly!

I look in the mirror and I'm awed by how beautiful I look. My father used to tell me stories of what my mother looked like. I've never seen a picture of her. My father used to say that I have a great mixture of both parents. I have the long hair, eyes, and lips of my mother. I have the nose and long neck of my father. My skin is a combination of the two; my father's milky white complexion, and my mother's smooth milk chocolate skin. In this light, in this dress, and in this beautiful place I, too, feel beautiful. I do my makeup carefully so that I don't mess up. When I'm done I step back and admire myself in the mirror. What I see takes my breath away, but it's not complete. I need jewelry.

I go back into the room and start looking in the drawers and finally I find what I'm looking for. Drawers full of necklaces, earrings, bracelets, and a whole drawer dedicated to crowns. I pick a gold crown that has a jewel in the middle that matches my dress. Now, it's complete and I go to find my husband.

I go down the spectacular staircase to see my Prince Charming waiting for me at the bottom of the staircase.

"I was beginning to worry about you," he says as he hugs me tightly once I reach the bottom of the stairs.

"I saw that you were upset at breakfast because of how rude Daniel was. Did he come and apologize to you?"

"Yes, he did," I say as I start to blush.

"I assure you, he is not going to disrespect you again."

He releases the embrace and looks at me.

"You look stunning. I see you found the clothes I had delivered here for you."

"How did you know my size, my make-up color, and the products I use?" I ask.

"All of them were guesses, plus, I had a little help from Ms. Hannon. All she had was a picture of you before the wedding and I gave her a budget to purchase you the best clothes, shoes, jewelry, and anything else she thought you might want or need."

"It is all so beautiful. Thank you."

"No, thank Ms. Hannon. I could not have done it without her. As a matter of fact, you can meet her now because dinner is almost ready."

We go into the kitchen and there stands a very pretty woman who looks as if she is in her late 40s. She has a very calming demeanor that makes anyone who meets her feel instantly at ease.

"So, you are the beautiful young woman that everyone is talking about," she says excitedly.

I blush.

"Turn around and let me get a good look at you."

I extend my arms and do a complete 360.

"I knew that dress would go well with your complexion. What can I say? When mama is right, mama is right!"

I smile. I've only known this woman for ten minutes and I'm already at ease. This woman knows exactly what to say and when to say it.

"Prince, can Ellie and I have a moment alone?"

The Prince looks baffled but complies and lets us know he will be back in a minute to eat dinner.

All of a sudden she turns back to me and her whole face has changed. Her eyes that were once joyous are now dark.

"You are trouble, girl."

"What do you mean trouble?" I ask with a shocked look on my face.

"Just as I said, trouble" she says as she looks me up and down. "By you being here, you have set off a series of events that is going to be the demise of you, the Prince, and my son."

I start to panic. Had she seen the kiss between me and Daniel?

"By the look on your face something has already happened. If you want to live, stay away from my son. I know he is persistent but I beg you, stay away from him. I keep seeing visions of floors covered in blood, with three babies sitting in the middle. The vision shows two boys and a girl. Now, I don't want you to think that I do not like you, or that I am trying to end the marriage between you and the Prince. In all honesty, that is the opposite of how I feel. I am happy for you, and I am happy for the Prince. He is like a second son to me, but, I am an Oracle first and my visions don't lie. Now, give me a hug."

The warmth returns to her face as I slowly walk toward the older woman to give her a hug.

As I start to hug her, she whispers, "stay away from my son, I will know if you did or not based on your first born." As she finishes her statement she releases me and kisses me on the cheek before she returns to the stove.

Just at that moment the Prince walks back into the room. Suddenly, I'm not hungry anymore.

"It sure does smell good in here!"

"I made your favorite meal; roast beef, mashed potatoes, vegetable medley, and for dessert, chocolate cake."

"Oh, Ms. Hannon, you sure do know how to spoil me," the Prince says with a boyish grin.

"Well, I figured I would cook your favorite so your bride could get a taste of what you like to eat," she says with the sweetest smile. "Now, go sit at the table so I can bring your plates."

My husband takes my hand and leads me into the dining area where there is a long, lavish table. He sits at the head of the table and I sit next to him at his right side.

In comes Ms. Hannon with our food. It looks and smells wonderful but my mind is swimming with so many thoughts that I can't possibly eat at this moment. Then I think if I don't eat I'll get sick and that is something I don't want to burden anyone with. So, I thank Ms. Hannon for the food, say grace with my husband, and eat. The conversation between us picks up and all of a sudden I feel better and lighter. He is my rock. Talking to him makes me feel whole again. Suddenly, the conversation turns risqué filled with recollections from last night laced with intimate language that instantly makes me blush.

With dinner finished, Ms. Hannon clears the table of the dishes and comes back with a huge slice of chocolate cake. I only eat about half before I'm so stuffed I can barely breathe.

The Prince's hand finds its way to my thigh. I look at him and he has a look of desire on his face. It makes me feel a tingle deep down in my stomach and I want nothing more than to indulge. He pushes his chair back; I get out of my chair and straddle him. He is surprised by my sudden move. So am I.

He lifts me up and does a repeat of last night, gripping me close as he runs up the stairs. I'm giggling uncontrollably. I'll never get tired of this. He miraculously opens the door and puts me on the bed; taking off my clothes. I am more than ready to please my husband. Everything is happening so fast that I don't know when all my clothes were removed or how he removed his at the same time. As he joins me on the bed my eyes are drawn to the dresser in the room. On top of the dresser are the most beautiful pink roses I've ever seen and in the middle of this bouquet is the brightest blue rose I've ever seen. A tear rolls down my face. Damn you, Fairy Godmother. Why did you have to be on vacation? This is the last thought I have as my husband shows me a whole new world.

CHAPTER TWO
I Put a Spell on You
Daniel

I can't believe none of my attempts to get Ellie to leave her husband have been successful. What am I doing wrong? I have tried roses, chocolate, and I've tried to get her alone again by luring her back to my lair; the garden. Nothing works! It seems like with my every attempt it only makes the love between her and the Prince that much stronger. Why can't I let this go? I can have any woman in the kingdom but there is something about her that makes me want to settle down, stop chasing women, and have a couple of kids.

I love a challenge but this is too much. It's been six months and their love is stronger than ever and it makes me sick. I can't even get close to her without that meddling Fairy Godmother always popping up for a visit whenever I come around. I wonder if she knows what I feel for Ellie and is trying to prevent me from doing something that will destroy her and the Prince's marriage. I don't care if she does know,

Ellie and I were meant to be together and I will not stop until I have her as my own. Suddenly, it occurs to me that I need to go see my mother.

I hurry and get dressed, then run down the hall to go see my mother. It's very early in the morning and most everyone is still sleep; everyone but Ellie and the Prince. The sounds of their ravenous love making echoes throughout the hall and I'm immediately disgusted. It won't be long now, I think to myself. I go past their room and down the grand staircase. Once I get down the stairs, I go out the main doors and across the lawn toward the servants' quarters. The Prince offered my mother a room in the castle, but she refused. She likes her little cottage that was built for her a couple of years back. A lot of the other servants are envious of my mother. They taunt her behind her back about the fact that she does not have to live in the quarters and that she is the Prince's favorite. None of them last long enough to do anything about it. After jogging most of the way there, I'm now standing at the front door of my mother's cottage. I raise my hand to knock.

"Come in," I hear my mother say.

I open the door to see her sitting cross legged on the floor with candles burning all around her.

"You have really got to stop with this voodoo nonsense."

"Isn't that why you've come here?"

I'm silent. I don't know how my mother does it, but she always seems to know what I'm going to ask before I can even formulate the words in my head.

"You don't have to answer; I know why you're here. The answer is no."

The whole time she addresses me she has not opened her eyes once. Her body is still except for the tell-tale signs of her breathing. In this moment, I hate this woman.

"Why are you protecting him?" I yell at this lifeless figure. "You've always loved him more than me!"

With those words her eyes flutter open, she gets up with an effortlessness that cannot be described and glides toward me; gripping me by my shirt.

"It is because I love you that I am telling you no!"

Her eyes scare me and, for once, I'm concerned. I don't see my mother, I see a witch in those eyes.

"You've done it before! You have helped me with a temporary love spell! Why is this different? Why can't I have her?"

"You cannot have her because her heart does not belong to you. I've helped you before because every time you came to me with a new infatuation with a woman I assumed my help would get you to settle down. I want grandchildren! I want to be able to hear giggles in this little cottage! Every time I help you, you become disinterested and then you throw them away as if they are a toy. What happens after that, Daniel? Tell me!"

"They die," I say, my words laced with sadness.

"How do they die, Daniel?"

She's now yelling at me with an intensity in her eyes that burns to my soul.

"Suicide."

"What makes you think I'm going to help you destroy something as beautiful as that girl's spirit? I have never in my life seen anything or anyone that pure. You, my son, are laced with hatred, envy, and selfishness. Your evil will be the utter demise of you, the Prince, the Princess Ellie, and me. If you interfere with the love and the bond between Ellie and the Prince you will die along with every other adult in this equation. I will not let your ruthless behavior result in the death. You will not destroy her life because you're having a tantrum. There are a lot of other women in the kingdom, go court one of them."

With those words, she resumes her position on the floor, closes her eyes, and starts slowly breathing again.

"None of them are as beautiful as Ellie," I say meaning every word. "I love her and I'll not stop until she's mine."

"Depart from me. I will not aide you in your demise."

With that she lifts her hand, points it toward me, and a strong gust of wind pushes me out of the cottage and slams the door.

"Oh you will help me whether you like it or not," I mutter to myself as I leave her cottage formulating a plan.

"Are you not hungry?" asks my mother as she looks at the uneaten food on my plate.

"Not really, I feel a bit sick," I say.

"What's wrong?" Ellie looks at me with a look of true concern.

"I'm fine, just not hungry."

"But blueberry pancakes, eggs, bacon, and cheesy grits are your favorite breakfast," my mother says as she comes towards me. She puts her hand on my head. "Hmm, you're not hot." She continues to examine me.

Finally she puts her hand over my heart and suddenly pulls her hand away as if she burned herself. Everyone is looking at her strange.

She then whispers to me, "You do love her, don't you?"

I nod my head.

"As much as it hurts me to see you hurt I still have to say no."

She picks up my plate and makes her way back into the kitchen. The room goes silent. Nobody knows what to say to the other. Everyone knows there is something lingering in the air but at this time neither Ellie nor the Prince have a slight clue as to what it is.

Finally, Ellie speaks, "Are you going to be okay? You're sweating. Here is my hanky to wipe it off."

I take the hanky.

"Thank you, but I'll be fine; I just need some fresh air," I say as I leave the table. I cannot stand to be in the same room with her any longer. It makes me sick that she's not mine. As I leave the table I do my best to not give my mother eye contact. She's part of the reason why I'm so angry. I don't understand why she won't help me. She is selfish. Can't she see that I'm hurting? That I long for Ellie? That my heart will not be complete without her?

"How do they die, Daniel? Tell me!" The words my mother yelled at me echoes in my mind. Those women were different. They were not worthy of a great man such as myself. They could not handle the pressure of being with me. I'm sorry they fell so deeply in love with me that they did not feel the need to live any longer. That's not my fault. If they were better companions, I would have been settled down by now. I'm mad. I'm envious. I'm jealous. And I'm hurt. These are a deadly combination for a man with a purpose. To the untrained eye it may seem as if I'm wandering to get some fresh air, but I knew all along where I was headed as soon as I got up from the table.

I go toward the servant's quarters toward my mother's cottage. As I near the cottage, I keep hearing snippets of the conversation we had earlier that day permeating through my mind.

"You will die. It's because I love you that I'm telling you no. I'll not aide you in your demise."

With each step the voices become stronger. I know this is an incantation that my mother has bestowed upon me. I start to block each of them with incantations of my own.

"Evoca la mia pace interiore. Non si prevarrà," I start to say this chant over and over again as I get closer and closer to the cottage. The more I repeat it, the quieter the voices get. When I get to the door the voices are no longer there, but I'm not fooled. I keep repeating the chant just to make sure that any other incantations my mother has spoken against me will not deter me.

I try to open the door using the doorknob but it won't budge. I try ramming the door a couple of times and it still won't budge. Finally, I step away from the door and close my eyes with my hands in front of me as if I am about to utter a prayer. I even my breathing.

Suddenly, I cry out "ABIERTO," and extend my hands. From my fingertips comes a gust of wind and the door flies open. When the door opens, several, horrific, ghost like figures emerge. They all charge toward me. I duck. "Evoca la mia pace interiore. Non si prevarrà," I start screaming the incantation towards the beasts. It does not slow them down. They keep coming from everywhere; attacking me, scratching me, wailing loudly. I press on. I fight against the beasts, trying to push my way inside the cottage. I must get to the book. I must get to the spell. I cannot fail. If she is to be mine I cannot quit.

I'm badly beaten and bruised. One of the cuts is bleeding profusely and my arm is limp. I want to turn back. I want to run but my heart wills me on. The attacks from the creatures get more violent. They're attacking me as if their lives depend on it. I keep screaming the chant. They can torture my body but they will not have my mind.

The creatures pile upon me and I can't breathe. Everything is going black. Just as I'm on the brink of unconsciousness I notice a stick not too far from me. I reach for it but I'm pulled back by the creature. I crawl towards the stick, each moment more painful than the last. Finally, I make it to the stick. I use all my strength to turn so I'm on my back. With the stick firmly in place I stab one of the creatures right through the heart. He makes a shrieking sound and tumbles backwards causing all the other creatures to fall off me as well. I hop onto my feet and make a dash for the door. The creatures have regained their composure and they're right behind me.

I fear I'm not going to make it. I can't breathe. This might be the end of me. As soon as I feel my body give out I realize that I have made it! I quickly leap through the threshold and close the door behind me. The wailing and the voices stop. Everything is silent. I've made it inside. One victory down, but the battle isn't over. I know now what I must do.

I go to my mother's medicine cabinet and start looking for a specific potion. Finally, I find the healing potion I was looking for. I dab some on my cuts, my bruises, and on my limp arm. I scream and double over in pain. I see nothing but white as I grit my teeth while my bones snap back into place and my wounds are covered up with new flesh. After a couple painful moments everything is restored back to normal. I put the bottle back in place. I clean up the bathroom so that any traces of my presence are no longer there. Finally, I go toward the spell book. I know better than to touch it with my hands. I get into a wide stance, close my eyes, even my breathing, and get into a prayer stance. Then softly and slowly I utter the words: "Abierto, Amore guida le mie azioni." The book awakens. It levitates off the mantle and then I hear a voice.

"You heart is not pure, son of Hannon, leave from this place."

"My heart is pure. I want love. I feel as if this woman is the one for me and I will not know for sure unless I have help."

"What is it that you seek?"

"Amore Fatal."

"That is a very powerful spell. You know that once I cast this spell it will be irreversible and if, for some reason, it does not work the repercussions will be fatal for both parties. Do you understand?

"I fought through mental and physical attacks to make it here to ask of this request. I understand the repercussions."

"As you wish, but, I need a sacrifice from you and something from the girl that you want to enchant."

I never knew about this part of the process. I quickly search my brain for something to sacrifice.

"I sacrifice my engagement ring from my first true love, Yanci. I have not taken this ring off since her death."

"Now, the object belonging to the person of whom you want to enchant?"

I smile.

"I give you her hanky."

"Please place the items on the mantle."

I place the items side by side on the mantle and step back. The book begins.

> *"Love is something to cherish and hold*
> *Love at first sight is a tale centuries old*
> *But fast forward time about three moons*
> *The woman you love will suddenly swoon*
> *You have three days to enjoy the bliss*
> *Seal her fate with just one kiss*
> *But beware, if by day four a kiss is not shared*
> *The love that was between you will suddenly disappear*
> *Now if the love proves to be true*
> *A child of two shall befall on you*
> *But beware if your eyes should suddenly sway*
> *Your wandering eyes will dig both graves*
> *As it is spoken, it is now completed."*

The book then places itself back onto the mantle and now all is still.

I'm smiling from ear to ear. It's now completed. She will be mine in three days. I must go and prepare.

I turn around to see my mother standing there. Her eyes are dark, her stance is rigid, and her demeanor reeks of anger and evil.

I am scared.

"What are you doing here?"

"I came to get some healing potion out of the cabinet."

"I have the ability to kill you where you stand. Now, do not lie. What are you doing here?" She steps forward. I step back. I hesitate before I am able to fix my mouth to give her an answer.

"Amore Fatal."

Her eyes get big. She looks deep into my eyes.

"Why?"

"I love her; she can be with no one else."

"So you jeopardize the home of yourself and your mother?" she screams.

As she screams, I feel sharpness in my chest and I fall to the ground. I look up and her hands are in a C shape twisting back and forth. With every twist my heart hurts that much more. I can't breathe.

"Please, don't kill me."

"I have to kill you before the book imprints your spell. If I do not kill you, everyone will die."

I'm on the brink of death.

"As it is spoken, it is now completed."

The hand she has been holding steady drops and I can breathe. I start gasping for air.

She goes to her book and silently says "Abierto" to her book. It opens without any hesitation. She reads the inscription. She steps back and then starts to cry.

"I cannot kill you because if I kill you it will instantly kill her, but I'm telling you now, son or not, if you for one second think that I'm going to let this pass, you are mistaken. The spell is going to take place as written. I have no choice but to allow the first part to happen. During those three days of love, be prepared. I will do everything in my power to prevent that kiss. Depart from me or I will kill you where you stand."

I get off the floor and scramble toward the door.

"Daniel!"

I turn back toward my mother.

"I hope you enjoy hell because you'll be going there soon. Whether it's by your hand or mine, I cannot tell you. I no longer have a son."

I leave the cottage and suddenly my heart is heavy. I gained the ability to have the one that I truly love but in the process I lost my mother.

Was this really worth it?

I walk toward the castle and start to smile. Yes, it is worth it. I will have the girl, my mother will have the kids, and I will have the kingdom if things fall into place. Oh yes, Mama, bring it on. I will be waiting.

As I get closer to the castle I'm very calm and elated. Suddenly, I'm whistling a tune. In an instant I go from whistling to singing. "I cast a spell on you, because you're mine." I laugh because the games have only just begun.

Ms. Hannon watches as her son skips away with a sense of accomplishment. She walks away from the window. An eerie smile creeps onto her face as she walks toward the back room. The room's door is always closed but today she opens it up. There is a young woman sitting on the bed with tears streaming down her face.

"I thought what you told me was a lie! I can't go through with this"

"We had a deal, little girl! You will do as you promised. You heard everything that just happened, you heard the spell! I told you that once you heard the spell you would be bound by its words until it came to fruition. I told you what was going to happen but you chose to remain naive. Well wake up! Everything I said was going to happen has happened. It is your job to try to prevent this spell from happening or you will die along with everyone else. But, if you're a good girl and do as you're told, I will spare your life. Do you understand me?"

The young woman nods.

"Good, now, the games begin."

With that, a slow cackle escapes from her lips and permeates the room. The young woman begins to cry harder with the full understanding of what she has just done.

CHAPTER THREE
As It Is Spoken
Anastasia
(Five months earlier)

It's been a month since Ellie left to be with the Prince and I'm in hell. I'm tired of my mother always bossing me around. I'm tired of my sister feeling as if she's superior. Once Ellie left, someone had to take over her chores and, of course, it was me.

Mother always loved Drusilla more. She thinks she is prettier, more talented, and a lot smarter. I'm tired of walking in their shadows; it's time for me to make my own way. I wonder if this is how Ellie felt when she was here. It doesn't matter, because she was not going to stay here forever. She is far more beautiful than me and Drusilla could ever imagine. She didn't have to do anything else but just stand there. It's people like her and my sister that make me sick.

"ANASTASIA!!!"

I roll my eyes. It's not enough that I have to cook, clean, mend things, take care of the animals, go to the store, and the millions of other things that Mother wants me to do. In addition to all that, I have to make sure my sister is happy at all times. If Drusilla is not happy, Mother is not happy, and if she is not happy I'm going to regret it. Most of the time Drusilla's requests are outlandish to say the least. She's always trying to find a way to get me in trouble because she likes to view the beatings I receive from Mother when things go wrong. Nonetheless, I make my way up the stairs to see what awaits me.

I walk into Drusilla's room and she is sprawled out across her bed looking at a fashion magazine.

"It took you forever to come up here!"

"I'm sorry, Sister, I was cleaning."

"What did I tell you about calling me Sister? I could never be related to someone so ugly and worthless."

The words cut me deep. I swallow as tears threaten to fall from my eyes. My gaze lowers as I stare blankly at the floor and answer her in a whisper.

"Yes ma'am."

"That's more like it. Now, I need you to go to town and pick up some things for me."

She then throws a huge list at me.

"But, Drusilla, retrieving these items is going to take me all day and I'll not have enough time to get back and finish the chores that Mother has assigned to me."

"That's not my problem. I need all of these things by the end of the day. If I don't have these things in my room by the end of the day, I'll not be very happy. We both know what happens when I'm not happy. We wouldn't want that, would we?"

"No ma'am."

"Good girl. Now run along."

I leave the room feeling defeated. There has to be something more for me. Why am I stuck here serving my sister when I should be waltzing around a big castle with a Prince? I can't dwell on it now. I have to hurry and get the stuff on this list and then try to come home early enough to finish most of the chores that Mother gave me. Hopefully, Mother will not go through the chores list with a fine toothed comb like she has been for the last couple of days.

I go to the stable and retrieve the cart. I then grab my horse, Misty, and hook her up to the cart. I saddle Misty, mount her, and I'm off to town.

As much as I hate serving my sister and my mother, I do love the ride into town. This is the best part of any day. The scenery is beautiful. I love the low hanging trees, vibrant flowers, and foliage. It usually takes me about thirty minutes to get into town doing a slow trot, but today, I do not have time to take in the scenery. I have to hurry and make it into town, purchase the items, and make it back in time to clean the rest of the house.

How did Ellie do all of this? I have no time to sit and ponder that question as I hurry along the road toward town. I've traveled this road many times before and I know every nook and cranny. At least I thought I did. I was daydreaming so hard I didn't see a low branch hanging from the tree. By the time I see it, it's too late. It knocks me off Misty and I land hard on the ground. The last thing I see is Misty stopping, turning around, and walking back toward me. Then I see nothing but black.

I wake up, confused, with a massive headache. It hurts to move. When I open my eyes it's dark.

Where am I? I realize that I'm in a nice comfortable bed with clean sheets and a nice comforter. The panic sets in.

This isn't my bed. My mattress is old and lumpy and my comforter is dirty and torn from years of use.

Was I kidnapped? I try to look around the room to get a better idea of where I am and possible escape routes.

What time is it? Mother is surely looking for me. If I don't hurry home I'm going to be annihilated.

As I lie there and pretend to be asleep, I realize that wherever I am is a lot better than where I could be. I could be at home, beaten within an inch of my life. I could be home, bloodied and bruised, with aches and pains whenever I move instead of a headache. I could barely be able to walk but still be required to perform the necessary house duties the next day. The worst of it all is the constant ridicule I receive from my sister. It's like her goal in life is to make me fail. I don't understand.

We were close up until Ellie left, that's when everything changed. I want my sister back, but she's so consumed with greed that she's become someone she wasn't in order to survive. I don't blame her, but a small part of me wishes I could die in this comfortable bed so she can get a taste of her own medicine. With that thought I smile. Death is better than torment. I welcome death with the sweetest embrace. With that, I stretch out my arms and decide to sit up. It's better to let my captor know I'm awake and willing to die.

"You're finally awake; I thought I'd lost you."

An older woman steps from the shadows. I didn't even know she was in the room. How long has she been there?

"I've been awake for a while, I just didn't move until I scoped out my surroundings," I say to the mysterious woman.

"Why would you do that?"

"No offense, the way I live now, I've learned not to trust anything unfamiliar."

"While cleaning you up, I realized that you have a lot of scars and bruises. If you are familiar with the pain that caused those bruises and scars I don't want to ever know what your version of familiar is."

I don't know why, but I'm offended by this comment.

"You don't know my story."

"I know more of your story than you think I know, Anastasia."

When she says my name a chill goes through my spine.

How does this woman know who I am?

"Who are you?"

"My name is Ms. Hannon, but you can call me fate."

With that sentence she gives one of the most eerie smiles I've seen.

"I don't understand."

"Sure, I figured as much. Let me explain."

She gets up and lights candles. She then goes to the stove to heat it and starts to remove things from the tiny refrigerator.

"Before I start, you must be hungry. Let me make you something to eat."

This whole situation was baffling. I'm confused and intrigued at the same time. I wish she would get on with the reason why fate brought us together. In the back of my mind I was a bit happy that she was cooking. I'm famished and can no longer deny my need for food. Even if I tried to deny it my stomach would have protested loudly.

"You hate Ellie, don't you?"

That question caught me by surprise.

"I don't hate her. I'm jealous of her. She has always been so happy, so carefree, and so beautiful inside and out even though my sister, my mother, and I treated her so horribly. I don't understand how someone can be so beautiful and remain that way even with all we put her through. I want what she has. I want the handsome prince. I want the happily ever after. I want the opportunity to show people that I am worth a lot more than what my mother says. I want to be loved."

"What if I told you I could give you all of that and more?"

I became more attentive.

"You mean you can give me everything that I envy about Ellie. How?"

"This will all be explained, child. Eat your food. Don't eat it too fast or else you'll get sick."

She put soup in front of me that smelled delicious and some bread for dipping. I look at her thinking she is about to poison me but she just gives me a genuine smile as she turns back toward the stove to clean.

I can't back down now. I told myself that I'd welcome death with open arms. So, if I'm to die from this soup, so be it. I take a spoonful of the soup and it is literally the best soup I have ever tasted in my life. It has all types of vegetables and little chunks of meat in it. I stop eating the soup and focus on the bread. It smells fresh, like it was just baked in the oven minutes ago.

How did she do this? I didn't smell bread, but yet, it tastes so fresh. I must have been a lot more famished than I thought and before I know it, both the bread and the soup are gone and I'm craving more. She must have read my mind because she refilled the soup and gave me another piece of bread. I get halfway through my second portion when I start to feel somewhat satisfied and instead of gulping down the food, begin to slowly eat as I wait for her to explain herself. She takes the cue and begins.

"I know that you are Ellie's stepsister."

"Yes, everyone in the Kingdom knows this."

"They also know what your mother and your sister do to you."

This information surprises me as I try to hold back the tears.

"Why hasn't anyone tried to help?" My question comes out as a whisper.

"No one knew how, until now."

"Is someone going to help me get away from that vile woman and my evil sister?"

"Yes, honey, me. I need you to do something for me. In exchange for your word, I will let you live in the cottage with me, rent free.

"What if I don't agree?"

"Then I will give you your horse and wagon and you can go back to your own personalized hell."

"What happens if I change my mind after the deal has been made?"

"The penalty for perjury is death."

Her eyes go black, the air around me goes cold and I become scared. I shiver. Not because I'm cold but because there is a chill somewhere in my soul. I feel like if I make a deal with her, I'm making a deal with the devil, but then again, my family seems to be his minions so this shouldn't be too far off from what I'm used to.

"Can I at least hear the proposal before I make my decision?"

"No. If I tell you, I run the risk of my plan being exposed. If my plan gets out before it is ready to be launched I will kill whoever is responsible. Make your choice, Anastasia, I don't have all night."

What kind of choice is this? I either choose to die a slow, painful death with my mother or choose to trust this woman and be bound, by an oath that I will have to fulfill no matter what it is. Based on what she told me she needs me to do something that could ultimately end in death.

For years I wished for this choice, either life or death. Now that it is being presented to me, I'm scared. I don't want to die, nor do I want to live with my mother and sister.

Life or death. Life or death. Life or death. It weighs heavy on my mind. If I live, and go back to my mother, she will surely kill me for being away for so long without explanation. This woman in front of me seems nice enough but at times I sense nothing but pure evil emanating from her. She did say if it is completed I could live and have all the things that I envy about Ellie. It sounds too good to be true. Do I deal with the Devil herself or her minions?

"Anastasia, choose!"

"I choose death! If I'm to die I'd rather die knowing that I did everything in my power to live the life I wanted to live instead of living with the fact that I'll die achieving nothing."

"What do you mean by death?

"If I chose to go with my mother, I would be choosing to live. With that choice I also have to live with the consequences of me being away all day with no explanation, my sister being upset because I didn't get any of her things, and my mother being upset because I didn't get the cleaning done. So, if I choose to live, I would have to live with regret and ultimately die. If I chose death, I am choosing to live by an oath that, depending on what it is, can kill me or cause me to wish death upon myself. But, if I succeed, it can open doors that I could only imagine. So, if I agree to your way it means the death of an old me and the birth of a new me. So, I choose you."

"That's a very wise decision, but it's not enough. I need to know that you're serious. You are to go back to your house, pack your belongings, and come back to me. If you face opposition you are to face it head on. It's time for you to stand up to your oppressors. It's time for you to get a backbone. If you go home and bring back your things then I will know you are serious and only then will I sign the oath with you and reveal my plan."

"What if I don't return?"

"Then I know you either died with dignity or surrendered like a coward. I'll never know the difference because I'll not seek an answer. My plan will go forward, just not with you. You have one moon to get your things and come back to me.

If you are not back here by the next moon I'll assume that you're not coming back at all."

With the end of her sentence she turned to leave the room.

"One moon. You will find your horse, wagon, and the things that you came with already packed and waiting for you outside. I wish you luck."

I watch her leave the room and my happiness suddenly turns to fear. I thought by me choosing to stay with her she would protect me and I wouldn't have to go back to that vile woman and my sister again. I was wrong. So, either way it goes I was going to have to die to live. I'm going to have to go to hell to get to the oasis that is waiting just beyond the fiery pit.

Truthfully, I'm not looking forward to this journey, but then again, who would?

I arrive at the house about an hour later and all the lights are on.

"Great, could this be any worse?"

I leave Misty outside along with the wagon. I don't tie her up because she's faithful and will not go anywhere. Plus, I don't plan on staying long. I get off of my horse and proceed to go up the stairs. I turn the knob and the door is unlocked. That means they are expecting me to come back. I open the door slowly and cautiously. I tip toe in the house looking right then looking left. Surprisingly the coast is clear. I go down the hall and down to the cellar where my room is located. I grab my bags and I start to pack. I do it slowly and deliberately. I want to make sure I don't leave anything of importance because I don't want to come back to the house ever.

"Anastasia, what are you doing?"

My nosy sister is now standing at the door trying to get

me riled up. I don't respond. I keep packing. She's not important to me anymore and nothing she says or does will change my mind.

"Anastasia, I am talking to you. Why are you ignoring me?"

Once again, I don't answer. I go to my jewelry box and empty the contents into the bag. I empty out of all of the draws, my small closet, my chest, everything. I can't believe my life and everything I own fits into two small duffle bags. Drusilla has been watching me the entire time, calculating my movements. Finally, I'm done. I pick up the bags to leave and Drusilla blocks the door.

"If you want to leave, you have to go through me first."

"No problem."

With those words her eyes get big as saucers as an evil grin engulfs my face. I don't know where I got the strength or what has gotten into me. All of a sudden, all of the torment, the pain, and the misery this woman has caused me comes boiling up and erupts. I wind my hand back and punch her square in the face. A light whimper escapes from her throat. She falls to the floor and curls up in a ball, her broken nose spewing blood everywhere. Seeing her sprawled on the floor infuriates me.

She was supposed to fight back! Why is she so weak? I quickly mount her and begin pounding her face with my fist. Every bit of anger and resentment that I have felt for the past couple of months is communicated through my fist. With each hit, my smile grows. I hit her until I can't feel her skin connect with my skin. I hit her until my hands become numb from the repetitive motion. I hit her until she stops breathing. I look at her lifeless body with blood splattered across her once beautiful face. I'm now satisfied. She can't hurt me anymore. I dismount her, stare at her corpse once more, casually step over her and laugh.

"Now who is the fairest of them all?"

I go up the stairs and walk through the kitchen and living room and am now crossing the corridor. I am almost to the door. I can't believe it was this easy!

"Anastasia!"

I stop dead in my tracks. I answer her without turning around.

"Hello, Mother."

"Where do you think you're going?"

"I'm leaving. I have no place here."

"Where are you going? You're far too ugly, fat, and talentless to go anywhere of importance. Why don't you just put the bags down? If you put the bags down I'll forget that you left this place looking like a pig sty and I won't punish you. I assume you have already had dinner wherever you were so just go down to your room like a good little girl and get plenty of rest. You are going to need your strength for tomorrow."

"No."

"What did you say to me?"

I turn around and face of the person who calls herself my mother right as her eye starts to twitch.

"I said NO!"

"Look here, you ungrateful little bitch. I didn't even want you. I wanted to abort you but your stupid father wanted to keep you. If it were up to me you wouldn't even be here to waste my time, breathing my air and carrying my name. You wouldn't exist. Your sister was and always will be my perfect child. You're just her ugly shadow. Now, you take your ungrateful ass downstairs and go to bed! You will repay me for the life that I gave you!"

With the harshness of her words I am deeply hurt. A single tear rolls down my cheek. All these years I did everything as I was told to make this woman happy, to make her love me! Now, I find out it was never possible to gain this woman's love. It hurts knowing this woman thinks of me as a burden and not a joy. With that, my sorrow turns to anger.

I taste vengeance. I hunger for blood, her blood. I'll not be happy until her head is on a spike outside of the house to warn people that this house is not to be entered.

"I. SAID. NO!"

I drop the bag and prepare myself for a fight. I turn around and stare into the eyes of a woman who is truly evil. Neither of us flinch. Time stands still. After some time I realize she's not going to do anything. I turn around, pick up my bags and start walking towards the door. Suddenly, I feel pain in the back of my head. I drop the bags only to turn around see my mother with her fist balled up in a fighting stance. I look at her and a smirk slowly comes across my face. This is what I want, I finally get my revenge and right now, it tastes sweet. My mother comes flying towards me with her fist flying. With quickness I didn't even know I possessed, I side step her advances and put my food out so that she can trip over it. She is coming at me full speed. Once she realizes what just happened it's too late. She trips over my foot and skids across the floor. Her ankle twists in a weird way. She screams in pain. I laugh quietly. She is sprawled on the floor, nursing her ankle and looking at me with a look of pure shock. In some sick twisted way, I am happy because she's right where I want her.

"Help me."

Her voice is barely above a whisper.

"Call your precious daughter. She's your perfect child, right? As you said, if it were up to you, I wouldn't even be alive. Well, your wish has come true. You're dead to me."

"I didn't mean all those things Anastasia. Please, help me! You can't leave me here like this. If you leave me here crippled I might surely die due to not being able to provide for myself. Your sister is lazy and I know in her hands nothing will get done. I can't bear to see…"

I don't allow her to finish her sentence before I slap her so hard my hand starts to sting. She grabs her face and looks at me with a look that could kill.

"Hurts, doesn't it?"

"You're a bitch."

"Oh, that's the mother that I know and love. I was starting to get worried that I lost her to a sniveling fool sprawled upon the floor."

I start to laugh as I start to walk around her.

"Ever since Ellie left I've become your maid not your daughter. For months I thought about leaving and for months you kept begging me to stay only to treat me worse. Listen to me and listen to me good. I'm leaving for good this time. There's no way to stop me. Now, I'm going to leave you here but I will leave the door open. Hopefully the mailman can help you in the morning."

With that, I turn to walk towards the door. I'm almost free of this retched place. Then, my mother speaks.

"You're worthless. I rue the day that you took your first breath. You will fail. No one will love you and you're nothing without me. You'll be back and when you come back I will not accept you. You. Are. Dead. To. Me. Bitch."

I am to door. Every word she says sparks a newfound anger within me and I feel a strength I didn't even know was there before. I turn around and I do not see a woman whom I fear but a woman whom I pity. She is so weak and feeble right now and I feel the need to rid the world of her existence.

"Funny you should say that, because you're dead to me as well, but, if you would have listened earlier you would have caught that statement, but you never listen to me. You don't deserve to breathe."

I quickly walk towards her, grab both sides of her face into my heads and stare at her long and hard. My mother has a look of anger, terror and sadness. I didn't know all three of those emotions could be displayed all at once, especially since this is my mother. She is known to be an emotionless creature. A tear falls from her face.

"Any last words?"

"Go to hell."

"After you."

I twist her neck quickly and hear an audible snap. The room gets eerily quiet. My mother is still staring at me but with lifeless eyes. I shake my head at her, laughing. I remove my hands from the side of her head and she crashes to the floor with a loud thud. I step over her and head out the door toward my horse. As I load the wagon. I have huge smile on my face. I should have done this a long time ago. I go back up the stairs after loading my wagon. I still see her lifeless body sprawled on the floor, eyes pleading with death for a second chance. I close the door ending one chapter and beginning the next. I go down the stairs to Misty; I saddle up and ride off toward Ms. Hannon's house, smiling all the way there.

I arrive back at Ms. Hannon's house in about an hour with all my stuff. It feels like I've not been gone that long, but when Ms. Hannon opens the door I feel as if it might be later than I expected. Ms. Hannon comes to the door and looks ravishing. She has on a teal night gown that looks dazzling next to her complexion. Her hair is no longer in her bun but is long and flowing in the wind, dark as midnight. Without her glasses you can see the full extent of her beautiful hazel eyes. She's gorgeous. Why do I feel like this? Why am I so mesmerized by this woman?

"I didn't expect you to be back so fast," says Ms. Hannon while tucking a piece of hair behind her ear. In this instant she looks vulnerable, not the evil woman I met earlier. She looks delicate and I'm attracted to this.

"I came back sooner, rather than later, so that you knew how serious I am."

"I knew you would come back."

She is now breathing slowly and her words sound husky. I wonder if she is feeling the same thing I'm feeling. She comes forward, places her hand behind my head, and kisses me slowly and passionately. I'm spellbound by this woman. I've never had the pleasure of a man or woman but I want to experience it tonight. I push her back into the house and close the cottage door. I'll get Misty later. Ms. Hannon stops kissing me and looks deep into my eyes and gives me the most genuine smile.

"Follow me."

She leads me to her bedroom in the back. It's immaculate! When I walked into the room I saw nothing but picturesque windows, a big canopy bed, and the high ceilings. I wouldn't have imagined this kind of room in this cottage. She instructs me to lie down and I obey. She goes to the chest at the foot of the bed and pulls out a long, crystal object. She then comes up to me and kisses me again, deeper than before. I'm falling for this woman. I have feelings I never knew were possible. She unbuttons my blouse and starts to plant kisses all over me.

"You're a virgin, right?"

"Yes," I say turning red from embarrassment.

"Don't be embarrassed, I have enough experience for the both of us plus five more," she said laughing. "It's a good thing because this blood oath wouldn't work if you weren't a virgin. Now, relax."

She takes off my pants and I feel a sensation I've never felt before, desire. She then takes my legs and spreads them apart. She then disappears. I feel the most wonderful sensation and then the most awful pain. I scream. What is she doing to me? Suddenly that pain turns into a slow dull ache and then from there it turns pleasurable. I'm enjoying this. All too soon it's over and I shudder.

She hands me a piece of paper and the crystal object.

"Sign this."

I oblige.

"Good girl, now the fun can really begin."

I get excited. Is this what intimacy feels like? Is this love? I don't know what it is but I'm ready for Ms. Hannon to teach me things I never knew about myself. The night turns into dawn and dawn turns into morning as Ms. Hannon is still teaching me new things and I, her hungry student, gobble up every lesson.

I wake up before Ms. Hannon. I feel like a new woman. I feel rejuvenated, refreshed, revived, and ready to take on the world. I decide I want to make breakfast for her to thank her for the wonderful night I experienced. I think I'm going to make eggs, bacon, toast, and oatmeal with some orange juice and coffee. That sounds like a nice hearty breakfast after some nice hearty exercise. I start to blush again. Mother would not approve of what I did last night, but then again, she never approved of my existence so I don't care what she thinks anymore.

I go outside to retrieve the paper and the front page stops me in my tracks.

**MOTHER AND DAUGHTER FOUND DEAD.
SECOND DAUGHTER MISSING.
BREAK IN AND FOUL PLAY A HUGE POSSIBLITY.
INVESTIGATION PENDING**

I read a little of the story. Most of the townspeople told reporters how evil my mother and sister were and how badly they treated me. They also expressed how they were glad I got away from the break in. Most people didn't feel bad for my mother and sister, but rather for me. Just reading that the townspeople had compassion for me makes me feel better. At least someone cares about me. They just never showed it. After reading a bit more of the article I read that someone just walked in the house and stole everything of value and didn't bother contacting the authorities to help the people badly hurt in the house. I smile. Karma is a dish best served cold. I take the paper back into the cottage and begin cooking.

"It smells good in here."

I turn around and she is smiling. The same teal nightgown from last night still hugs her body and her hair still hangs loose around her shoulders. I shudder again. She takes a seat.

"I want you to know that I have never done that type of thing with anyone before. Yes, I have had sex but the blood oath between two women has never been performed, until now. It is known as the most powerful blood oath there is. The only way for it to work is one party, usually the person signing the oath, has to be a virgin. The other person, usually the person, who is delivering the oath, has to have some type of attraction. You're special, Anastasia, and I hope once this is all over it will continue to be special and we can remain together. I have met a lot of men and women in my life but none have affected me the way you have in this short amount of time."

Tears threaten to moisten my cheeks. No one has ever expressed a want to remain in my life. Everyone who has ever loved me left me in some way, shape, or form. Now, here is this beautiful woman who wants to be with me even after everything has been accomplished.

"There's something about you that makes me want to love you. I've never felt this way before except with one other person, a man. I've never felt these emotions with a woman before, but there is a first time for everything."

Ms. Hannon gets up, crosses the kitchen, and gives me one of the sweetest kisses I've ever had. My heart is so full of joy right now.

"Now, what are you cooking? It smells so delicious!"

"I'm cooking eggs, bacon, toast, oatmeal, and your choice of either orange juice or coffee."

"That sounds so yummy, I'm starving! Is this the newspaper for today?"

"Yes, I got it off the porch this morning."

She lifts up the paper and takes a look at the front page and the color drains from her face.

"Did you do this?"

She looks at me with a kind of sadness in her eyes that I can't explain. I stop cooking and turn towards her, taking her hands in my hands. I look deep into her eyes as I try to keep the tears from escaping from mine. I feel as if her eyes are interrogating my soul and I'm obligated to tell her of my wrongdoing.

"While I was there, I felt liberated. I felt a power that I've never felt before. I felt like it was my duty to rid the world of the filth that lived in the house, and that is what I did. I didn't go there planning to kill them. It just kind of, happened."

I start to choke up. In the midst of me telling my story, Ms. Hannon starts to smile. It is that same eerie smile that I saw the other night and instantly I'm uncomfortable.

"So it worked?"

"What worked?"

"The potion I gave you last night in your soup! I gave you a small dose. It was meant to give you clarity. It was meant to give you a sense of bravado. It was meant to give you the initiative to take charge and go after what you wanted, and it did all of those things. It's the side effects that intrigue me. The side effects listed are increased strength, emotional numbness, and finally an insatiable sexual appetite. I have never seen all three side effects come to fruition after taking a potion except for in some rare cases.

"What does that mean?"

"Only time will tell. Right now, I will have to watch you closely to see how you react to some other tests. I should know something about what is going on in about a week or so. Never mind that, let's eat!"

We sit down at the table and begin to eat the food I've prepared.

"Anastasia, this is good!"

I smile. I'm happy that she is enjoying her food but I can't help but to feel a little uneasy.

What did I sign? What did I agree to? Why am I not remorseful that I took two lives? Why is Ms. Hannon suddenly happy after she found out how I killed my mother?

"Anastasia, why are you not eating?"

She looks genuinely concerned.

Maybe I shouldn't be worried, but I need to know what all happened last night. If that potion was really as strong as she said she might have had a hand in me killing my family.

Why wouldn't she tell me that she gave me the potion so I could be more cautious? Did she want me to kill the only family I had in order to make sure I would be completely hers with nowhere else to go?

Suddenly, I feel sick.

"What did I agree to?"

She stops eating her meal and looks at me as if she is studying me.

"I was waiting for you to ask," Mrs. Hannon says as she pushes her plate away from her. "I can finish the food later. I feel as if this explanation can't wait."

She takes me by the hand and leads me into a room where a big book in the middle of the room. Surrounding the book are big black pots that look as if they are brewing something. There are jars containing liquid, body parts, and some even contain live bugs or animals. There are books galore. So many books, in fact, that I don't know how one person can read all of these books in a lifetime. With all of this stuff around me I get uneasy. I feel as if I don't belong here and right now I feel panicked.

Suddenly, Ms. Hannon grabs my hand and I am instantly calmed.

"I know this is a lot to take in, but I promise you, with you living here, it will come as second nature to you in no time. You can't live here and not dabble in the arts just a little bit."

That same eerie smile returns. I shudder.

She goes to the book and utters the word "*Abierto*" to the book softly and sweetly and the book opens with ease.

"Not everyone can utter that word and have the book open with that command. If you are not me and utter those words the guardian of the book will come forth and ask what it is that you seek. If you do not come with a pure heart then the guardian has the power to reverse the spell you are trying to cast or strike you dead. That is very important to remember. Do you understand?"

I nod my head.

"Good, now I'm looking for something very specific in this book. This book not only contains spells, but also prophecy."

She starts flipping through the pages, intensely looking at all the pages that pass through her fingertips.

I'm getting antsy. Is there really a prophetic message written about me in the book? I never thought my life had importance and look at me now. Mother would be so spiteful to know that her mistake is now the anchor to an even bigger plan.

"Aha!"

Her sudden sound and movement causes me to break free of my sinister thoughts.

"What does it say?"

She looks at me with the most quizzical facial expression.

"Are you sure you want to know, Anastasia? Once I read this to you there's no turning back. See prophesies are pre-destined to come to fruition, whether we want it to or not. Ignorance is bliss and with that you don't have any responsibility of knowing what is going to happen. Do you really want to get a glimpse of your future or do you want to stay ignorant in the present?"

I think about this long and hard. Do I really want to know what it is that she is talking about? Do I really want to know my role? I don't have to think long before I come to my conclusion, yes. All my life I've never had something to live for. All my life I wasn't important, but now, I am a pertinent piece of a puzzle. I want to know what is being formulated before all the pieces are put together.

"Yes, please, tell me."

With those words the room goes dark. Then there's an eerie green light that emits from the book, illuminating Ms. Hannon. She looks purely evil and now I regret my decision. There's no turning back now. I asked for the truth and now I'm going to get it. Her eyes roll to the back of her head and she levitates, becoming one with the guardian of the book. Her hair flows wildly around her. I want to run and scream, but my legs feel heavy and I can barely move. I don't know if I'm paralyzed due to fear or if the magic is forcing me to stay in place. Either way, I don't like it.

Suddenly Ms. Hannon looks right at me and points her finger. I'm mesmerized as I begin to listen to the prophecy.

"Once a kid and now she's grown
Neglect in life has made her loathe
The person that gave her life
Coached to be obedient, but never taken as a wife
Jealousy rages through her soul
As she longs for things that are out of her control

> *When enough is enough she'll kill the oppressor*
> *For once in her life, becoming the aggressor*
> *Sweet at heart and soul just as clean*
> *But with her first kill she will turn mean*
> *An insatiable appetite to seek what is lost*
> *to put her mind at ease*
> *This is the person who will fulfill the prophecy."*

I can't breathe. This sounds just like me and I need to know more. What is this prophecy? What am I supposed to do? I feel faint, but I can't fall. My legs are glued in place and I feel rigid. Is it my fear that paralyzes me? Something in me knows that it is not my fear that's keeping me in place.

"What does the prophecy say?"

After I speak I suddenly regret it. Why did I have to open up my mouth and say anything? It could have been over and I could have lived in ignorant bliss and fulfilled the prophecy without my knowledge.

> *"Ignorant is as Ignorant does*
> *Ellie is the one that has fallen in love*
> *With a prince but lo' and behold*
> *She will suddenly swoon for a friend who is really a foe*
> *A spell will be cast and will fall on two ears*
> *A bond will be formed between the two that hear*
> *It can only be broken with the death of one of the afflicted*
> *One will die, while the other will walk conflicted*
> *When the spell is casted; by the one who feels discontent*
> *It will surely set off a catalyst of events*
> *But lo, with the death of one before a three day kiss*
> *Will ensure that the other four parties affected will exist*
> *But lo' if the kiss shall happen before the third moon*
> *Then that kiss will be fatal and seal each life with doom*
> *Two innocent lives will be forever changed*
> *By this spell that will leave both parents slain*

*With nothing to lose and nothing to gain
The blood shall be shed by the one who was previously name
As it is spoken, it is now completed."*

All the color has now drained from my face.

Slowly, she descends until she is standing upright in front of the book as she was once before. Her eyes go back to normal and her hair lies flat against her body.

All is quiet in the room.

I can't speak; I don't know what to say. After a couple of minutes of just standing there staring at each other I finally can speak.

"What if I don't want to do it? What if I refuse?" I whisper.

"Anastasia, as it is spoken, it is now completed. As much as I want to say that this prophecy does not pertain to you I would be lying if I told you so. It is prophecy and it is going to come to fruition with or without your help. I told you in the beginning, ignorance is bliss."

"What did I sign last night? What did I agree to?"

"I was wondering when you would ask about the blood oath. I read the prophecy some months ago and I had no idea who these people were at the time. When the Prince married Ellie I knew that the prophetic message was starting to take shape. I was waiting on the other person mentioned in the prophetic message. At the time I had an inkling that prophecy was speaking of you. The only other possibility was your sister and she didn't seem to be docile enough. So, I devised a plan with the little bit of information I had waiting for the chance for me and you to meet. Never in my wildest dreams did I think that our encounter would be so fast! The oath states that you will become a Lady in Waiting to Ellie and become her confidant. From there, you will gain knowledge of this foe and ultimately kill him. The oath states that if you do not kill him or aide in his death you will walk among this earth forever alone. You will never love, you will never marry, nor will you ever bear a child, which, to me, is worse than death."

I shudder at her words. I was so wrapped up in the bliss of last night that I didn't even think to sit down and read what I was getting myself into, but what other options did I have? I'm pretty much alone now. As she said, this would have happened with or without my consent. I wish I didn't know as much as I now know.

"I need to lie down," I say as I rub my temples.

"Do you want me to lay down with you?" Ms. Hannon looks at me with a very sinister look and I'm instantly perked up.

"Maybe for a little bit," I smile as I go toward the bedroom. My headache is suddenly gone. I now have a new outlook on life. I was already deemed a killer in prophecy, so if I can't beat them, I might as well join them. I feel a bit more relaxed as I realize that there's no escaping fate. I'm now all smiles as I lead her by the hand into my own, personal, customized, blissful, hell.

CHAPTER FOUR
Am I My Sister's Keeper?
Anastasia

I've been living with Ms. Hannon for the past four months and I've never been happier. She's been teaching me all about the castle and the various duties, preparing me to be Ellie's lady in waiting or whatever job is available at the time. We've settled into a routine. We wake up after a blissful night, I cook breakfast, she goes to work, comes home, I have dinner prepared, and then we retire to the bedroom and do it all over the next day. It was fun at first and I'm still happy but honestly, I'm getting bored. I basically wander around town when she's not around and even then I get tired of seeing some of the same people and the same things every day.

One day, while she was gone doing duties for the castle, my curiosity was piqued and went to the book. I felt along the edges and felt a weird sensation, as if I shouldn't be here. I step back. My mind is saying to go away but my heart is gravitating toward the book. I sit there and stare at the book.

I wonder how it opens. I stare at the book some more as I try to remember what I saw Ms. Hannon do so many times before. Suddenly, I remember. I stand in front of the book, feet apart, and arms resting at my sides. I look directly at the book and utter the word "*Abierto*". The room goes dark, the book levitates and I'm scared. What have I gotten myself into?

"What is it that you seek, o ye pure of heart?"

The voice is deep and loud and resonates around the entire room. He is handsome and has eyes full of purpose and sadness. His face looks as if it has been carved by the hands of gods. His lips are perfectly plump; his hair is waving effortlessly within the green hue of the smoke as he crosses his arms across his perfectly chiseled chest. If I weren't terrified I would be in awe.

"I require the truth."

"Dear child, you have already received the truth."

"I know about that truth, but who am I? Why was I chosen? Is there anything written in there dealing with just me? Or does my life always revolve around someone else"

"Dear child, everyone's life revolves around the action of someone else, whether it's an ancestor or someone near and dear to the person's heart."

"I understand that, but all of my life I've been that person who has never had a meaning. I have never had purpose. Show me what my purpose is! Please do not keep me in the dark. Why am I pre-destined to die even before I have had a chance to fully live?"

The room goes silent as tears trickle down my face. The guardian of the book has no expression on his face, which makes me even more upset.

"Love is the meaning of your life
For in one year's time you will be a wife
Life will be filled with purpose and laughter

With the conclusion of this wretched chapter
You will bear three children with the conclusion of this task
Protect Ellie and you'll have everything that you ask
But if you fail you will still be a wife
You'll bear the children but your life will remain in strife
For if you don't do as prophesied in one years' time
You will be married but not to whom you have in mind
As it is stated, it is written."

I start to panic now. Does this mean that I am not going to end up with Ms. Hannon? I know we couldn't have children but I figured there was a spell around that. I never thought I could see my life without her. Now I really regret opening up this book.

"Does this mean if I do not help Ellie, Ms. Hannon will die?"

"I cannot predict the future; I can only speak of prophetic messages. I am sorry, o ye pure of heart."

With that, he returns to the book and the room goes silent.

I cannot believe this! My life is starting to make sense. My life is actually going great. I am loved! Why is this happening to me! I cannot believe that she will be taken away from me if I do not help Ellie! Once again this stupid wench is ruining my life! Why did I have to open that book? Why did I have to know my purpose? I could have been naïve and blissfully happy.

I run into the room and throw myself on the bed, fitfully crying myself to sleep.

Sometime later, Ms. Hannon comes barging into the room. She is yelling frantically and pointing at a piece of paper in her hand. I'm still a bit groggy from my bad nap and I have a bit of a headache. I look at Ms. Hannon jumping up and down and I become disinterested. I roll over and pull the covers over my head. Right now I don't want to be bothered. I have to figure out a way to get close to Ellie so I can have a future filled with no regrets. Suddenly the covers are ripped away and are now levitating above me. I turn to face Ms. Hannon and there is a scowl on her face.

"I will not be ignored."

"What is it, Ms. Hannon?"

"Look at what has been posted today!"

She hands me the paper and I read it slowly, taking in all the words. After reading it through once, I get excited and read it again more expeditiously. After reading the posting several times I look at Ms. Hannon with tears in my eyes. This is exactly what I have been waiting for, a posting to be a Lady in Waiting to Ellie. This will provide me the cover I need in order to get close to her and prevent the inevitable from happening. I jump up and give Ms. Hannon a kiss. Things are finally going right and, now, I can focus on my future with Ms. Hannon. I smile. I love what my life has become.

"You start training in the morning and it will last for three days."

Today is the last day of my Lady in Waiting training. Ellie has no idea that I'm here and what I'm training to be. I would like to keep it that way until I can talk to her face to face. So far it's only me and one other person. Her name is Noelle and she's very beautiful. I can't place it, but she looks very familiar, like I have met her before. Surely I would have remembered someone so beautiful. I know if I was Ellie, I would not want her anywhere near my husband. She is tall, fair skin, very dark, long hair and piercing green eyes. I can already see this being a problem in the future and we have only just met.

Essentially, our training consisted of three days. One day for etiquette, one day for proper hygienic techniques to keep the Princess properly groomed at all times, and finally, maintaining acceptable appearance so that we may represent the Princess in a very respectable manner. To me, all of this stuff comes easily. I have been doing it most of my life. That is one thing I thank my good for nothing mother for. She at least taught me how to behave like a lady. I find it truly ironic that now I'm training to do the exact same thing Ellie did for us for so many years. We are now on day three and I'm bored out of my mind. Noelle just can't seem to grasp the idea we have to look presentable at all times. She'd rather be comfortable. She doesn't understand this is a job and in a job we don't have a say. I wonder how long before Noelle has a Prince Charming willing to whisk her away? She's not as beautiful as Ellie, or as smart, but she is a close second.

"Anastasia, pay attention,"

I hear the crack of a ruler and I instantly straighten up. I've had the unpleasant feeling of that ruler once before and it's not a feeling that I want to relive.

"Now that I have both of you lovely ladies' attention I want to congratulate you on graduating from the program. Your work will set the tone for how all future Ladies in Waiting will be trained. Please treat this job with respect. Now, each one of you will have the opportunity to meet with the Princess for an hour before your official work begins. Not everyone gets along with their employer so if you feel as if working for the Princess will not be a good match for you this is your opportunity to opt out before the job actually begins."

There's no opting out for me. I need to be in this position, no matter how much I hate the ground she walks on. I need to be in place for the prophecy to take place. What would have happened if I didn't know what was to come? Would my mother and my sister still be dead? Would I still be doing chores with people secretly feeling sorry for me? I can't think about that now, I have a job to do.

"Noelle, you're first."

She gets up and graciously follows the instructor to meet the awaiting Princess.

I wonder if she looks different. I wonder if she looks as if she's made of money. I wonder if she looks as if she's royalty now. I guess I will find out sooner rather than later.

Noelle comes back and she looks angry.

"What's wrong," I asked with a concerned look on my face, even though I really didn't care.

"I can already tell that I am not going to like working for her, but, I need the money."

This piqued my interest.

"How can you tell?"

"When I went in there she barely spoke to me, as if her mind was pre-occupied. She just waved me off as if I wasn't important! Never in my life have I been so disrespected!"

I just laughed. If only she knew that in actuality, her life was insignificant, she would not feel as if she belongs on this high, fictitious pedestal. When she realizes that I'm not going to give her a suitable answer to fuel her anger she stomps off, mumbling under her breath. With an attitude like that I can see why she hasn't been approached by a suitor. I still can't shake the feeling that I know her from somewhere. I shrug it off. I can't let her negativity rub off on me. I have a job to do.

I take a deep breath as I gather my courage and walk toward the door. I stand in front of the door for a couple of minutes trying to rehearse the script I've created in my mind. Finally, I turn the knob and press on the door while lightly knocking. As expected, she is not looking in my direction, but rather out the big picturesque windows lining the study. I go to the middle of the room and examine her. She is so beautiful. It seems like since she left the house her beauty has been enhanced. Suddenly, I hear her speak to me with a soft voice.

"What brings you here, Maiden"?

All the while she has never looked away from the window.

"I'm here to serve you, as you have served me."

"Dear Maiden, you speak of tales. I have never served anyone in my life but my wicked step mother and my two step sisters! Now, all of them are dead! Why would you come in here with lies only to make me feel worse?"

With that sentence she starts to cry. "I despised them, but I also loved them. They were the only family I've known and I'll not rest until I find the killers. Have you ever had that feeling before? Have you ever had that feeling of hating someone so much you loved them?"

"Yes, I have, but in the end I found myself. I learned to love myself, and by loving myself, I learned to accept the love of others."

She still has not turned from the window.

"You're very wise, Maiden. What is your name?"

"My name is Anastasia."

The room goes quiet. The sobbing turns to quiet whimpers.

"That was my step sister's name. I always thought her name was so pretty. She was such a smart girl, but my step mother and step sister always held her back. It's awful what they did to her once I left."

"It was awful."

"How would you know, you don't even know her!"

She turns around quickly with fire in her eyes; ready to pounce.

I stand there ready for the physical abuse I'm about to receive. I close my eyes and tense up, ready for a blow. All of a sudden I feel arms around me. She's not hitting me but is hugging me and sobbing loudly in my shoulder.

"Oh, Anastasia, it really is you! I thought you were dead!" She sobs louder until her words are nothing more than incoherent babblings.

At this moment I feel loved. I wish I could bottle this

emotion and keep it with me forever. I wrap my arms around her as well as I start to sob. I start to apologize for how badly I treated her, how I always loved her, and that I was sad when she left. We stayed like that for a while until we both were exhausted from crying and could no longer stand. We collapsed on the floor; still holding each other expressing our love for one another. Eventually we both went to sleep curled up in each other's arms with dried, tear stained faces.

I awaken a couple of hours later feeling very refreshed. I can't believe she received me so well even after how horribly I treated her. If I would have known how she felt for me I would have stood up for her. It would have been two against two. We could have survived together, but that's not how fate works. Now, fate has brought us together again, but this time I am preventing her death instead of trying to cause it. After so many years of taking her through hell it's only right that I try to give her some solace so she can actually have her happily ever after. I open my eyes expecting to see Ellie lying beside me. She's not there. I sit up and panic sweeps over me. I look around the room and I see her sitting a couple of feet away from me, staring. I get an eerie feeling that I just cannot shake.

"What happened to Drusilla and your mother?" She is very still. Her words come out as a whisper as her eyes search my face for some sort of answer.

"They died."

"I know that, Anastasia, I'm not stupid. It's plastered everywhere around the news. I have people out there searching for you as we speak. Tell me what happened."

I don't want to speak. I don't want to move. I don't want to tell her the truth. I know if I tell her what happened she can have me confined to prison, or worse, put to death. If

I'm put to death I'll not feel so empty and unfilled, but, at the same time, if I die, so will Ellie. I've always been told to tell the truth even when the outcome might not be so great. Although I want to lie to her, something in my heart decides that I need to tell her the truth. I take a deep breath and I tell her everything. I tell her about me hitting my head as well as the blissful night with Ms. Hannon. I tell her what happened in the house and I told her Ms. Hannon's promise for me to stay there if I help her. I left the part about the prophetic message out. I don't need her to know why I'm here and what I'm protecting her from. After I complete the whole story she sits there for a couple of minutes, not saying anything.

"You know I can hang you for this."

Her words are cold.

"Yes, I know. Do as you wish."

"I'm not going to do that. You've already gone through enough torture. You got a small taste of what I've been going through since both my parents died. I also believe their deaths will forever haunt you. I do not need to punish you further. Your secret is safe with me, for now. Understand, if you in any way, shape, or form disrespect me, speak blasphemy against my name, become physical with me, or do anything outside of what you are supposed to do I will have you killed. Fate has spared you this time because you are my sister and the people you killed were purely evil, but there will not be a second time."

"Yes ma'am."

"Go fetch my scribe so that I can send updated information to the paper."

"Yes ma'am."

I go and fetch the scribe and return immediately to Ms. Hannon's cottage. I'm exhausted after today's events and all I want to do is go to bed. I go toward the bedroom and

Ms. Hannon is lying across the bed, her hair hanging wildly around her shoulders with two wine glasses in her hand.

"I heard what happened. I think congratulations are in order. You are truly amazing."

She gets to her knees on the bed and comes closer. She hands me the wine and it taste so sweet. It is gone in seconds. Ms. Hannon takes my glass and pulls me onto the bed with her. I'm tired but I go along for the ride. I guess my work is never done. As I prepare for yet another blissful night I can't help but wonder how she heard about what happened so fast? Her lips are so soft and so moist, I soon forget the question.

The next day, I'm summoned by Ellie. I have no idea why I'm being summoned, but if I don't go I risk losing my job as a Lady in Waiting. I roll over and Ms. Hannon is already gone. I smile as I get a whiff of her scent. Who knew love like this existed? I quickly take a shower and get dressed before making my way across the grounds toward the castle. I go to the kitchen and Ms. Hannon is cooking with a big smile on her face. Our eyes meet and I instantly start to blush. I don't know what it is, but there's something about Ms. Hannon that drives me crazy, and I love it.

"Do you know where Ellie is?" I ask Ms. Hannon.

"I think she's up in the study where she was yesterday. When you go up there can you please take her breakfast?"

I nod and take the tray. It has tea, biscuits, eggs, and bacon. It smells delicious. I go toward the grand staircase. I don't know how I am ever going to get used to these stairs.

Finally, I make it up the stairs. I stand outside the study balancing the tray in one hand while trying to knock with the other. It was hard, but I do it. I catch the tray right before it falls.

"Come in."

Once again I balance the tray, turn the knob, and slowly nudge myself in.

"Close the door behind you."

I do as I'm told. I take the tray to the desk and wait for instructions.

"Please, Anastasia, sit."

I sit down. At this time I am nervous. I don't know what to expect. Has she decided to renege and punish me for the death of my mother and my sister? Will I be confined into the deepest, darkest dungeon for the rest of my life? I start shaking. I would rather be put to death then be left in solitude with my own thoughts. The room is quiet as Ellie sits in front of the same picturesque window she sat in front of the other day.

"May I ask what this about?"

"I feel like you're the only person I can talk to about this."

"About what?"

"I need to speak to someone about my feelings. As I see it, you have a secret so I know what I'm going to tell you will not leave this room. You are the only person I have complete trust in at this moment."

I get goose bumps. I have no idea what she wants to talk about but I feel as if it's not good.

"Sure, go ahead and tell me, your secret is safe with me."

"I'm in love with Daniel."

All of the air goes out of my lungs. All I can do is think of the prophetic message I received only days before. The words keep circulating in my head. Ignorant is as Ignorant does, Ellie is the one that has fallen in love; with a prince but lo' and behold she will suddenly swoon for a friend who is really a foe.

"How do you know?" I ask Ellie, not really wanting to know the answer.

"It was in the garden. We kissed. I felt so much passion in

that kiss, but ever since then I have felt conflicted. I love the Prince with all of my heart, but I cannot describe this feeling I have with Daniel. It's like he was made just for me."

I get sick. The food in the room no longer smells good but is nauseating. This is out of order! Where is the spell? Am I too late? I start to pace the room thinking of how to possibly break it to Ellie that she might be in danger.

"What's wrong, Anastasia?"

"You have to break this off with Daniel. You can't see him anymore."

"You're not my mother, Anastasia!"

"No, I'm not, but I'm the closest thing to a mother that you will ever have."

"I love him!"

"You lust him! You've only had the pleasure of one man. You're just going through a phase where you see something else and you wonder what it will be like. You have everything you want and more with the Prince. Please don't endanger your livelihood by sneaking around with a man you barely know!"

"Don't you think I know that? I've stayed away from this man for a whole month. Every time he comes into a room I leave. I make sure I'm not alone with him for more than two seconds. I can't stand to be in a room with him because every time I see his hazel eyes my heart aches for him. I know this is love. What I have with the Prince is not as deep as what I feel for Daniel."

The room goes silent. I don't know what to say next. She starts to cry. I go to her and wrap my arms around her, trying to console her from the internal pain and turmoil I know she is experiencing.

"I don't know what to do, Anastasia. Please, help me."

She's now weeping into my garments and I don't push her away, instead I welcome the tears. I'd rather have her cry over something she can't have than ruin her life trying to obtain something that will destroy all she has.

"I will help you. I'll do everything in my power to keep you away from him, if it's the last thing I do," I say that meaning every word. If I have to die to ensure that she and her unborn children will have a full life with her in it I will gladly do it.

She stops crying, pulls herself from me, and she suddenly has the biggest smile.

"Thank you. I'm going to promote you to my assistant. I want you by my side at all times. The only times I don't want you near me are when I am bathing, utilizing the facilities, sleeping, or servicing the Prince. That will prevent Daniel from trying anything."

I'm relieved. This is going to be easier than I thought. Hopefully we both can deter the advances from Daniel and help her be more focused and devoted to her husband.

"You'll start in the morning. You are dismissed."

I bow to Ellie and leave with a skip in my step. I can't believe that almost five months ago I was being oppressed by my sister and my mother and now I'm here. Who knew change could happen this fast! I start whistling as I make my way to the servant quarters to prepare for the first day I will officially be Ellie's assistant. I head downstairs to get my area ready and prep myself for the big day ahead of me tomorrow. I mingle with some of the new and old employees. I get so lost in my tasks and conversation that it's dark when I'm done.

I go back to the cottage and Ms. Hannon is waiting there for me with dinner ready and a glass of wine as soon as I enter. I thank her and slowly sip on the wine as I go toward the heavenly smells emitting from the kitchen. I see a big spread of food: turkey, mashed potatoes, gravy, and corn. The whole array of food is lined out perfectly on the table. I sit down and begin to dig in.

"Why did you make so much food?"

"I made a lot of food because I figured that I would not have time to prepare home cooked meals as often as we would like. Also, I know being a Lady in Waiting can be a bit demanding at times."

"Why wouldn't you be able to cook?"

"I've been promoted to head staff leader. I oversee all hiring and make sure everyone is doing what they are supposed to do."

"When did this happen?"

"Today!"

"I'm so happy for you!" I smile.

"Now, tell me what happened with Ellie today. What did she want?"

"She has promoted me to her assistant."

Ms. Hannon stops eating.

"Did she give you a reason why?"

I thought about what Ellie said about not telling anyone her secret.

"No, she didn't. Well, not a full one. She said she liked being around me and that she feels like I'm the only person she can trust right now. She wants me near her at all times unless she is bathing, sleeping, utilizing the facilities, or servicing her husband."

Ms. Hannon gives me a look that says she doesn't fully believe me. She picks up her fork and begins eating again.

"I guess we aren't going to have time to cook like I thought. To promotions!"

She lifts up her glass for a toast. I lift up my glass and the clinking sound echoes throughout the cottage.

I take a big gulp and the wine calms me. I can barely keep my eyes open.

"I think I need to go lie down, I'm really tired and I have a big day tomorrow."

"I understand, love."

I stumble toward the bedroom and fall on the bed. I'm too tired to take anything off or to even crawl under the covers. Today has been a very emotional day. With that thought, I'm fast asleep.

I awaken a little while later to Ms. Hannon levitating above me speaking strange words. Her hands are slowly moving in front of my face. I can't breathe. I can't move. Flashes of today play before my eyes. Suddenly the reel stops with Ellie telling me about being in love with Daniel. I can't talk. Am I dreaming? I feel pain in my skull. I can't describe it, I just want it to stop! I can barely recognize Ms. Hannon. She is green, her eyes are totally black, and her hair, which is white instead of the beautiful dark color it usually is, is floating wildly around her. Why is she doing this to me? She leans closer to me as if she's going to kiss me. I'm now able to breathe but what comes out is shocking. It's like a movie reel coming out of my mouth and going into hers. I feel like I'm going to be sick. My eyes are pleading with her to stop. She leans closer, kisses me, and all I see is darkness.

I sit up in bed. My body is drenched in sweat and all I'm wearing is a T-shirt. When did this happen? I look over and Ms. Hannon is sleeping soundly next to me. I can't shake this eerie feeling. I stare at Ms. Hannon for a little while longer to make sure that she's sleep and I calm down a bit. There's no way that could have happened. It was just a bad dream. I roll over, pull the covers back over me and drift back to sleep. As I'm falling asleep I swear I can hear Ms. Hannon silently laughing.

I awaken the next morning bright and early. The bad dream I had last night is still permeating through my mind. I look at the clock and it reads 5:30 AM. I sit up in bed and Ms. Hannon is still sleeping. God, she looks so beautiful when she sleeps. There's no way she could have ever morphed into the hideous creature I saw last night.

I look around the room and, for the first time, I actually

take in the beauty of this room. Even though the cottage is small, this room is enormous. The floors are of a dark wood quality. The dresser is placed directly in front of the bed with a huge mirror attached. The bed is a canopy style bed with sheer curtains going around. For the past five months I've not had a chance to examine the beauty of this bed. The delicate wood work going around the frame is immaculate. The headboard is breathtaking and the railings attached to the top of the bed are astounding. This bed was made for a Queen. Other than the furnishings, the room is really plain.

I get up, go to the bathroom, and start to run a bath. While my bath is running I look in the mirror. I look tired. I have no idea what happened last night but I don't have a good feeling about any of it. I don't think Ms. Hannon would intentionally harm me to get information, would she? No, she wouldn't. I don't know why I would be dreaming that.

"You weren't dreaming; it was real."

A strange face appears in the mirror. I want to scream but no sound is coming out of my mouth.

"I'm sorry, dearie, for startling you but I had no other way of talking to you other than waiting for you right here. This mirror can be a cramped place for a girl to wait. Now, if you promise not to scream so that Ms. Hannon does not come in here I promise I will allow you to speak. Do we have a deal?"

I nod my head furiously.

"Good, please do not go back on your word."

I feel the tightness leave my throat and I can now speak. I've never been so happy to be able to talk.

"Who are you?"

"Well, my name is Samantha, Sam for short, but you probably know me as Fairy Godmother."

I get angry. I can't believe she has the audacity to show her face after what she did to me! If Ellie had never married the Prince, I would not have been oppressed. If I hadn't been oppressed, I wouldn't have killed. If I had not killed my family, I would not be mixed up in this weird prophecy. As far as I can see, she is responsible for everything! As I go to scream profanities I can't speak once again.

"Just by the look on your face I have some explaining to do. Believe me, I owe you an explanation but now is not the time, nor the place. I don't have a lot of time but I came to warn you, Anastasia, you are in danger. You are mixed up in some very dark magic. I've come to help you and to protect you as I have with Ellie. The supposed prophecy you heard from that book of dark magic is only part of the story. That prophecy is not all real and if you do what that book says you will die along with everyone else mentioned in that message. If you allow me to talk to you and give you the rest of the prophecy you will be able to possibly save your life and one other. The choice is yours. If you tell Ms. Hannon what you and I have spoken of then there will be dire consequences to you, but not from me. That dream you had last night was not a dream at all but rather it is an ancient art of black magic. She basically gave you the kiss of knowledge. She wanted to know everything you know up until this point. If she would have held on to that kiss for just a second longer you would have been dead. Is that someone you want to entrust your life to? Now, there are parts of that prophecy that cannot be overlooked. There are parts that are going to happen, but there are some parts you can fix. If you want to know the truth, Anastasia, meet me tonight in the room of roses. I have to go now. Remember, do not tell anyone of this conversation or else it will be detrimental to you."

With that, she leaves. I feel the tightness leave my throat and I can now speak. Just a few seconds later Ms. Hannon comes into the bathroom to use the toilet. I don't look at her. I don't know who to believe, the love I have for Ms. Hannon or the Fairy Godmother who spoke common sense. I quickly go to the bathtub and stop the water. I undress and get into the bathtub. Ms. Hannon finishes her business and proceeds to brush her teeth.

"Did you sleep well?"

"Like a baby."

"Good, you were tossing and turning so much last night I feared that you would wake up grouchy."

"No, I'm fine. I just want to take a bath and get ready for my first day of being an assistant."

"You don't have to worry about that. Ellie has fallen ill. I got a call from her just a couple of minutes ago. She said you are to report to her first thing tomorrow morning. All she is going to do is stay in bed for the rest of the day.

I relax just a little. I'll go and check on her in a little bit. Right now, I just want to relax. Ms. Hannon offers to get into the tub with me. I decline. I have a lot on my mind and right now I just want to be alone. She finishes getting dressed and goes out to the main room of the cottage. After a couple of minutes I smell the tell-tale signs of her burning candles. I sink further into the tub. After the incident with the book I don't want to be anywhere near Ms. Hannon when she's doing her voodoo rituals. All of a sudden, I hear a male's voice. I look out the room to see Daniel. What is he doing here? I listen in on the conversation.

"Come in."

I hear my Ms. Hannon speak to her son in such a cool and calm manner.

"You've really got to stop with this voodoo nonsense."

I tell her that every day! I smile because at least someone is on my side.

"Isn't that why you've come here?"

Everything goes silent. My heart is beating rapidly.

"You don't have to answer; I know why you're here. The answer is no."

The whole time she addresses him she has not opened her

eyes once. Her body is still other than the tell-tale signs of her breathing.

"Why are you protecting him?" Daniel is now yelling at his mother.

She does not move an inch. I'm impressed.

"You've always loved him more than me!"

With those words her eyes flutter open, she gets up with an effortlessness that can't be described and glides toward Daniel and grips him by his shirt.

"It's because I love you that I am telling you no!"

Her eyes scare me and, for once, I'm concerned. I don't see a witch but I see a Mother in those eyes.

"You've done it before! You've helped me with this temporary love spell! Why is this different? Why can't I have her?"

"You cannot have her because her heart does not belong to you. I've helped you before because I thought each time you came to me with a new infatuation with a woman if I helped it would help you settle down. I want grandchildren! I want to be able to hear giggles in this little cottage! Every time I help you, you become disinterested and then you throw them away as if they're a toy. What happens after that Daniel? Tell me!"

"They die."

His words are laced with sadness.

In an instant, I feel sorry for him.

"How do they die, Daniel?" she is now yelling at Daniel with an intensity in her eyes that burns to my soul.

"Suicide."

I silently gasp. This is way more serious than I thought. I recuperate and continue listening.

"What makes you think that I'm going to help you destroy something as beautiful as that girl's spirit? I've never in my life seen something or someone that pure. You, my son, are laced with hatred, envy, and selfishness. Your evil will be the utter demise of you, the Prince, the Princess Ellie, and me. If you interfere with the love and the bond between Ellie and the Prince you will die along with every other adult in this equation. I will not let your ruthless behavior result in the death of three innocent people, including myself. You will not destroy her life because you're having a tantrum. There are a lot of other women in the kingdom, go and court one of them."

With those words, she resumes her position on the floor, closes her eyes, and starts slowly breathing again.

"None of them are as beautiful as Ellie," Daniel says and I really believe the words he is speaking. "I love her and I will not stop until she is mine."

"Depart from me. I will not aide you in your demise."

With that she lifts her hand, points it toward him, and a strong gust pushes him out of the cottage and slams the door.

"Anastasia, you can come out now."

I hesitantly come out of the bathroom with nothing on but a towel. She is still sitting crossed legged on the floor with her long, luxurious black hair falling all around her. Hey eyes are still closed and I get an uneasy feeling in my stomach.

"Anastasia, please don't be alarmed. You knew what I was when we first met. I love you and I will not let any harm come unto you. Now, go in the room and lie down. You need your rest."

I go into the room and lie down, she's right, I do need my rest. I can't believe the night I had and now this. I'm beyond tired and all I want to do is sleep. I go into the room, cross the wooden floor, and collapse in the oversize canopy bed. I'm asleep in seconds.

I awaken to screams. Some of the screams are not of this earth and instantly sends a chill down my spine. I hear another scream, a man, and I spring into action. I get up, throw on some clothes, and try to get out of the room. The door will not open. I push and pull and bang on the door, screaming for someone to help the gentleman that's in so much trouble. Suddenly, a horrific ghost like figure comes up under the door and stops right in front of the door. I'm scared. The figure is not moving. I try to find another way to exit the room, but every exit I come to, the ghost like figure mysteriously appears before it. Finally, I give up. I sit on the bed and stare at the beast. He stares right back. I still hear the man screaming. I want to go to him, but I'm confined to this room. This creature is so big he makes this normally grandiose room seem petite in nature. The man's screaming intensifies. I hope he's ok. I hope when this is all over I can help him the best way I can, but for now, I sit.

Twenty minutes go by and the figure has not moved. Then, in a flash, it disappears. I watch in astonishment. How can something so big and terrifying disappear so quickly? I wait a couple of minutes and cautiously ease my way to the door. I crack the door open to make sure none of the ghost like beasts are there. Once I crack the door, I see Daniel coming in, bloodied, with his arm hanging loosely. He goes toward the bathroom and is in there for a couple of minutes. I hear a blood curdling scream and seconds later he is out of the bathroom looking refreshed. The only way to tell anything was ever wrong is the blood on his shirt. Once he's out of the bathroom he makes his way to the book and whispers, "Abierto, Amore guida le mie azioni". The book awakens and levitates off the mantle and the same powerful being that addressed me only days before emerges. Then I hear a voice.

"Your heart is not pure, son of Hannon. Leave from this place."

This is new; I've never heard the book address anyone in this way.

"My heart is pure. I want love. I feel as if this woman is the one for me and I will not know for sure unless I have help," replies Daniel.

"What is it that you seek?"

"Amore Fatal"

"That is a very powerful spell. You know that once I cast this spell it will be irreversible and if, for some reason it does not work, the repercussions will be fatal for both parties. Do you understand?

"I fought through mental and physical attacks to make it here to make this request. I understand the repercussions."

"As you wish. I need a sacrifice from you and something from the girl you want to enchant." Daniel looks baffled.

Good, I hope he has nothing and this nonsense can end.

"I sacrifice my engagement ring from my first true love, Yanci. I haven't taken this ring off since her death."

"Now, the object belonging to the person of whom you want to enchant?"

"I give you her hanky."

How did he get that! She hasn't spoken to this man so how did he get something so personal. Everything in my body wants to go and hurt Daniel but my feet won't move. I try harder, it doesn't work.

The ritual continues.

"Please place the items on the mantle."

Daniel places the items side by side on the mantle and steps back. The book begins.

As the book begins, I'm levitated. Light is shining all around me as the words circle around me paralyzing me.

"Love is something to cherish and hold
Love at first sight is a tale centuries old
But fast forward time about three moons

The woman you love will suddenly swoon
You have three days to enjoy the bliss
Seal her fate with just one kiss
But beware, on day four if a kiss is not shared
The love that was between you will suddenly disappear
Now if the love proves to be true
A child of two shall befall on you
But beware if your eyes should suddenly sway
Your wandering eyes will dig both graves
As it is spoken, it is now completed."

The book then places itself back onto the mantle and I am suddenly dropped from the air. I land hard on my arm. I start to panic. That was the spell! The prophecy is now happening!

"A spell will be cast and will fall on two ears. A bond will be formed between the two that hears. It can only be broken with the death of one of the afflicted. One will die while the other will walk conflicted."

This can't be happening! I thought this was a lie. I thought I was only supposed to kill Daniel. I didn't know I was going to be the one bound by the spell as well. I get up to leave so I can find Sam. As I open the door, I see Ms. Hannon standing there. Her eyes are dark, her stance is rigid, and her demeanor reeks of anger and evil. I am scared. I close the door a smidge so that I can see through the crack. Ms. Hannon addresses Daniel.

"What are you doing here?"

"I came to get some healing potion out of the cabinet."

The air is heavy with anger. She speaks to him through gritted teeth.

"I have the ability to kill you where you stand. Now, do not lie. What are you doing here?"

She steps forward.

He steps back.

I gasp.

"Amore Fatal."

Ms. Hannon's eyes get big. She looks deep into Daniel's eyes. It looks as if she's hurt.

"Why?"

"I love her; she can be with no one else."

"So you jeopardize the home of yourself and your mother?" she screams.

As she screams, Daniel falls to the ground. He is in a lot of pain while she cups her hand in the air before him twisting her hand back and forth.

"Please, don't kill me." Daniel chokes. Blood is now oozing from his mouth.

"If I do not kill you, everyone will die."

Daniel is turning pale, I am frightened. What he did was wrong, but he should not be killed. I go to save him but before I can open the door he whispers.

"As it is spoken, it is now completed."

The hand she has been holding steady drops. Daniel can breathe. With every cough I feel a sigh of relief.

She goes to her book and silently says *"Abierto"*.

It opens without any hesitation.

She reads the inscription, steps back, and then starts to cry.

"I cannot kill you because if I kill you it will instantly kill her. But I am telling you now, son or not, if you, for one second think I'm going to let this pass, you are mistaken. The spell is going to take place as written. I have no choice but to allow the first part to happen. During those three days of love be prepared. I will do everything in my power to prevent that kiss. Depart from me or I will kill you where you stand."

Daniel gets off the floor and scrambles towards the door.

"Daniel!"

As his name is yelled he turns back and faces Ms. Hannon.

"I hope you enjoy hell because you will be going there soon. Whether it is by your hand or mine I cannot tell you. I no longer have a son."

Daniel leaves the cottage and I'm flabbergasted. I don't know what to do, so I stand there.

Ms. Hannon watches as her son skips away. She calmly walks away from the window. An eerie smile creeps onto her face as she walks toward the back room. I silently close the door and scramble toward the bed. She opens the door and tears are streaming down my face.

"I thought what you told me was a lie! I can't go through with this," I cry to Ms. Hannon.

"We had a deal, little girl! You will do as you promised. You heard everything that just happened, you heard the spell! I told you once you heard the spell you would be bound by its words and you were to do the complete opposite. The spell was not meant for you, but since you heard it, the opposite is true for you. I told you this was going to happen and if you don't do what you're supposed to do you will die along with everyone else. But, if you're a good girl, and do as you were told, I will spare your life. Do you understand me?"

I nod.

"Good, now, the games begin."

With that, a slow cackle escapes from her lips and permeates the room.

I begin to cry harder with the full understanding of what I've just done and who this woman really is. How could someone who loves me allow this to happen? I thought she would protect me. I guess I was wrong. Now, I'm frantic. Now, it is time to see Sam. It might mean life or death.

CHAPTER FIVE
Do You Know the Muffin Man?
Anastasia

I have to check on Ellie. I have to make sure that she is okay. I want nothing more than for her to be lying in bed sleeping soundly. I have to check on her before I can go see Sam. For my sanity, I have to check. I wait until Ms. Hannon leaves to attend to some staffing issues and I run out of the cottage to the castle. I go through the foyer toward the big staircase and start running up the stairs. When I finally reach the top of the stairs, I'm sweating and out of breath, but I have no time to waste. I turn right and run straight into their bedroom. Ellie is sitting up in the bed.

"Hi, Anastasia, I was wondering where you were all day. Weren't you supposed to start work today?"

"I was on my way here this morning when Ms. Hannon said she got a call from you saying you were sick."

"I didn't make a call."

My stomach churns. Ms. Hannon lied? Why would she

do that? Suddenly, it hits me. She wanted me to hear that spell! She wanted me to be bound to her son, but why? This realization just makes me want to go see Sam that much more.

"I'm sorry for the miscommunication. I'll definitely be here tomorrow. I came to see how you were doing. Are you feeling okay?"

"I feel a little under the weather, but I'm fine, nothing too serious. It just started not too long ago, actually, so I decided to come upstairs and lie down."

My stomach churns again. I hope it's not the spell already taking effect.

"My head's hurting, I feel dizzy, my chest feels like it's about to cave in, and I'm hot. I have no idea what this is but I sent for my husband to see if it's something we need to call the doctor about."

It sounds like the spell is taking a toll. I feel bad for Ellie because she has no idea what's going on right now. She's so oblivious to the evil that surrounds her. She can't help that she's a naturally beautiful person inside and out. If she was born plain, she wouldn't have to worry about half of the problems she is facing now. Ellie suddenly lets out a scream that gives me goose bumps. I look over and she is slumped in her bed. I run to her side and she's burning up. I quickly remove all the covers from her and try to wake her. Nothing is working. I try to take the water on the nightstand and force her to drink, but she's not responding. I start to panic. I feel her pulse and her heart is still beating but it's beating slowly and her breathing is slow and shallow. I panic even more. What am I supposed to do? Just then Daniel comes bursting through the doors.

"What's going on here? What's wrong with Ellie?"

I narrow my eyes at him. I don't want to answer him but I feel like I must in order to keep Ellie safe from the truth.

"She has a fever and just slumped over. I have no idea what's going on with her, but I'm worried."

"My mother has a remedy that she used on me when I was young and used to have fevers. It may work for her now."

He walks toward her and I hold her closer.

"We're just going to wait for the Prince. You don't have any type of remedy that could help her now. Who knows, your remedy might make things worse for everyone involved."

I give him a mean scowl. There is an air of awkwardness that passes between us.

"You know, don't you?"

I stare at him with the meanest look I can muster.

"Know what?"

Ellie wakes up and her voice is so soft and weak that it doesn't even sound like her.

"It's nothing. You have nothing to worry about," I say as I glare at Daniel. "Actually, Daniel was about to leave. Weren't you, Daniel?"

He looks hesitant, as if he doesn't want to leave the room. I dare him to come near her. I might not be as big as he is but I sure can pack a mean punch. If he comes near her it will be a replay of what happened at my house many months ago.

He edges toward her and I prepare myself for battle.

"Daniel?" Ellie calls out to him.

I instantly feel sick because I know what is about to come.

"Yes, Princess?"

"You said you know a remedy, right?"

"Yes, I do, my mother used it all the time."

"Can you please do it? I'm in so much pain, help me."

"Sure Princess."

He looks at me with a smug look on his face.

All I want to do is slap that look right off his face. I reluctantly get up and Daniel slides in behind Ellie. He pulls her close to him. His lips are very close to her lips.

"What are you doing?"

Her voice is weak.

He keeps inching closer.

"It's okay, Princess, it'll all be over in a couple of seconds, just trust me."

He leans closer and his lips are practically brushing against hers.

I'm sweating now. I've failed within the first couple of minutes of the spell being active. There's nothing I can do. If I attack him, I will have to explain why I was so violent toward him. That's only if I'm not whisked away to be hung. I can only stand there and hope some divine intervention happens and the kiss can't happen. He gets closer. I close my eyes. I can't watch.

"What's going on? Daniel, what the hell are you doing?"

The Prince comes bursting through the doors. I have never been happier to see him. Daniel jumps up from the bed. I'm laughing silently on the inside.

"James?" Ellie whispers his name and it's the sweetest name I have heard in a long time.

"Yes, baby, I'm here," says the Prince.

I didn't know the Prince's first name was James. Right now, that doesn't matter. The only thing that matters is he's here on time. One day down, two more to go. He automatically takes his place with Ellie in his lap, rocking her back and forth.

"Daniel, we'll talk about what I've seen later. For now, can you please go and fetch the Doctor."

"Right away," says Daniel as I start to snicker.

Daniel leaves the room and I'm now able to breathe. That was too close of a call.

"Anastasia, what happened? What was he trying to do to my wife and why were you just sitting there letting him do it?"

"It was out of my control. He said he had a remedy that

his mother used all the time and when I told him we would wait for you Ellie opposed and asked him to try."

"Is this true, Ellie?"

Ellie nods.

The Prince looks hurt. I can tell by his face he doesn't know what's going on but he feels as if he's losing his wife physically and mentally.

Ellie passes out in his arms.

I run to her side and check her pulse. Her pulse has slowed down again and her breathing is slow and even. She's still burning up. The Prince starts to cry. I don't know if the tears are from the fact that she's slowly fading away or if he's crying because of what he saw with Daniel.

The next instant the doctor enters the room and begins examining Ellie and taking vital signs. I take this as a perfect opportunity to leave the room to go find Sam. I'll check on Ellie later.

After about half an hour and a lot of stairs later, I finally find the garden. I don't know who's responsible for putting this together, but it's breathtaking. I didn't know some of these flowers even existed! I'm particularly drawn to this bright, vibrant, yellow rose. When I look at this rose it makes me feel calm. I touch the petals and it feels soft and delicate. I pick the flower and smell it. It smells sweet and pure. If only my life reflected the life of this rose.

"Beautiful, isn't it?"

I jump and quickly turn around, ready to face my aggressor, but I see Sam standing there smiling.

"Don't do that!"

"I'm sorry; I've been waiting for you to join me. This was a lesson, you should always keep your guard up, especially when it comes to the people that you have associated yourself with."

I'm annoyed. I didn't come up here for a lecture. I came for information. I place the yellow flower in my hair and sit down on a nearby rock, ready to receive whatever this woman has to tell me.

"Yes, Anastasia, I know you are annoyed right now, but I promise I'm not telling you something I wouldn't tell my own daughter. You have to trust me when I say that you are inadvertently involved with a lot of things that are beyond your realm of thinking. Ms. Hannon is not who you think she is."

"I've already figured that out. Tell me something I don't know."

"I'm Ellie's mother, that's why I need your help. I don't want to see my child dead before she can even start to live."

I'm floored. I wasn't expecting this. Ellie's mother is a Fairy Godmother? If that is the case why does she not possess any magical powers? Why didn't she retaliate when we treated her so badly? My head is spinning with this new information.

"Why didn't you come for her sooner?"

"Believe it or not, she had to go through what she went through with your family in order to be put into the position she is in now. Her life and what happens hence forth deals with a lot more than what you humans can see. I had to leave her father in order to try to destroy Ms. Hannon. I knew what was to come and I had a chance to stop it if I killed Ms. Hannon. So, by me leaving him, it kept him and Ellie safe for a while. When the turmoil between me and Ms. Hannon got too heated I sent word to my husband that I died trying to protect them. It broke my heart watching him remarry and have other children while I was still alive. When he died, it killed me more because I had never had a chance to say goodbye. To this day I still do not know what happened to him."

She stops and wipes a tear away from her eye. After she regains her composure, she continues.

"If I had my way I would have killed you guys the night my child was made into a common slave in order to accommodate all your selfish needs. Watching you tear her to shreds the night she wanted to go to the ball almost made me lose it. Everyone almost lost their life that day, instead, I interceded. I wasn't supposed to, but I had to if everything was to go back to normal. Now, because I interceded, it has allowed witches with ill intent to gain more power. To know who Ellie really is. It has thrown off the balance of good and evil. You are the only person who can help her. As much as I don't like it, I'm stating facts."

I don't want to believe it. I'm in the same room as Ellie's mother. She's a gorgeous woman, a little on the plump side, but other than that really beautiful. I see where Ellie gets her looks. The garden becomes awkwardly silent. I find it ironic that we are having such a dark and ugly conversation in a place that is so beautiful.

"Anything else I need to know?"

"I don't have anything else to tell you, but maybe you can help me. What is her first name?"

At this question, I'm speechless. I never really thought about it. I always seem to call her honey, baby, or sweetie. These pet names embodied the way I feel about her. Come to think of it, I've never heard of another name besides Ms. Hannon. How could I give someone the most sacred part of me and not know her first name?

"I don't know."

"Nobody knows. This has been an ongoing mystery for hundreds of years. It's said if you utter her first name it will strip her of all her power and all of the curses and spells that have been administered by her will be destroyed."

"What good is that for Ellie? The spell was administered by her son, not by her."

"Her spell book is an ongoing spell. Do you think there is a guardian that comes out of all spell books? No, that whole book is a spell. She has some powerful dark magic in that book. That book is able to spit out messages that become prophetic and eventually into fruition. When you got your first prophetic message from that book it was not written into the book of prophecy until a day later."

"So you mean to tell me that I could have had a normal life? You mean to tell me that I had a choice to be involved?"

"Yes and no. You see, although that prophecy was not written into the book of prophesies, there is another one in there that deals with you and this situation. It has been written that you are to guard Ellie with your life. Her life is now your life until you die, she dies, or she is out of imminent danger."

"Why didn't you come to me sooner?"

"Name one time you were away from Ms. Hannon long enough for me to approach you. I'll wait."

She's right. Ms. Hannon and I have been inseparable for these past five months. Now, I see why.

"Does every witch have access to the book of prophecy?"

"Yes, and I really think she used what she read about you to her advantage."

How does she do that? She's able to read my thoughts as if they are plastered on a billboard and then address them in her next statement. Weird.

"What should I do?"

"I'll tell you what you need to do. You need to go on with life as usual. Also, you will need to go see the Muffin Man. Do you know the Muffin Man?"

"The Muffin Man?"

"The Muffin Man. He lives on the corner of Drury lane."

"Yes, I have been to his cart a time or two to get bread. What about him?"

"Not today, but sometime this week you need to go see

the Muffin Man. He will not only have information on how to defeat Ms. Hannon, but he might have some information you may find interesting."

"Why can't you go? Why does it have to be me?"

"I know where he lives, but he has taken himself out of the magical world so that he may live as a mortal. He has all kinds of charms and spells surrounding his place so that no one of magic can step foot into his house. Believe me; I've tried to contact him for years. I can only speak to him if he contacts me first and in this case, I need you to get in touch with him a little sooner than that."

"What is he?"

"He is a wizard. "

"Why did he leave the magical world?"

"That's something you can ask him. I will be back in touch with you, If you want to live until then, you need to remember three things: One, you did not see me. Two, act as if everything is normal. Three, go see the Muffin Man."

Before I could ask any other questions she disappeared.

"What are you doing up here by yourself?"

I turn around to see Ms. Hannon standing behind me watching me intently.

"I was just wandering around the castle and found this place. I'm kind of sad for Ellie and the fact that I cannot do anything for her at this moment."

"But you can do something for her! Stop that kiss! The Prince told me what happened. He is really upset with Daniel."

"I don't blame him."

"I'm glad I found you though. There is something I want to talk to you about.

"What is it?"

"I need you to go see someone for me tomorrow. I need some more bread and he has the best bread in town. He is known as the Muffin Man and he lives on the corner of

Drury lane. Not only do I need bread but I need you to take this note to him as well."

This is working out better than I thought.

"Sure, I can do that for you. Why can't you come with me?"

"The Muffin Man and I have history. I don't want to disturb him, just give him a message. Besides, I have a lot of work to do around the castle. I will look after Ellie. I need you to go early in the morning."

I nod. I guess I am off to see the Muffin Man who lives on Drury Lane.

I awaken the next morning and the house smells heavenly. I get up, take a shower, and brush my teeth. I put on my clothes and prepare to go see the Muffin Man. I don't know what to expect. I'm nervous and excited at the same time. Sam's voice is going through my head. I keep hearing her say "He might have some information that you will find interesting." Just by her saying that I have a feeling that she knows something that I don't, but this seems to be the norm around here. When did my life become so important? I wonder if when my mother gave birth to me she knew what she was giving birth to. That I would grow up and be someone who has the lives of so many people in the palm of her hand.

I walk into the kitchen and Ms. Hannon has cooked so much food. She has made eggs, bacon, toast, cheesy grits, coffee, fresh squeezed orange juice, and a plethora of other things that make my mouth water as soon as I walk into the room. I sit down at the table and Ms. Hannon sets a plate down in front of me. I immediately start to eat. This is some of the best food I have ever had in life. If she wasn't such a manipulator I could really see myself growing old with this woman, but I know it will never happen. I finish my food and am now sipping on the orange juice. Ms. Hannon sits down in front of me sipping coffee. There is an air of awkwardness between us. Someone needs to break the silence and I feel as if it needs to be me.

"What is your first name? Don't you find it awkward that I keep calling you Ms. Hannon after we have been damn near married for the past five months?"

She shifts uncomfortably in her chair.

"I don't have a first name."

"Bullshit. I have been nothing but honest with you. I have given you all of me and I can't know your first name?"

"Where is this question coming from, Anastasia?"

"I've been thinking about it for a while. I mean, I'm supposed to save Ellie and I'm supposed to stop your son? Has anyone stopped to think that maybe I don't want to do all of these things? That maybe I want to be normal? I'm supposed to give up my life for another and all I want is for the person with whom I'm intimate to tell me her first name! I don't think I've asked for much out of this whole ordeal. All I want to know is what to call my lover. I'm not your child, I'm not your servant, I'm your woman and every time I call you Ms. Hannon I feel as if I'm working for you rather than lying in bed with you every night. I want to be able to call you something other than "Sweetie" or "Baby." I don't think that's too much to ask. Do you?"

Ms. Hannon is staring at me with a weird look. I don't know if she's happy, mad, or turned on. It's the kind of look that makes you want to do naughty things and then cry about it later. For the life of me I cannot figure this woman out. After a long silence she finally speaks in a whispered tone.

"I cannot tell you my first name. As much as I want to tell you, I can't."

"Why?"

"There are some things that happened in my past that I'm

not too proud of. Because of my actions, my first name has been laced with a curse."

"Why not give people another first name to use?"

"It's a little more complex than that, Anastasia."

Her nose starts to flare, but I'm no longer afraid.

"Then simplify it for me."

"Leave it alone, Anastasia, you're treading on dangerous ground and you will not like the outcome. Now, for the last time, leave it alone if you know what's best for you!"

There is electricity in the air. Ms. Hannon's eyes flash and they are now black as coal. Her sweet demeanor has left and is now replaced with the heart of a killer. If looks could kill I would be fading into ashes at this point. I'm not afraid. If anything, this has just confirmed what Sam told me and helped me pick a side. If I wasn't sure before, I am sure now. I will just keep playing the field until this has passed. Hopefully, I can find my happily ever after once this is done. But I do know one thing; it will not be with Ms. Hannon.

I hold her icy gaze letting her know that I am not afraid of her. I casually grab my plate, take it to the sink, go to the refrigerator to grab a carrot, and walk right past Ms. Hannon out the front door. I have to go and find the Muffin Man.

I walk toward the stable and get my trusty horse, Misty. I start to saddle her so I can prepare to go see the Muffin Man. I give her the carrot I got out of the refrigerator. She happily chews the carrot as I do my routine inspection. Why is he called the Muffin Man? Are his muffin's spectacular? That is just a weird name. Then again, I thought that calling Ms. Hannon by just her last name was normal and look where that has gotten me. I'm finally done with my inspection and ready to take Misty into town. I climb on top of this magnificent beast and pull the reins so I can steer her in the right direction. I didn't fully get out of the stable before Ms. Hannon steps right in front of Misty.

"Anastasia, please, don't leave yet, let's talk about what just happened."

"What is your first name?" I ask her coolly.

Again, she gives me that icy glare.

"I can't tell you my first name nor why I can't give you my first name."

"Then we have nothing to talk about."

"Please, don't be mad at me. I'm sorry. Let me make it up to you."

"No, I have to go and see the "Muffin Man" as you call him. As far as I can see, you cannot say, nor do, anything to erase what just happened. If looks could kill and if you would have had your way, I would have been dead just now."

I give Misty the signal to trot forward. Ms. Hannon moves out of the way and allows me to pass. I let out of a sigh of relief because I didn't want to run her over with Misty, but I was prepared to do so if necessary. As I ride off toward town I turn around briefly to see Ms. Hannon standing in the middle of the road watching me leave. A couple of months ago I would have thought it was sweet, but now, it leaves an eerie feeling that something is about to happen; something that she cannot control.

It takes me most of the day, but I finally find the whereabouts of the Muffin Man. He is nestled right between the woods and the outskirts of town. To the untrained eye it would look like an old cottage, but to me there is something odd about it. It's pretty dated but there is a beautiful creek right next to the house and the water is being moved by a working watermill that looks oddly new. There's a path that looks as if it has been freshly laid and although it looks as if no one has set foot in cottage due to the cobwebs and the weeds popping up along the path; the cottage itself looked shabby chic. I have to give it to the Muffin Man, he has mastered the art of low key decorating.

I inch Misty closer to the cottage. I tie her to an old tree trunk and walk toward the house. As I walk closer, the air gets thicker and thicker and the cottage gets more and more updated. Suddenly, I'm just mere feet from the door when I discover that I'm frozen in place. I can't move an inch. I can't move forward or backwards. I'm just stuck. Suddenly, the door swings open. I try to call out to the inhabitant but no words come forth. As I'm trying to find a way to communicate, a gorgeous man appears in the doorway. He is the color of cinnamon with short black hair. Although he wears tattered clothing it doesn't take away from his handsomeness. He is gorgeous. He is over six feet tall, chiseled arms, and a baby face that could make any mother forget about her wayward children at home. His eyes are the color of jade with full lips and perfect teeth that only make you imagine what it would be like to be bitten by him. He is nothing short of a god and I'm instantly smitten.

He walks straight up to me and I couldn't help but to go back and forth between his eyes and his lips. I have a weird mixture of sensations. I'm both terrified and aroused. He starts chanting something slow and steady. Although I can't hear him I can tell it's serious because of the scowl plastered on his face. Suddenly, I feel a pain in my stomach that rises to my chest and then to my throat. Without sound, a strange being erupts from my mouth. The stranger's mouth begins to move faster as his face becomes more intense. The being is levitating before me, squirming in pain. As his mouth moves faster the being squirms harder. Suddenly, the being explodes in midair with a tiny pop. As soon as I hear the pop I fall onto the ground at the feet of this stranger. He helps me up and looks me in my eyes. I feel as if I will melt.

"Do you know what that was?"

"What, the being?"

"Yes, do you know what it was?"

"No, I have no idea."

He steps backs and rubs his meaty hands along his chin.

"That was a Linx. It has the ability to insert itself inside of you and link your emotions, thoughts, and actions to another person. So, in essence, everything you say, think, and do is on display to whoever inserted this being in you. Also, they have the power to control your actions and make it seem as if it was your intention."

I'm flabbergasted.

"Do you know who would have done this?"

"I have an idea." I say, instantly thinking of Ms. Hannon. "Before I give you that name, tell me, how long can those beings live inside of you?"

"They can live in you forever and you will never know. By the look of the one that I just killed, I will say that it had to have been at least six months old."

I'm floored. That is around the time I killed my mother and my sister. Could I have just been used to kill my family to make it seem as if I had no one so I could fulfill this prophecy? I feel sick. My life has become nothing more than a puppet show. I have no idea who to believe at this moment. I'm shattered. I look up to see him studying my face. I feel inclined to ask him if he knows about me and why I'm here. Instead I ask him something else that's weighing on my mind.

"Do you know someone by the name of Ms. Hannon?"

"Yes, she is not permitted to enter my grounds. Why do you ask?"

"Because, I think that might be the person who gave me the Linx."

A flash of anger is shown through his eyes.

I'm now afraid.

"What are you here for? Are you a friend of Hannon? I do not serve her kind here!"

He grabs me with his big hands and starts shaking me.

"Tell me why you are here or I will kill you with my bare hands!"

"Sam sent me!" I say through tears. I'm now regretting coming here at all. With the mention of her name he puts me down gently and instructs me to stay here.

I don't want to stay but I know I must in order to find out what I need to know. If it was just my life at stake I would have run until I got home. All I want to do is go home and curl up in the bed I share with Ms. Hannon and sleep. I want to pretend like my life is normal and I'm not caught between the forces of good and evil. I want to be a normal woman again where all I have to worry about is cleaning, organizing, and what is going to be for dinner. I want a real romance where I don't have to worry about whether the person loves me or not. In my heart, I know this will never be.

My life was forever changed the day that Drusilla sent me on that errand. Maybe she knew I was destined to fail. Maybe, she's watching me from wherever she is now, cackling at all the pain that I'm going though. He returns a couple of minutes later and approaches me to give me a hug.

"I'm sorry for how I treated you earlier. I just spoke with Sam. She told me she sent you. Come inside. I have some fresh bread that I just took out of the oven and some soup I made earlier. You can eat while I tell you the story of the Hannon's and where you and I fit into this ordeal.

"You and I?"

"Yes, you and I. Anastasia, I know you're tired of hearing of prophecy, but it is written that you are to be my wife."

I'm stunned. How can I be the wife of this gorgeous man? I'm short, I'm frumpy, and I have stringy hair and features that are not so memorable. How can I ever compare to any woman that could possible want this man?

He motions for me to follow him.

As I sit at the table I see my reflection in the glass plate.

Recently, my mother made me think of myself as not beautiful because of my weight. I've heard people tell me that I have a gorgeous face but an ugly waist, but my mother, when Ellie lived with us, told me it was lies. When Ellie left that all changed. She started repeating everything that the townspeople were saying. It never matter that people said that I only had an ugly waistline. I only heard the word ugly and applied it to my entire being. After months of being told that I'm hideous, stupid, and worthless by my mom and my sister, I slowly started to believe it. But, then again, they said the same things to Ellie for years and look at her now.

Maybe there is hope for me. I must be important. Look at how many prophecies are revolved around me! I think they knew what my life would be and tried to break me down, but it hasn't worked. I've actually become stronger than I thought I would ever be. Maybe I need to just open my heart and start to live for me instead of the approval of other people. Maybe I could start with him. I start to smile at the thought of those chiseled arms picking me up and handling me in a more gentle way. I shiver slightly.

"Are you cold?" He asks me as he comes in with a tray that has two piping hot bowls of soup and a loaf of bread. He sets the tray down and sits across from me at the table.

"No, I was just thinking of something." I start to smile and blush.

"What were you thinking about?" He also starts to smile.

"Nothing important."

"Everything about you is important."

I blush a deeper shade of red.

"I thought I would never meet you. The prophecy has so many forks in it that it was a big possibility we would not end up together. Secretly, I hoped we would. I have watched you for years, Anastasia. I never approached you because you were always with your mother or your sister. I've always thought you were beautiful.

"You're beautiful, I'm plain."

"Everything about you is beautiful. You have just had some bad influences that made you think differently."

"You can say that again."

"Here, eat."

He takes one of the bowls off the tray and hands it to me. It looks so delicious. It has chunks of meat, vegetables, and a dark broth. He then takes the knife off the tray to slice the bread before placing it on a tray and handing it to me. I look at him and the food with a quizzical look.

"Why are you looking at me this way?"

"Last time I accepted food from a stranger I ended up with a lynx killing my mother and my sister. What will happen this time?" I raise my eyebrow for effect.

He does not look at all phased by what I've said.

"What you did was not done by you. There is no judgement here." He takes a piece of the bread for effect and eats it. "I ensure you, it is safe. Please eat. In my culture it's rude not to eat when food has been offered. While you're eating I'll tell you my story. Is that okay with you?"

"Sure."

"Alright, first off, let me start by giving you my name. My name is Jesus De La Rosa but I'm known to most as the Muffin Man. I'm considered one of the best bakers around. I actually have a cart that sells my bread and baked goods to the townspeople every day. I took a young boy that was without parents and a place to stay and I made him the face of my baked goods. Have you ever heard of Bread of Life?"

"Yes, that's my favorite place to get…"

"Scones, I know. I used to not bake them as much but when I realized that was your favorite thing on the cart I made a special batch for you every morning."

I'm shocked as my face turns bright red. I can't believe someone would go out of their way to make sure I was happy. I get hungry thinking about those scones. They are literally the best baked goods around. I really like the young man who works the cart; but something told me that he was not the one baking all those goods.

He continues with his story.

"I'm what you call a wizard. It's like a male witch. I left the magical realm years ago after Hannon came to power. Sam and I actually put our powers together to try and defeat the one who calls herself Hannon. We were really close. We researched old prophecies and found the one that mentioned a spell that was put on Hannon when she was a young girl. Apparently, someone knew what she was going to become and put a curse on her first name. It's said that whoever says her name three times will instantly kill her and her descendants. It's also said that if you say her name three times backwards it will only kill her and not her descendants."

Now the conversation from this morning makes sense.

"Can't you just reach out to the woman who initially put the curse on Ms. Hannon?"

"I would, but it's not that easy, she has disappeared from the face of the earth. That's where you come in. The story suggests there is a locket that has a picture of her mother and father. On this locket, her name is engraved. If we find the locket, we kill the witch."

"And if we do not find the locket?"

"Then we find the woman who casted the spell or we're in trouble."

This is too heavy. My mind cannot comprehend what is going on right now.

"I see that your mind is overloaded with questions. It's written all over your face. Let me start from the beginning."

"That would be best."

"A long time ago there was a King and a Queen who ruled the magical realm. They ensured that peace and harmony existed between the different species. Well, one day, the King and the Queen both fell suddenly ill and died. At the time no one made any connections until it was discovered that Hannon was the cook. Hannon was always a bad egg and was widely hated throughout the whole magical realm due to her constant trickery and scamming. The whole magical realm went into an uproar but Hannon fought with her army of followers and won. She overthrew the kingdom and began to rule with hate. Evil began to flourish and eventually annihilated any good left in the magical realm. There were talks of rebellion but the leaders of these movements always ended up dead so everyone stopped trying and lived under the thumb of Hannon."

"That's awful!"

"I know; there's more. Hannon thought that she was untouchable and that no one could dethrone her and she would be the ruler of the magical realm forever until one of her prophetess came to her and told her of a problem."

"What was the problem?"

"Sam. Sam was the problem. At least that is what my father said; I was too young to remember any of this. My parents did a good job sheltering me. No one thought she could get pregnant by a mortal. She was, and still is, one of the most beautiful fairies known in the magical realm. Once Hannon gained control, Sam fled. Hannon was jealous of her looks and the attention she always received. She thought Sam was a threat and offered a bounty for her head. Sam then fled to the mortal world with the help of my father after an unfortunate run in with Hannon. My father taught her how to bake and she started the bakery cart. My father gave her the money, she sold the goods. She met her husband while working as an attendant for my bakery cart. He was a wealthy man so she never had to worry about money after that. He courted her, they fell in love, got married, and lo and behold she got pregnant with Ellie. It took Hannon six long years to find out about Ellie only because my family threw Hannon off of her scent. During the time she was looking for Ellie there were people who wanted to overthrow her. Eventually there were enough people to run her out of the magical realm and put things back in order, kind of."

This story is getting more interesting by the minute. I'm intrigued.

"How did she find out?"

"She found out from her son, Daniel. One day he was playing around with the infamous spell book of Hannon and accidently came to the page that foretold of the prophetic message regarding both him and Ellie. She kept sneaking back into the magical realm and searching all throughout the land for Ellie, not knowing whose daughter she was. She thought if she could find Ellie and have her and her son marry she could use that marriage to gain favor back into the magical realm and eventually rule again. Finally she summoned the powers of dark magic to reveal more information about the child. The child was protected by a spell so that her whereabouts were not known, but it did show who her parents were. Sam found out and left her family behind in hopes of killing Hannon before she destroyed her family.

Sam left her husband and a young Ellie with the excuse that she was going to go help family. She knew she could never return because Ellie would die if she did. So, she sent word that she died. Years later, after your father married and had your sister and then you there was another prophetic message that foretold of your involvement with Ellie. Once again Hannon tried to find you but could not because you were not born with magical abilities. I don't know how, but she found out that your father was Ellie's father as well and planned on killing all of you except Ellie. She planned on keeping Ellie locked up until she was able to wed her son, bear a child, and then kill her. The trouble with that is simply that your father traveled a lot for business. So, she killed your father out of anger because he would not lead her back to you and Ellie. She never gave up looking for either one of you and in the end, both of you just fell into her lap."

I'm shocked, I'm angry, and I'm hurt. *Ms. Hannon killed my father? How was I supposed to take that information and digest it? Am I supposed to go on living in her cottage thinking that we are the perfect couple, all the while knowing that she killed the one person in my life who loved me unconditionally?* Rage is boiling over and all I have on my mind is death. There is an uncomfortable silence between us.

Finally, he breaks the silence. "Do you want to talk about it?"

"No."

"It'll make you feel better."

"I said no!"

I start to cry. Jesus comes around the table and wraps his big arms around me as he comforts me. I wail harder. It feels like an eternity when I finally stop. I look up at him and he is looking down at me with a look on concern on his face. My face turns red. I'm embarrassed as I detangle myself from his arms.

"What's wrong?"

"Nothing,"

I turn my back toward him and look out the window. It is such a pretty view. From there, I can see Misty casually grazing. I feel his presence behind me. He places his large hands on my delicate shoulders and turns me around. He then places his finger beneath my chin and lifts it up so that our eyes meet.

"You have nothing to be ashamed of. I think you're beautiful even when you cry. I know what you're feeling and everything will be made right in due time."

I nod my head slowly as I look deep into his grey eyes. I don't know what comes over me. I don't know if it's simply the fact that I'm emotional or if it's due to the fact that he is just so handsome, but I kiss him. I kiss him like there is no tomorrow. He places his arms around me and he kisses me back just as hard. There is electricity in the air and something in my body tells me that this is right. This is where I'm supposed to be and whom I'm supposed to be with.

The kiss gets deeper, I feel that same sensation that I felt with Ms. Hannon on the first night and I like it. He picks me up and I place my legs around his waist. With one swift movement he pushes everything onto the floor and places me on top of the table. I help him take off his shirt. His muscles look even more tantalizing with no clothes. He helps me unbutton my blouse and pulls down my pants. I'm in front of him naked and unashamed. He slowly takes off his trousers without his eyes ever leaving mine. Finally, I break the eye contact as my eyes travel lower. I am surprised by what I see. *Is it supposed to be that big? That thing is supposed to go where?* I look at him with panic in my eyes but all he does is smile.

"Mi Amour, you have nothing to worry about, trust me."

He lays me down on the table and kisses me slowly and caresses my body with kisses. I'm going crazy. My body is yearning but I don't know what for. This is the first time I've ever been with a man and I feel after today it won't be the last.

He positions himself between my legs. Suddenly, I feel some of the worse pain I've felt in my life, worse than the night with Hannon. I scream. He hushes me with kisses and ensures me it's going to be okay. He takes it slow. The pain subsides and now it's pleasurable. This is the best feeling I have ever felt in my life. He changes up the tempo and I vibe with him. I feel this weird sensation bubbling up. I can't control it. I. Need. To. Release. This. The sensation comes forth and it is the most beautiful feeling in the world. I cannot begin to describe it. All I know is that I want more. He picks me up and carries me into the bedroom. It's dark so I can't see the décor but I don't care about décor right now, I just want him. He lays me on what I think is the bed and continues to take me to a place where there is no good, no evil, no death, no hurt, nor any pain. It's just me, him, and this feeling that keeps erupting over and over again.

Hours later we are tangled in the covers. I'm lying in his arms and he's caressing my head.

This feels so right yet so wrong.

"How do I know that you are not trying to use me?"

"How do I know that you are not trying to use me?" He asks, chuckling. "I am the one with the best goods around in and out of the house."

"No, I'm serious. How do I know that you are not going to end up like Ms. Hannon? How do I know that you are not going to use me as a pawn to get to your ultimate goal? How can I know that your feelings are real?"

"Anastasia, I have loved you since I first saw you. Even before I saw the prophecy I knew you were mine. I don't know what everyone else has done to you, but let me love you, please?"

Tears start rolling down my face. No one has ever been this genuine before. Ms. Hannon was like this at first but she changed. I don't know why, but I trust this man.

"What does the prophecy say?"

"To summarize, it says, that once this is all over we will be together with kids. Now, I can show you the prophecy if you want."

"Maybe another day; right now, there are more pressing matters. I have to go back to Ms. Hannon and act like nothing happened, don't I?"

"Unfortunately, yes. If Ms. Hannon knew what we did and what I told you she would kill you without any remorse. What did she send you here for anyway?"

"Bread."

"I'll get the bread ready. Go ahead and wash up and get dressed. You have to leave soon."

He grabs my hand.

"Just know that if it was up to me, you would stay here forever."

He lets go and heads into the kitchen. I look around the room; same as all the other rooms. Spacious, with mostly brown coloring, but in this room the accent color is red. It gives the room a very sensual feel. The bed is huge. I could get lost in it for days. I mean, he has to have a big bed, he is a big man. I go to the bathroom which is accented with white and wash up. I get dressed and come out ready to go. He's waiting for me by the door with the bread.

"Why do they call you the Muffin Man?"

"I live on Drury Lane. I know you've heard the song."

We share a laugh.

"Seriously, why?"

"I'm called the Muffin Man because those are my specialty. Also, because I'm a small tempered guy but if you apply heat I expand just like a muffin. Depending on what kind of heat; it could be a good or bad thing. Moral of the story, don't ever apply heat unless I apply it first."

His look confuses me. I don't know if it's a sensual look or if I'm supposed to be slightly scared. I'm both.

"By the way, I was serious about not serving Hannon. The only reason I'm giving you this bread is because she is involved with you."

I blush.

"Oh, by the way, she told me to give you this note."

"Who?"

"Ms. Hannon."

He takes the note from me and as he reads it, his face turns white.

"You may have to come and live with me sooner rather than later just so I can protect you."

"Why?"

"Read this."

He hands me the note. Written on it is some of the most beautiful handwriting I have ever seen with the words:

> *"I know who you are,
> your time has come."*

CHAPTER SIX
Kiss of Doom
Ellie

As soon as the pain starts, it stops a short while later. I can't explain it but it feels as if my heart is wrenching. It feels like every emotion I have ever known comes rushing at me at once and it's too much to bear. All I can do is think about Daniel the entire time, which I know is wrong. My husband has been waiting on me hand and foot but I feel like my love for my husband is wavering. I don't know why. He has done nothing wrong. He has been the ideal husband, but he lacks the spontaneity that I have come to admire in Daniel. I know it's wrong, but I cannot help how I feel.

The doctor came in to see me and has put me on bed rest for a day just for observation purposes. It has been two days since I've felt Daniel's arms around me when he offered to give me a remedy that his mother performed on him years ago. Truth is, I didn't want the remedy, but I wanted a kiss.

I wanted to kiss those soft, succulent lips. I've never wanted something so bad in my life. What is wrong with me?

"How's my favorite patient?" James asks as he walks into the room.

"Fine."

"What's wrong?"

His constant questions are annoying me. I wish he would leave me alone.

"Nothing, I'm just tired."

As I say this I see my husband hang his head in defeat and my heart wrenches just a little. I don't mean to hurt him, I just don't love him like I love Daniel and I think he knows it. He knows I'm sitting here lying to him right now, but what else can I do? I don't feel like myself at all. How did I go from loving this man with all my heart to not standing the sight of him? I look him over and realize his hands are behind his back.

"What's behind your back?"

"Nothing, I just got something I thought would make you feel better."

He then takes his hands from behind his back and presents me with the most beautiful array of pink roses I've ever seen in my life and, instantly, I know where they are from.

I start to cry. That's all I can do. I'm so confused right now. I know for a fact these roses came from Daniel's garden on the roof.

He rushes to my side and tries to console me. I'm inconsolable and push him off as I scream for him to leave the room. He takes his time releasing me and then just stares at me with a look of defeat as I keep yelling for him to get out of the room.

As he looks at me I can see tears welling up in his eyes, but an angry scowl on his face. He turns on his heel abruptly and leaves the room, slamming the door behind him. I know he's angry. I'm angry too! How could he bring these flowers to me? It's like a cold, bitter, slap in the face. These roses remind me of the fact that I can't be with the person I truly love. If I can't have him, I'd rather die. I don't want to go through life if I can't have Daniel. I can't go on living a lie with the Prince. I decide that today will be the day I cease to exist. This room has become a prison to me and I refuse to be imprisoned any longer.

I get up and go to my closet. There are hundreds of gowns lined up there. I just need to find the perfect dress to die in. I search the racks and find a simple pink dress. It is an A-line cut and is very light and airy. The dress is very proper, yet casual. That's how I want to be remembered, the casual Princess.

I get undressed and go to the adjourning room which is our bathroom. It's lily white with gold features. It's truly an amazing bathroom. I decide to not take a bath because it will take too long so I opt to take a shower which is easier and quicker. If I'm going to die there's no need for me to smell bad while I do so. I get out of the shower, dry off, put on my feminine products, and finally spray myself with my signature fragrance. I then put on the dress and admire myself in the mirror. Gorgeous. I look in the mirror again and realize that I really should do my hair and makeup. If I don't do my hair and makeup people will look at my death as if someone else planned it. I need to look put together.

I walk out of the bathroom, onto my plush carpet toward my vanity. It's a cherry wood vanity with different jewels plastered around the large mirror. It's truly a sight for sore eyes and I love it. It literally takes up a good portion of the room with all of the makeup and jewelry that's contained in it. I sit in front of the vanity and put my hair in a high bun. I then put on blush, eyeshade, mascara, and nude lipstick that gives my lips just a little color. I look in the mirror and I look gorgeous. I wish Daniel could see me now.

I need jewelry. I look in one of the drawers and pull out

a gold necklace leading to a pink jewel. I then find a gold bracelet in the drawer to compliment the necklace. I then cross the room one more time to go back to the closet into the shoe section, where I pull down a pair of golden flats.

I go back into the bathroom and look at myself in the mirror. I twirl around a bit and I love what I see. I walk out of the bathroom and take one last look around the room. I will miss the big canopy bed the most.

I slowly walk across the room toward the large balcony doors. I open the doors and walk out onto the huge balcony. I go over to the railing and look at our Kingdom. I have everything a girl could ask for. I live in a castle, married to a handsome Prince, soon to be co-ruler of this big Kingdom, and I am a Princess. So why am I not happy?

I climb onto the railing as tears start to stream down my face. There is no point in living if I can't be happy. I outstretch my hands to either side of me. I open my eyes to take a mental picture of my Kingdom. It really is a perfect place to die. I close my eyes, takes a deep breath, let it go, and jump.

I come to and everything is white and I am elated. Am I dead? Did it work? Slowly, my vision starts to return and I see my Fairy Godmother looking over me with a concerned look on her face. Slowly my vision allows for the room I'm in to come into focus. I stare upward and see the tell-tale sign of my canopy bed. I look to the right and see the balcony doors still open. I look back at my Fairy Godmother and see that there are tears streaming down her face. I don't care if she is hurt, I'm angry.

"Why?"

I can't really say much else. My mouth is very dry and my

throat hurts. I want to scream, but the pain I'm in forces me to remain silent.

"I should be asking you the same thing, Ellie. Why would you do something so foolish as to try to take you own life? I gave you everything you wanted and you repay me with this disrespect for life!"

"I love him."

"Love who?"

"Daniel! I can't live my life without him! If I can't have him I don't want to live!"

"Ellie, what is wrong with you? This is what you wanted! You are telling me that you want to throw it all away for some fling with someone who is known around the Kingdom for breaking hearts!"

"It's not some fling, it's love!"

I try to sit up in bed to emphasize my point but it only cripples me. I am in so much pain.

Why did she save me?

"Come here, child."

She puts her hand underneath my chin and looks into my eyes. She gasps and whispers the words, "Amore Fatal."

"What is that?"

"A very powerful spell used to invoke love."

"You're lying!"

"I'm not lying. Just like I'm not lying when I say I thought you were dead. You jumped and landed sprawled on the ground. You were unconscious, but still breathing. I got you back up to your room, did some healing incantations then changed you into a night shirt. You might be sore for a few days, but other than that you will live."

"What don't you understand? I don't want to live!"

"Yes, you do, Ellie! This is not you talking, this is the spell! Don't you see! You were happy before today. You and the Prince were in bliss!"

"I've never been happy! He bores me. I want excitement

and that's what Daniel gives to me. I knew that I loved him from the first kiss."

The room gets quiet. It's a couple of minutes before she speaks.

"When did you kiss him, Ellie?"

"Some months back, but I knew then and I have never been surer of anything in my life!"

She gets up and paces the floor. She's making me nervous. I don't know what she's thinking.

"You have to understand me when I say that being with Daniel is not going to be sunshine and roses. If you leave the Prince for Daniel there are a lot of lives at stake. You have to believe me when I say that Daniel and his whole family are toxic. If you kiss him within the next day or so, you are signing your death certificate. Don't do it."

"Why should I believe you?"

"Ellie, just please believe me. You have to fight this."

"What if I don't want to? I have nothing to lose! I don't have any family left. The only person who is close to family is Anastasia and, even though I've forgiven her, I don't trust her. I love Daniel. He completes me. If I can't have him or the life I want I don't want to live. You're all knowing; tell me one reason why I have to live."

"For me, Ellie, live for me."

"Who are you? A magical person who goes around granting wishes? Someone who put me in this compromising situation? My Fairy Godmother! Nothing more! You will never be anything more to me than that! There is an uncomfortable silence in the room for a moment. Tears are welling up in her eyes and I am confused. Finally, after a couple of moments, she speaks.

"Ellie. There are some things I have not told you. First off, I would prefer for you not to call me Fairy Godmother anymore, but Sam, if you choose to not call me by my other name.

"What other name?" I ask.

"Mother."

The room goes silent.

"I don't understand."

"Ellie, I am your mother."

The breath leaves my body. Did this woman just say that she is my mother? For years I've gone through this world alone and I've had family all along? I'm sick to my stomach. Tears start to stream down my face. How could she come to me and tell me that lie? My mother died when I was young. I don't even remember what she looked like. I don't even remember her name. My father died some years later. Even if she is my mother, why would she wait so long to say something to me?

I'm so confused. I want Daniel, but having him could potentially mean that I will die. I love the Prince, but he's not as exciting as I'd like him to be. Anastasia and I have reconciled and are on the verge of a great friendship, but I don't trust her. Ms. Hannon flat out does not like me for whatever reason. It just seems like all the people surrounding me either wants me for something or I have mixed feelings about them. I'm tired. All I want to do is lie down and forget this day even happened. I want to die and I resent Sam for saving my life. Isn't her job to give me what I want?

"Why are you telling me this?"

"Because I love you and I want you to live. I want to have grandchildren. I didn't do all of this fighting for you to just die."

"What were you fighting for because it certainly wasn't me? Where were you when I was scrubbing floors? Where were you when I was getting beat whenever I didn't do something right? Where were you when I was crying into my pillow at night? Where were you when I wished I was dead because no one loved me? WHERE WERE YOU?"

The room is silent for a while before Sam finally speaks.

"I couldn't come to you, but I watched you. I was there when you cried. I was there when you were doing the work. Those times when you felt you could not go on, it was my love and power that kept you going. The mice you spoke to, I created them. You were never alone, I just couldn't come to you. I'm sorry I didn't tell you sooner. I just needed to make sure you were ready to hear the information."

"You tell me this *after* I try to take my life? You sure do have some great timing, Mother!"

I instantly regret the words as soon as they leave my mouth. She has a look of pure defeat on her face. Then, she starts to cry. I didn't want to make her cry. I don't even know why I'm crying right now. I should be dead. Dead people don't cry and that's how I feel right now, dead.

"I deserved that."

She wipes away her tears, clears her throat, and starts talking to me again.

"There are some things I need to explain to you. Once I explain things to you it will all make sense why I did what I did. It's not safe right now. It's not safe for you to even know I'm your mother. There are some powerful beings who are after me and if they knew you were my daughter it would be very detrimental. Please, just take heed to what I'm about to tell you.

The first thing is Ms. Hannon is not your friend. Please don't look at her as such. She has some ulterior motives that I don't have the time to explain. If she asks, you haven't seen me. If you want to live, you need to know that you can't tell her that you've seen me, for the sake of you and your future children. Secondly, please don't put yourself in a situation where you and Daniel are alone. I understand right now you are confused, but this spell that has been put on you is bigger than whatever feelings you may be having right now. Third, Anastasia is the *only* person you can trust right now. Believe me, what she did to you when you were younger was not her doing. When someone watches someone for a long time they mimic what they see. Anastasia has a pure heart that was clouded by the hatred of other people. Last, but not least, know that I love you. I know right now you don't understand why I did what I did but, I promise you, you will thank me for it when this is all over."

She leans over, kisses me on the forehead, and disappears. Not even two seconds later Ms. Hannon comes bursting through the door with a tray in her hands.

"Are you ok, Princess?"

"Yes, I'm fine, just a bit sore."

"I was coming up here to bring you breakfast as instructed by the Prince and I thought I heard another voice in here."

"No ma'am. It was just me. I was just reading and sometimes I like to read aloud so that is what you probably heard.

"Then where is the book?"

"Right here on my bed."

Sure enough there is a book there. I silently thank Sam in my head.

"Why are you coming in here questioning me?"

"I am not questioning you, Princess Ellie, I was just concerned. I'm sorry if you were offended, I just have your best interest at heart."

I really want to believe her but something in me is telling me not to.

"Thank you for breakfast, but I really just want to rest right now."

"Sure, I will leave your food right next to your bed. If you need anything else, let me know."

"Yes, I do need something. When you see Anastasia can you please tell her to come and see me?"

"Sure, she has not returned from an errand I sent her on earlier today, but as soon as she comes in I will send her up."

"Thank you."

With that, I snuggle in my bed and get some much needed rest. I mean, I did just die and was resurrected all in the same day no thanks to my mother, so I would think that rest is essential at this point. That is weird to say and to think about. My mother is alive and she's a fairy? Does that mean I have magical powers? I'm so confused with life. Although I tried to take my life today I'm kind of glad that she brought me back. I need to be here for the Prince. She's right; I need to forget about Daniel because it will be nothing but trouble for me. I keep telling myself that I don't love Daniel and that I will be perfectly fine without him and content with the Prince. As I lay down I keep telling my heart to believe the lie that my head is repeating, but my heart refuses to listen. Finally, with a mind full of problems, a heart full of pain, and eyes full of tears, I fitfully fall asleep.

I awaken hours later and it's dark in the room and I have the feeling someone staring at me. I instantly start to panic until I hear the Prince's voice.

"I came up to check on you, love. How are you feeling?"

"I am doing better than before. Thank you for checking on me."

He kisses me on my forehead and I feel an ease of tension.

"Anything for you."

He smiles at me and I feel the butterflies in my stomach. I love this man and I don't know why I ever doubted it.

"I wanted to come up and tell you goodbye personally."

"Where are you going?"

I start to panic. Sam's words resound in my head. I can't be left alone with Daniel and I can't prevent that if James isn't here.

"I am going to the next town for business. I'll be back later today, I promise."

He leans down and gives me a kiss on the lips.

"Bye, I'll see you when you get back."

"Alright, lie down and get some more sleep. You'll need it when I get back. I love you"

"I love you, too."

He winks at me as he leaves the room. I pull the covers up to my chin and tuck myself into bed. I decide I need more sleep. As I'm snuggling back into my bed I hear the door open and I start to smile. I guess he wanted to come in and get another kiss. I choose to stay nestled in the covers to see if he will try to wake me with a kiss. Instead he gets into the bed with me, snuggles with me in the covers, and puts his arm around me. I feel at home. I feel loved. How could I ever choose Daniel over this? He starts to nibble on my ear and then my neck. He has never done this before. I don't know what has come over him, but I like it. He slowly takes his hand and caresses my curves until his fingers find my most personal area. I gasp. His fingers feel so good against my skin. I don't want it to stop. I close my eyes to savor this moment. He turns me over onto my back. He lifts my shirt and starts planting kisses down my body. My body is on fire. I have no idea what he is going to do next. I love this spontaneity! Maybe he should have pressing matters in other places more often.

He goes down lower and now I'm curious. He has never done this before. He gets down to my area and blows. I shiver. What is he going to do? Suddenly the soft, brisk, wind is replaced by a firm, thick tongue and I go crazy. My brain doesn't know how to comprehend the pleasure that I feel at this moment. I feel myself getting to the peak. I'm almost there and as I'm about to enjoy my bliss, he stops, flips me over and inserts himself inside me with a hard thrust. It hurts yet feels so good at the same time. Why has he never done this before? He goes slower and his member goes to regions that I didn't even know could be explored. That same feeling comes erupting up again, but this time I plan to let it come to fruition. I press back into him letting him know that I'm on the edge. In the heat of passion, I yell out that I want to have his child. He answers me with a grunt. He then grabs my hips, thrusts deeper and harder, and finally we explode together. I see stars, I see angels, and I feel butterflies all over. This is honestly the best I have ever had. I can't keep my eyes open as I lie down and go to sleep directly afterwards.

I wake up some hours later and I still feel his body next to mine. Wasn't he supposed to be at a meeting? I untangle myself from the covers and turn toward my Prince but what I see shocks me. It's not the Prince at all, but Daniel. Now it all makes sense! What he did to me could not have been done by the Prince. I'm disgusted, yet elated at the same time. This is what I wanted. This is who I wanted to wake up next to for the rest of my life. This is who I want to grow old with and have children with. This is my love. I love him and now it's time to seal it with a kiss. I lean over and look at him closely, admiring the handsome man lying next to me in bed. Sam's voice is ringing in my head but, at this point, I don't care. I love Daniel and I want to be with him. What harm can come from one little kiss? I inch closer and plant one of the sweetest kisses onto his lips. Suddenly, I feel pain in my chest, and I can't breathe. My head explodes with pain. I want to scream but the words won't come out. I see an eerie glow around me. I try to wake Daniel but I can't move. Finally, I pass out in the midst of the worse pain I have ever experienced in my life.

I'm awakened some time later with a kiss on my forehead. I smile. Daniel has come back for round two. I open my eyes to see that the Prince is there. My stomach drops but I keep on smiling. I don't love this man. I don't want anything to do with him, but I know I have to keep him happy in order to stay close to Daniel. So, I accept his advances and let him have his way. Usually I'm content with James but now, I'm bored. After what I experienced with Daniel I don't know if

I can be truly content with James ever again. He mumbles something about having a child as he explodes inside me. He then collapses on top of me and is asleep in seconds. I stare up at this beautiful canopy that I'm sleeping in and start to cry knowing that one of these men might be a father in the next nine months but I honestly don't know whom it's going to be. In my heart, I hope it's Daniel's. I cry silently as this man I do not love wraps me in his arms.

CHAPTER SEVEN
And Then Comes a Baby Carriage...
Ellie
(Three months later)

I don't know what's wrong with me. One minute I'm angry. One minute I'm sad. One minute I'm happy and want to do a musical dance number. One minute I want to throw up and the next minute I want to eat everything in the kitchen. I'm hot, I'm cold, I have a little bulge in my stomach that won't go away, and I'm always uncomfortable.

Anastasia has been a dream. She has been at my beck and call the entire time. She doesn't seem as happy nowadays, but I'm sure that has something to do with her personal life with Ms. Hannon. Everyone is talking about it in the castle, but who am I to judge? Speaking of judging, I haven't seen Sam in three months. This is around the time when I need my mother. I'm pretty sure she can wave a wand over me and make me feel better, or at least tell me what's wrong with me. With all these changes to my body I know one thing is certain; I love Daniel. We have spent every moment I can get away from the Prince together. Our favorite spot to meet is in the garden upstairs. I'm surrounded by beauty as he whispers beautiful words to me as we make love. It's the best feeling in the world and I don't want to give it up.

We just got through making love for the third time on the roof garden and now I'm nestled in his arms looking up at a big full moon and twinkling stars. A girl can get used to this. I can feel Daniel's hand on my stomach and I feel a flutter of butterflies.

"You're gaining weight."

I'm slightly insulted even though I have realized it myself. It's one thing to realize it for yourself, but it's another to have someone else point it out.

"Is that a bad thing?"

"No, it just concerns me. You're so petite and this sudden weight gain is just in your stomach and nowhere else."

"What are you saying, Daniel?"

"Ellie, I think you might be pregnant."

My stomach drops. I can't be pregnant. If I'm pregnant I can honestly say that I don't know whose child it will be. I've been with both Daniel, out of love, and the Prince, out of obligation.

"What if it is not yours?"

"I would understand. Would I be happy? No. Would I still love you? Yes. There is nothing in this world that can change the way I feel for you."

I smile.

He gives me a kiss and I feel the butterflies in my stomach again. This is the exact thing that I wanted and needed to hear. I love it when he reassures me.

"But you really should get it checked out, just to make sure."

I smile.

He's worried about me and I think it's fantastic. With each passing day I love this man more and more and I know that he is the one for me. I don't need anyone but him. We slowly get up and get dressed. I'm just now getting everything on and zipped up when someone bursts through the door. Daniel hides. It's my husband and he looks angry.

"Ellie, I have been looking for you for hours! Have you been up here the whole time?"

"Yes, love. I love it up here; don't you think that it's beautiful?"

He calms down just a bit and kisses me.

"Yes, it is beautiful but not as beautiful as you."

I blush.

Even though my love is not with this man I still like him. He has the ability to make me feel good even when I feel crummy about myself.

"Now, Ellie, I will only ask this once. Were you up here with someone?"

His eyes are bloodshot as if he has been drinking, but I can't smell alcohol, so I am assuming he's been crying. His clothes and hair are disheveled. I feel bad for him, but I can't help who I love.

"I was up here by myself, why do you ask?"

"You know, everyone is talking about it, you and Daniel. They say they see you guys spending more and more time together. Some have even said that they have seen you kissing! Why, Ellie? I love you so much. I want to have children. I want you to reign with me when I become King. He can't give you what I can give you. So why entertain it? Do you love him? Are the rumors true?"

I divert my eyes from his and look at a really pretty rose right next to me.

"Do you love him?" he screams.

I jump. I've never seen him this irate before.

"No, I do not love Daniel. He's a great friend of mine. I

haven't been spending alone time with him. I'm not stupid. I know there are eyes and ears everywhere. Isn't that what you wanted? Didn't you want your best friend and your wife becoming great friends as well so that our encounters with each other wouldn't be awkward?"

He stops and thinks for a minute. I can see my words etching themselves into his brain.

"Then why haven't I seen Daniel in a couple of days?"

"I'm not sure."

The roof becomes awkward as we try to find out what to say to the other. He knows I'm lying but he just continues to stare at me as if I didn't say a word. It's eerie.

"Ellie, I love you. Why don't you love me?"

He starts inching toward me in a zombie like manner. I'm officially scared.

"I do everything for you. I've made a great life for you. What does he have that I don't? Tell me. What do I have to do in order for you to love me again, Ellie? What do I have to do to make it like it was our first night here? Baby, please tell me."

He keeps inching forward looking at me with those bloodshot eyes.

I am scared. I don't know what to do. Right now, the way he's acting I'm not sure what he's going to do to me. All I know is that I can't bear to be away from Daniel so I need to make this work out with the Prince somehow. Daniel needs to stay employed here so we can keep our relationship going. I need to find out who's telling my husband these things so those people can be fired.

As he inches closer my heart starts beating faster. I look for ways to escape but I can't. His bloodshot eyes now look crazed. I fear for my life. He is so close I can smell what he had for dinner on his breath.

"I might be pregnant," I say in a whisper.

He stops dead in his tracks and instantly the craziness has left his eyes.

"What?"

"I might be pregnant. I haven't been feeling good. I'm hot, cold, irritable, and on top of that, I am gaining weight. See?"

I turn to the side and pull my clothing tighter on my stomach. I see a smile slowly creep on his face. I'm relieved. I then decide to milk this cow for all that its worth.

"See, how could I possibly be having an affair with Daniel if I'm pregnant with your child? I love you and I can't wait to start this new chapter in our lives."

I hug him and it takes a minute but he hugs me back. He starts crying as he wraps his arms around me, babbling apologies. I look toward the door and I see a fully clothed Daniel sneak out. Right before he walks out he looks at me with the most hurtful look I've ever seen. My heart breaks. I didn't mean to hurt him. Can't he see I am doing this for us? I start to cry right along with my husband. Not because I'm happy for this baby, but because I might have just watched the love of my life walk out the door forever.

A couple of days later it is confirmed. I'm pregnant. The doctor then went on to say that from the looks of it, I'm about three months along. I get sick hearing the news. It was about three months ago when I had relations with both Daniel and James in the same night. I don't know whose child it is and feel myself starting to panic. I can't ask the doctor how I can tell who the father is before the child is born because he will surely report the news to my husband.

As he starts to tell me the list of things I can and cannot do for the duration of my pregnancy I start to cry. How could I ever think to bring a young one into this world without knowing who the father is? How is that fair to the child?

I look over at my husband and he is elated with tears in his eyes, mouthing the words "I love you." I can't consider mouthing the words back so, instead, I give him a nod. He is celebrating with the staff and all I can think about is where Daniel may be. He should be here celebrating with everyone else because the child I'm carrying may in fact be his. I cry a bit harder at the thought of Daniel being so angry at me for what I said yesterday that he doesn't want anything to do with me. I might have just lost him forever.

After everyone finished yelling and jumping for joy my husband ushers them out of the room and sits down on the bed with me.

"You don't have to worry about a thing. You don't have to lift a finger. I will be at your beck and call."

"Thank you."

I smile at him even though inside I'm silently crying.

"I'm going to leave you alone right now. I'm pretty sure all that excitement tired you and the baby out."

I didn't actually realize how tired I was until he mentions it. I yawn really big and snuggle deep inside my covers. He comes around, tucks me into the bed, kisses me on the forehead, then leaves the room. As he leaves the room I fall asleep before he can even close the door.

I suddenly wake up somewhere other than my room. I'm surrounded by wilderness. It's dark, dreary, and eerie. I call out and all I hear is the sound of my own voice. I'm panicked now. How did I end up in this place? I realize that panicking is not the best thing. So I get off of my bed, which is now a pile of leaves, and decide to go exploring to see if I can find a way out.

As I'm looking around, I realize there are two of everything. Two squirrels, two trees that look alike, two snails, it's two of everything! The funny part about this is they are identical. It seems whatever one thing does the other one does the exact same thing in perfect synchronization. I don't know what's going on, but I'm getting really freaked out. I find a path and get happy. If there's a path it must lead to civilization! I'm happy at the thought of someone being able to help me and my baby. I stop. My baby. I put my hands on my stomach and realize that the bump is not there and that my stomach is perfectly flat. I start to panic even more. Where is my baby? Did I lose it on the way here? I'm so confused! I need someone to help me.

I start running down the path. I see a faint glowing light in the distance. My heart leaps into my throat. I'm elated. As I get closer I hear voices softly chanting. I slow down to a creep so I do not disturb them and decide I will ask for help when they're done.

After waiting for an eternity, the chanting finally stops. I get up from my hiding place and go into the lighted area. There are men dressed in cloth material tied around their waist like diapers and they are surrounding two objects in the middle of a circle. I can't see what these figures are. I decide I need to get closer in order to figure out what's going on. As I'm walking I step on a twig and it breaks. It is the loudest twig in the world. Everyone turns to look at me. What I see is horrifying. I see all of these random mythical creatures who look evil praising two children! A boy and a girl! What they do next haunts me. They slowly get up and come toward me saying, "All hail the Mother of the dark Lord and dark Lady!"

I didn't give birth to these monsters. I'm not evil. They surround me and bring me to the babies. I look at the children and they look like me. They can't be more than a year old; cooing and blowing spit bubbles. I'm instantly in love with these children and I want to save them from this insanity. I pick both of them up and run. I run as hard as I can. When I look behind me the mystical creatures are right behind me, begging me to bring the children back. I have no idea where I'm running to. I only know I need to protect these children.

As I'm running, the children start to disintegrate. I look at my hands as sand falls out of my palms. *Where did the babies go?* I turn around and the creatures have now catching up to me, running full speed. I scream as the creatures run right into me and start cramming themselves into my body.

I awaken with a loud scream. I'm sweating. I can't catch my breath. *Why can't I breathe? What did that dream mean?* I reach down and feel my stomach. I'm relieved when I feel the tell-tale signs of my baby in my stomach. My joy doesn't last long as I get the strange feeling that I am not alone. I look over to my right and see Ms. Hannon. She is staring right at me with a look of concern. I scream. She jumps.

"Are you alright? I came up to bring you some food since you missed dinner and I heard you screaming."

"Yes, I'm fine. I just had a bad dream. That's all."

She looks a bit concerned.

"Describe this dream to me."

The way she asks me to describe the dream is a bit haunting. I'm not entirely sure I can trust this woman. As I'm weighing my options she grabs my hands and gives me one of the sweetest smiles. She assures me she is only trying to help and if I don't want to reveal the contents of the dream it's completely fine. It's funny how one gesture can put your mind at ease. I tell her everything. I tell her about the fact that everything was double, the mythical creatures, the twin babies, and the creatures cramming themselves into my body. She sits there and listens intently as I tell the entire story. When I'm done, she looks like she is in deep thought.

"Did you leave anything out?"

"No ma'am. I told you everything that I remember from the dream."

"This is not good."

"Why is it not good?"

I'm starting to panic all over again.

"I remember hearing something about this dream from an

old friend of mine. Let me contact her and I'll get back to you as soon as I have an answer."

She gets up to leave. For some strange reason I'm drawn to her and don't want her to leave. I don't know if it's the hormones or if it's the fact that she is the mother of the man I truly love. She must have sensed that I didn't want her to go because she comes back to the bed, smooth's my hair down, and tucks me in.

"Don't worry, Ellie, you're fine. The dream shouldn't come back. If it does, ring the servant's quarters and I will be right back up here. Now, get some rest."

I lie down and watch her leave the room. I roll deeper into the covers as I think about the dream again. I'm terrified. *What does this dream mean?*

The door to my room opens and closes gently. I feel someone get in the bed with me, get under the covers, and wrap their arms around me. I turn around to get a good look at the person and it is Daniel. I start smiling. He smiles back.

"I missed you," I whisper the words to Daniel and his smile gets bigger.

"I missed you, too."

"What took you so long to come and see me?"

"I didn't want to run into the Prince. He still has it in his mind that I'm sneaking around with you and that you love me more than you love him. That's simply preposterous, right?"

I giggle.

"I love you, Ellie."

"I love you, too."

"Run away with me."

"What?"

"Run away with me. We'll wait until the baby has been born and then we'll leave the Kingdom together."

I think about this for a moment.

"Where will we go?"

"Wherever love takes us. Just say yes and I'll take care of you, Ellie."

I think about it for a long time. I love Daniel but I'm not sure if I'm ready to leave. I don't know what to say, but I do know we cannot keep this up much longer. Once this affair is found out he will be put to death. As much as I want to stay, I want to keep Daniel more. So my answer is obvious.

"Yes."

With that, he has the biggest smile I have ever seen. He kisses me on my lips, he kisses me on my neck, and his tongue leads the way to my belly and kisses it.

I blush. Something in my heart tells me that the baby I'm carrying is his. His tongue leads its way back to my mouth and we indulge in passionate kissing.

I stop.

"What if he comes in? What if he catches us?"

"He won't. When I snuck in the room there was a do not disturb sign. If we are quiet no one will even know I'm here."

He kisses me again.

I kiss him back harder.

He pulls me on top of him and he starts to strip me out of my clothes. The kisses get deeper, the clothes come off quicker, and the heat is getting insatiable. All I want is for him to touch my body, to caress it with kisses. He complies with my desire. I don't want this to end. As he takes me to ecstasy we are completely oblivious that there is someone else in the room.

I am sleeping in Daniel's arms, feeling content. I feel happy and loved and absolutely nothing can mess up this moment.

"Hi, Ellie."

I jump at the sound of my name. I untangle myself from a sleeping Daniel and the covers and look directly into my mother's eyes. I'm shocked and I'm embarrassed that she is seeing me like this since she fought so hard for me to be married to the Prince. So much for this being a perfect moment. I have a panicked look on my face.

"Don't worry, love, I'll not tell the Prince, but you and I need to talk."

With a wave of her hand it seems as if time is going slower. It is truly amazing.

"Ellie, what are you doing?"

"I'm sleeping with Daniel."

"Yes, in the bed that you share with the Prince! I know that spell has taken a toll on your heart but it doesn't have to take a toll on your mind. You're digging your grave, that is what you are doing, but I didn't come here to tell you about that. I came to warn you."

"Typical. You only show up when I'm in trouble, and like I told you, I'm not under a spell. I loved Daniel before all of this happened. Where were you when I needed you?"

"I don't have much time. I'm not going to sit here and argue with you about my presence. I'm fighting for more than just you right now. So if that means I'm not here, that means you get to live another day in this blasphemous life you have created!"

There is a moment of silence. I feel like I was just slapped in the face with her words. I'm getting angrier by the minute. I feel nothing but rage toward this woman. If looks could kill, Sam would be on the floor right now. I would end her wretched life right now if I could.

The moment passes and she continues, "Now, listen to me. The baby you're carrying is evil. It has a lot of pure evil energy that is both powerful and dangerous that a lot of people want to control. You are to remain with someone at all times. Please, don't go off by yourself. These creatures and people will only try to attack you if you are by yourself. I know of your dilemma, not knowing who the child belongs to. Unfortunately, I can't give you that answer. There is a strong magical block surrounding you. It will not let me see the sex of the baby or who it belongs to. I will tell you that when you give birth, if it is one child it is James' child. If you have two children, they are Daniel's. If you give birth to two children we are all in grave danger, especially you."

I'm getting really scared. I don't know what's going on. Maybe this is what my dream meant.

"I had a dream last night."

"What was it about?"

I spend the next couple of minutes telling her about the dream. As I get deeper into the dream her face turns white.

"Who all did you tell this dream to?"

"I only told Ms. Hannon. She told me she's going to talk to her friend and get an answer for my dream. What does my dream mean?"

Her facial expressions are unreadable.

"Don't go around Ms. Hannon. Do you hear me?"

"Why? For some reason I want her around me all the time. When she's around me I feel happy. Why are you trying to make me unhappy? Don't I deserve to be happy and do what I want with my life?"

"Yes, you do, Ellie. That's all I've ever wanted for you, but if you want to keep your child and use his or her magic for good you're going to have to do what I say, sweetheart. There's a lot of power surrounding you now. Right now, the evil is taking over the good, but that can change! There's still time to sway the magical influences of that child. Just please trust me."

"Why should I?"

"Ms. Hannon is a witch, Ellie. She's a very evil witch. She's the reason I had to leave and your father is dead."

I'm shocked. How can someone so sweet be so evil? How can she give birth to such a wonderful man?

"I don't believe you."

"You don't have to. It will be revealed in time. If you value your life, you will not tell Ms. Hannon of the conversation we just had. She will kill you and take that power away from your child."

I start to cry. Why do these things keep happening to me? All I want is to have this baby and be happy. I don't think that is a lot to ask, but apparently it is. I feel myself getting angry again. I get up from the bed and lift up my hand slowly and point it at Sam. Her eyes are panicked. I cup my hands slightly and Sam starts to choke. I lift up my hand and Sam goes into the air, kicking her feet and flailing her arms. My actions are not my own. I have no idea what's going on right now, but all I know is that it feels good. Sam can't breathe. She's basically trying to talk to me in between breaths.

"Ellie, control it. You have to control your child. Don't let this child make you into an evil person! Control it!"

With that I snap out of it and drop my hands. Sam slams to the floor. I look at my fingers in pure astonishment. *How did this happen?* I look up at Sam and she is staring at me with a scared expression on her face. I want to hug her and tell her I'm sorry for everything and that I love her, but I feel right now is not the time to touch anything or anybody. She slowly gets off the ground.

"That child is more powerful than me and I'm one of the most powerful fairies known in the magical realm. Ellie, please be careful. Control it."

She goes towards the window, opens it up and steps on the ledge.

"Also, please know that even when I'm not here, I am here. I see everything. I love you and just know that everything I do is for you."

"What does the dream mean?"

"My dear child, I'm no fool and I don't think you are one either. I believe you know what it means."

She waves her hand and time resumes. She jumps out of the window and she is gone.

As soon as she leaves I feel my anger leave my body. Maybe she is telling the truth about my baby being evil. I've never felt so angry in my life. I'm pretty sure this is not your typical mood swing. I look at my hands again. I could have killed her and the way I feel right now, I would have not had any remorse.

I hear footsteps outside of the door followed by knocking.

"Ellie!"

I hear the Prince calling out my name.

"Is everything alright in there? We heard a commotion downstairs."

"I'm fine, I promise."

"I'm coming in."

I panic. Daniel is now up putting on his clothes. I lift my hands toward the door and it locks. No time to contemplate what just happened. I start putting back on my clothes and hop into bed.

"Just a minute!"

I sit in my bed and lift my hand toward the door. It unlocks. I signal for Daniel to hide in my closet. He does.

"Why did you have the door locked?"

"Ms. Hannon locked the door when she left the room earlier."

"Okay, that makes sense. What have you been up here doing? All I heard was yelling and then some thumping sounds. Are you sure that you're ok? Are you sure that there is no one in here with you?"

He walks toward my closet and I panic.

"No baby, no one is here. So, you know what that means."

I start to crawl across the big bed toward the side that the Prince is standing on. His mouth drops and I see a little drool coming out of his mouth. He slowly walks toward the bed taking off his clothes. He is right next to the bed and I kiss him. I kiss him with everything that I have as I motion for Daniel to leave the room.

He darts out of the room to safety. I continue to kiss James. The longer I kiss him the more I want him. He lays me on the bed and starts to take off my nightgown. When he gets it off he starts kissing me again but, this time, it's different. My stomach is not behaving well. I'm hot, I'm cold, and I all of a sudden don't feel well. I push him off me and hurry to the nearest trashcan where I release all the food I ate earlier that day.

Of course James is right there rubbing my back calling me beautiful while holding my hair. How could I not love this man? Come to think of it Daniel doesn't do any of these things for me. He doesn't call me beautiful. He doesn't come to my rescue when I need him. Matter of fact, the only thing he is good for is good loving and running away. My chest starts to hurt. I can't breathe. It's like whenever I think about the possibility of not loving Daniel I feel as if I'm going to die. In my heart I know I'm supposed to be with Daniel but in my mind James is the best choice for me. I'm so confused.

After releasing my lunch I'm tired and want to lie down. James swoops me up into his arms and carries me back to the bed, lays me down, tucks me in, and then climbs into the bed with me and wraps his arms around me. I turn toward him, stinky breath and all, and I smile at him genuinely.

He mouths the words, "I love you."

I look at him and mouth the words right back to him. Tears start streaming from his eyes. For the first time in months I'm happy. That's the last thing I remember before feeling excruciating pain in my chest and blacking out.

Several months go by and I get as big as a house. I've never been this heavy before in my life. My feet are swollen, at least

I think they are because I can't see them. My back aches. I'm always angry. I'm just not myself.

My love for Daniel is starting to confuse me. I love him but, in my mind, I don't know why. It seems like whenever I want to call it quits I get a pain in my chest that feels worse than anything I could have ever imagined. It's only when I remember that I do love Daniel that the pain stops. This love is going to kill me. I just know it.

During this time the Prince and I have gotten closer than ever. He runs my bath water and rubs my feet. He makes sure I'm well taken care of and I love him dearly for that. Everything I could possibly want and need, I've found in this man. How could I have ever strayed from him?

I've been to the doctor and listened to the heartbeat and even had a sonogram done. It's confirmed. It's one child. I'm having healthy baby boy. I can breathe. So now I know the baby belongs to James instead of Daniel. I don't know why this makes me feel elated, but it does.

As I get closer and closer to my due date strange things seem to happen. Every night I go to bed swear someone is watching me outside my window. I'm able to do strange things magically that I have never been able to do before, especially when I'm angry. Things levitate around me. When I cry, it rains and when I'm happy, the sun shines brighter than it ever has before.

I'm getting used to being waited on hand and foot. Everyone in the castle is buzzing about the new baby as they prepare the nursery. The royal subjects are ecstatic as they wait for the day I go into labor. I've never been adored by so many people yet felt so alone. I wish my mother was here. I miss her and I have so many things to ask. Why didn't I have magical abilities until I got pregnant? Why did she leave? I know it was to protect father and me, but I want to know why the fighting started in the first place. I want to know why she wasn't there for me when I was crying in my pillow. I just want to know why.

I start to cry and the weather outside changes from a perfectly sunny day to raining hard. I'm crying so hard that I need to sit down, but I can't move. It feels as if I'm glued in place. All at once I feel so much pain it's ridiculous and in the midst of this pain a liquid shoots from between my legs. Is this what the doctor was talking about? Am I going into labor? I waddle over to the service phone and call an attendant to inform them that I think I'm having the baby. It's too early! I'm only seven months!

I go down to my knees, holding my stomach. I'm in so much pain. I open my mouth to scream out and no words come out. Instead white and black shadows emit from my mouth. I'm confused and scared. What does that mean? After the shadows are released into the air they start to bounce off the walls. I don't know what to do. I just want the pain to stop and for these shadows to stop playing in front of my eyes. The pain stops, at least for a couple of minutes I can breathe. I pick myself up off the floor and try to make it to my bed. The pain comes back. This doesn't feel good. I don't want another child after this! Why is it so hot in here? Why can't I breathe? I feel like all my insides are going to fall out. Finally, the white and the black shadows collide and temporarily form the yin-yang symbol before the whole room erupts in a blinding white light and forces me to pass out to escape the pain.

I wake up and I have nurses surrounding me along with Daniel, Anastasia, and Ms. Hannon on one side and the Prince, his mother, and father on the other side. If only they knew the irony of their placement they would see why I find it so hilariously terrifying.

There is a cold cloth being applied to my head and the doctor is down at the foot of the bed while my legs are hiked up and spread apart.

"We have to deliver the baby now. The cord is wrapped around his neck."

I start to panic. I don't want my baby to die. I grab James' hand, Daniel looks upset. He's going to have to get over it. If I grabbed his hand instead of James' then it would have caused problems and right now, that is not a problem I need. I grip James' hand tightly as the next pain starts. I scream. It hurts so badly.

"Ellie, I know it hurts, but I don't have time to give you any drugs. I need you to push when I tell you to push. With any luck you'll be holding your new baby soon."

The pain is so awful I feel as if I'm going to pass out again.

"Ellie, remember your breathing."

James is coaching me through the process. Anastasia grabs my hand on the other side. I smile at her. I've really come to love my sister. She has done a lot for me. Too bad I'm dealing with all my problems or I would show her how much she really means to me. The pain is starting again. The doctor then yells for me to push. I push with all my heart, mind, body, and soul. He tells me to rest. I'm already tired and I just want this to end. The pain comes again and it is unbearable. The doctor yells for me to push again. I push with everything in me. Still no baby. I rest. The pain comes back faster than it did before. I push harder. I grit my teeth. I crush the hands of both James and Anastasia as I give it everything I have. I'm pushing all my anger, all my love, all my pain, all my anxiety, and all my fears.

Finally, I hear the sweetest sound I could have ever heard, my baby crying. James brings the baby to me and when he puts him into my arms I already know his name, Jayson. Prince Jayson has a nice ring to it. He looks at me with his beautiful green eyes and I'm in love. Just a couple of seconds later the pain is back but worse than ever. The baby is taken from me and given to James. Daniel looks as if he wants to jump across the room and kill James.

The doctor assures me that I'm just passing the after birth. It will be over in just a minute. I push and push and nothing is happening. Finally, I feel the urge to do a hard push. I grit my teeth and grab my legs. Then I hear it; another cry. Everyone in the room goes silent.

"It's a girl," the doctor says.

He looks just as shocked as I feel. He puts the baby in my arms and I love her just as much as Jayson. Her eyes are the color of wheat. My heart wrenches a bit. How is this possible? She wasn't on any sonograms nor did I hear her heartbeat. It's like she appeared out of thin air. I look toward James and he looks as if he wants to pass out. Anastasia looks as if she has seen a ghost. Daniel looks confused and Ms. Hannon has a creepy grin on her face. No one knows how to react to her. Princess Jaylin. Twins.

CHAPTER EIGHT
Wandering Eyes
Daniel

Twins. Both my mother and Anastasia have expressions that lead me to believe there is a bigger explanation and I plan on getting to the bottom of it, but not right now. I leave the room as the Prince and Ellie rejoice with their twins, Jayson and Jaylin. They're cute, very cute. But something tells me that those kids are not his. I decide I need some air and I'm going to go into town. Maybe conversing with some normal, everyday people will take my mind off of the drama that is building in the castle.

I go to the stables and see this majestic looking horse that I have never really paid attention to before. I look at the plaque above the stable and the name reads "Misty." I decide I want to take this horse. I'll be the talk of the town riding in on this beast. I take her out and feed her some oats that were in a bag in the stable. As she eats, I saddle her. I pet her and once I'm done attaching everything, I ease myself into the saddle and make my way into town.

Misty runs so smoothly and I love the fact that she looks so powerful. At least people in town will be able to appreciate a good man when they see one, unlike Ellie. How dare she look so happy with the Prince? She's supposed to be rejoicing with me! She's supposed to be telling me that she loves me! She's supposed to be mine! If I can't have her then I will find someone else that I can have. I need to find someone who appreciates me for who I am and what I have to offer. I regret doing that spell now.

I estimate I've been riding for about twenty minutes when I reach town. All the townsfolk are hustling around trying to get their errands done or trying to make a quick sale. I take Misty to the post and tie her with the other horses. She outshines all of them. People start to take notice of her and hoard around her, feeding her carrots and oats and petting her mane. Misty looks to be satisfied and in good hands so I decide it's time to explore.

I go toward the jewelry and perfume shops in town. I know a lot more women will be hanging around those stores, women that fit my taste. I'm a person who loves beautiful things. If she can't do her womanly duties such as cleaning, housework, or mending clothing, there's a spell for that. There's a spell for just about everything. I'm a man who loves beauty and I'm also a man who gets what he wants either magically or physically.

I walk around the shops, randomly going into stores and talking with the shop keepers about different prices. I end up buying some perfume for Ellie as a gift, lavender for my mother, and some baby gifts for the babies. Although I don't like James at this moment, I'm happy for him and think his kids deserve a gift. He is my best friend at the end of the day. As I'm leaving the baby boutique I see a very beautiful woman go into the perfume shop I just left.

She is the color of cinnamon with hair that is so long and thick it could be braided and used as a rope. Her eyes are the color of coals yet very enticing. Her thick lips accentuate her round face. Her body is a very perfect hour glass petite frame. She kind of reminds me of Ellie but untarnished, unattached, and just mine for the taking. As I follow her into the store I can't imagine being with anyone else but her. I walk into the store and overhear the last part of the conversation between her and the shopkeeper.

"So, do you have any more lavender?"

"I'm sorry, a gentleman came in earlier and cleared us out."

"I thought you said you were going to hold them for me, Nate!"

She put her hands on her hips and I'm easily taken with her feistiness.

"I'm sorry, Layla, but I have to pay this place off somehow. He had the money right then so I took it. I should have another shipment in a day or so."

She rolls her eyes. Silently, I'm jumping up and down because I hold the very thing she wants and she has everything I need. I feel as if this meeting was meant to be.

"I'm sorry, I couldn't help but overhear," I say as I casually walk up to her. "What is the lavender for?"

"I put the petals in my bath. It makes me smell nice and keeps my skin soft. I'm running low."

"What if I told you I knew where some was?"

"I would kiss you."

"Now, do you want to kiss me because I know where the flowers are or because you think I'm attractive?"

She blushes a deep red. I have her in my trap I'm clicking my heels in my mind.

"You are bold, Mr.-"

"Hannon. My name is Mr. Hannon but you, my fair lady, may call me Daniel."

"Daniel. I like the way that feels on my tongue."

She gives me a wink and then walks away.

The shop owner just looks at me and smiles. I wink at him and proceed to follow her; watching her hips sway back and forth. I start to drool. I run to catch up to her so that we are walking side by side.

"So, where are we going, Layla?"

"How do you know my name?"

She whips around fast and looks at me with that same feisty look and her hand planted on her hip.

"The shop keeper said your name."

"Oh, okay. That's fine."

She becomes visibly more relaxed as she starts to walk away again.

"You never answered me. Where are we going?"

"Well, Daniel, I'm assuming you were the gentleman that came in and bought all of the lavender, correct?"

"You would be correct."

"I just wanted to make sure I was right."

She still has not answered my question. I'm a bit turned on by this. Normally a woman would be all giddy when she met me, but she is in control and I love it. Right now, I would gladly follow this woman to the moon and back. I catch up to her and we talk about random subjects. After walking for about ten minutes we come to a very nice looking cottage. She walks right to the door, takes out a key, unlocks the door, and walks in. She motions for me to follow. I do.

Her house is nicely decorated with earthy colors throughout. She has some good taste. When I walk in I don't see her anywhere so I take a seat on the sofa. It's firm yet soft. That's how I like my women and I'm hoping I get those same feelings when I touch Layla. A couple of minutes later I hear water and out comes Layla in a robe.

"It's time for my bath, Daniel. If you would follow me with the lavender," she says as she turns around and sways those hips toward the back room.

I grab the lavender out of my bag and hurry behind her. She drops her robe as soon as I get in the room and dips her body into the hot water. I'm now at attention. I slowly pick off the petals and drop them into the water. One falls on her breast, another on her knee, and another on her stomach. She moans every time one touches her skin. I decide to take it a bit further and take one of the petals and use it to trace along her body. She goes crazy.

"Get in."

She doesn't have to tell me twice. I hurriedly strip out of my clothing and join her in the bath. She pulls me close to her and gives me a kiss. I'm breathless. Her hands travel along my body as my hands travels along hers. Things get heated and we end up making bubbles in the bathtub for quite some time. The water never ran cold because our bodies kept it hot.

I arrive back at the castle four hours later. That woman was passionate and so giving. I didn't want to leave her, but duty calls. I left with the promise that I would be back soon. She is so beautiful. Not as beautiful as Ellie, but a close second. If I can't have Ellie then she will be a great substitute. I put Misty back in the stable and walk toward the castle, whistling a tune of happiness when, all of a sudden, I hear my mother call my name from her cottage. I roll my eyes. All the happiness I once had is now gone as I begrudgingly walk to her cottage. As soon as I get into her cottage she motions for me to sit down at the table. I do so. She then takes her book and sets it down in front of me. I'm nervous.

"Where were you, Daniel?"

"I went into town."

"You smell of lavender."

"I brought some for you," I smile, thinking I have gotten away with it.

"You also smell of a woman. Once again, I will ask you what you were doing and who you were with."

I'm really nervous now. Why does it matter who I'm with? Why does it matter what I was doing? I remain silent. I feel if I give her an answer it will only get me in more trouble.

"By you not answering me it has answered my question."

She then turns to the book and speaks to it.

"*Book, Abierto!*"

The book opens and out comes the book guardian looking menacing.

"Please repeat spell numbered 854754."

"As you wish, Mistress."

The book levitates and starts repeating the spell in a loud, booming voice.

> *"Love is something to cherish and hold*
> *Love at first sight is a tale centuries old*
> *But fast forward time about three moons*
> *The woman you love will suddenly swoon*
> *You have three days to enjoy the bliss*
> *Seal her fate with just one kiss*
> *But beware, on day four if a kiss is not shared*
> *The love that was between you will suddenly disappear*
> *Now if the love proves to be true*
> *A child of two shall befall on you*
> *But beware if your eyes should suddenly sway*
> *Your wandering eyes will dig both graves*
> *As it is spoken, it is now completed."*

My face goes white. This is the same spell I begged her to perform. I forgot about the whole spell. What have I done? I look toward my mother.

"Does that mean..?"

"Yes, Daniel, the children are yours."

I want to pass out. I didn't mean for it to go this far. I just wanted her for a time. I was going to leave her alone once I left. Now, I'm stuck with her and those kids, my kids.

"Daniel, I see everything. Layla just sealed your doom. I told you if you went through with the spell then everyone's lives would be in danger. You didn't listen to me."

"There has to be some other way to reverse this! You always have an answer!"

"Not this time, Daniel, not this time. All I can say is just ride it out. Just know your day is coming and you have no one to blame but yourself. Your wandering eyes will dig both graves."

"That's fine. You don't have an answer for this. Well, let me give you another riddle that you can't solve. What is white, tall, and deceitful? No answer? I'll give you a clue. It's Anastasia. While I was in town I heard that she has been frequenting a certain male's house. According to my sources, she has come out looking very satisfied. I bet she wasn't happy at home, was she?"

With that I turn to walk out the door.

"Don't you dare walk away from me!"

I feel myself being turned around and I'm pinned to the wall. My mother's hands are fixed on me. She has a look of death on her face.

"You're lying!"

"I have no reason to lie. I have nothing to live for, remember? As it is spoken, it is now completed." I grin. I know I have her in a bad position. I can tell by her eyes she wants to kill me. A small part of me wishes she would. She releases me and I fall to the floor.

"Leave."

I turn to leave. As I'm stepping out the door my mother gives me one more message.

"Watch the kids. One is evil, one is good. If you can figure out which one is the evil one and find a way to harbor its soul, you may be able to save your life. You better find out before I do."

She starts cackling and my blood turns cold as goose bumps rise on my skin.

I go to Ellie's room with the gifts I've purchased. The traffic has died down a lot; mostly it's just servants and people there to tend to the babies. I walk into the room and Ellie instantly beams. She looks beautiful. I want to kiss her but all the servants are staring. Ellie dismisses them and asks them to close the door.

Once they are gone I kiss Ellie with as much passion as I can muster. How could I ever step out on this girl? How could I be so naïve? She's the one for me! I sit down on the bed and tell her everything. I leave out the part about one of the babies being evil and my mother deciding to kill one of them to harbor its soul. I'll deal with my mother. There's no way I'm going to allow her to kill one of my children.

Ellie, after hearing everything, calmly tells me that she knew they were my children when she looked into their eyes. We make plans to leave the castle when the children are one year old. That gives us time to save up and decide where we'll all go. In the meantime, she has agreed to let the Prince keep thinking that Jayson and Jaylin are his. We kiss and bid each other farewell. As I leave the room and close the door, a single tear falls down my face. I wipe it away before anyone can see it. I look up and standing right in front of me is the Prince. My heart leaps in my throat. He looks angry and hurt at the same time.

"What were you doing in there?"

"I was giving your wife my gifts."

"Why didn't you give them to me to give to her?"

"I thought both of you were going to be in the room."

His eye twitches and his frown deepens.

"I don't know what you and Ellie have going on, but it stops here. You're not to be in the room alone with her for any reason. Do you understand me?"

"Or what? I'm just as much her advisor as I am yours. I have no intentions of doing anything to your wife. How can you accuse me of this when we have been best friends for so long?"

"I see the way you look at her. I'm warning you, Daniel. Stay the hell away from her."

He walks past me and bumps me hard on my shoulder. I stumble as he enters the room with Ellie and slams the door. I snicker as I walk away, whistling a tune of happiness. Nothing can dampen my mood now. The Prince doesn't know that I have one up on him. His woman is already gone to him and now belongs to me.

For the next six months the babies grow into the cutest things. Each of them has its own personality, but I can't tell which one is evil and which one is good. I'm hoping and praying this information isn't discovered before Ellie and I leave the Kingdom. If I'm not at the castle helping with the twins, I'm at Layla's house engulfed in passion. Right now I'm in love with both of them. I know the love Layla and I have is genuine and the love Ellie and I have is circumstantial. A part of me wishes I had found Layla before I got mixed up in this voodoo, but I can't change it now. If I'm going to die, I'm going to die a happy man.

One day while I was at Layla's house wrapped up in her arms, she asks me the most terrifying question.

"What would you say if I told you I was pregnant?"

"I would say that it's not something that fits into my life right now and that it needs to be terminated."

She looks up at me with a serious expression that I can't read.

"You don't want to have a baby with me?"

"I would like to have a child, just not right now. It would complicate things."

She gets up from the bed and goes into the bathroom. I get up and follow her. She is sitting at the tub running water for a bath. She takes her lavender petals and puts them in the bath.

"It's her, isn't it?"

"Her who?"

"Ellie. You're in love with Ellie and that's the only reason why you won't commit to me."

I'm shocked by her words.

"What makes you say that?"

"If we aren't talking about us or random people in town or things we want to do in the future you're talking about her and those damn twins! If I didn't know any better I would say they are your kids as much as you talk about them!"

I have a look of shock on my face.

She studies me and then slowly comes to the realization. "Those are your kids, aren't they?"

"No, they're not my kids!"

"Yes, they are! That explains everything! It explains why you feel the need to always go back to work after we make love. How you always want to spend time with the twins! How you can't stop talking about her and comparing me to her! You're worthless!"

She stops the water and goes towards the kitchen, I follow her. She goes to the cabinet, pulls out a piece of paper, and throws it at me.

"I wanted this to be a special occasion. I wanted you to be happy for me; for us!"

She starts crying hysterically, goes into the bathroom, and slams the door behind her.

I look at the paper that was thrown at me. The paper states that she is pregnant and is about four months along. What have I done? I knew coming here was a mistake. This can't get back to Ellie. This can't get back to my mother. This can't be spread around the Kingdom. I can already tell that if she does not get her way, the whole Kingdom is going to know about me, Ellie, and the twins. That's a risk that I just can't take. I know what has to be done.

I go into the bathroom, strip down, and get into the bathtub with her. I sit behind her and massage her shoulders and kiss her neck, telling her that I'm sorry for everything and that everything will be okay. I explain that I read the letter and I'm really happy for us. I tell her I can't wait until the baby is here and I vow to spend more time with her. I also explain that the twins are not mine.

"Yes, they are, but I'll not tell anyone. There is no way that I'm going to sit here and let you lie about it. Those are your kids."

"You know what? Yes, they are my kids. Ellie is my woman and no one will ever find out about it."

"How do you figure? Someone will eventually find out."

"Yes, but when they do find out it will not be from you."

With that I press her down into the water and hold her under. Her legs are thrashing and her hands are grabbing and scratching my skin, but I don't let go. I know this is for the best. She starts to weaken as tears fall down my face. I really liked Layla, I wanted to be with her and have my child, but this thing with Ellie is too complex and I can't let it get out or I will die as well.

She starts to slow down significantly. I speak soft words to her, letting her know that it's okay to let go and we can be together in the next lifetime. I can see her eyes under the water asking me why. I cry harder. I never wanted to hurt anyone. Suddenly, the life leaves her eyes. I let go of her shoulders and get out of the tub. She floats lifelessly in the water surrounded by lavender petals. The thing that brought us together is now the same thing that surrounds her in death. I will never forget the significance of the smell of lavender. I get dressed, gather my things, and remove all evidence that I was ever here. I go back to the water, kiss her lifeless lips for the last time, and close the bathroom door. I walk out of the cottage, never to return to the sweet smell of lavender. I walk back to the castle knowing I have a long journey ahead of me. I wipe the tears that are streaming from of my eyes, never knowing that I was being watched.

CHAPTER NINE
Downhill from Here
Anastasia

"Oh Jesus, this is so good!"

We had just finished making love for the fourth time and now he's feeding me one of his freshly baked muffins.

"I now know why they call you the Muffin Man!"

"Who lives on Drury Lane."

We both share a laugh. He then stops and looks into my eyes.

"Anastasia, I love you."

My smile gets wider. I can't believe this handsome man actually loves me. I've been to his house every day for the past six months. I can't get enough of this man. Everything about him is perfection.

"I love you, too."

He kisses me softly and sweetly on the lips.

I instantly feel like melting. I look at the clock on the wall and realize I was supposed to be at the castle an hour ago. Ms. Hannon is not going to be happy.

"Don't worry. I've gotten everything the list called for in your cart. You can blame the elongated time away from the castle as just browsing. I'm pretty sure she is not going to do anything to you."

"Are you sure? Ms. Hannon isn't stupid and she did send you that note stating she knew who you were and warning you that your time has come. Doesn't that worry you in the slightest?"

"Not really. I've defeated her before and I'll defeat her again. Plus, I now have more to fight for. It would take all the witches, wizards and fairies of the magical realm to keep me away from you because I love you that much."

I blush a deep red. I love this man more than words can describe. I can't explain it, but this love just feels so right and it hurts me every time we have to part. We decided after he read the note that it was best if I went back to the castle and lived as normal as possible. There was no need for Hannon to know that I knew what she was about to do. Every time I leave him I think it is the last time I will be able to look into his bright green eyes and I panic.

He reassures me every time that he will see me the next day at the same time.

I'm becoming more and more doubtful. I put on my clothes and realize my clothes are a bit snug. I shrug it off and figure it's from the all of the delectable treats that I've been having. I plan on cutting back my portions and being a bit more active.

He gives me a hug and kisses me passionately as he bids me farewell.

I try to fight tears. I don't know why I'm so emotional. Maybe it's because I love him so much that I don't want to leave. Either way it goes, I have duties to fulfill and I'm already late.

As I'm leaving the cottage I turn to my left and see Daniel silently closing a door with tears streaming down his face. He then starts to run away from the house. I get goose bumps on my skin. Something isn't right. I've never seen Daniel run. I give Misty a carrot and command her to stay. My stuff should be safe. If someone messes with it then Jesus will come out and defend it. I need to go to that cottage to see what's going on.

I get to the cottage and it's very well put together. It seems like everything is in order and I decide there is nothing to look for; until I look on the floor. I see a wet lavender petal on the floor. I look around for another one and spot one a bit closer to the back of the room. I pick it up and it's wet as well. The only two places I can think of that would have water are the kitchen and the bathroom. I go into the kitchen and all the dishes are cleaned and put away with the exception of a cup; other than that there's nothing weird. I decide the next place I need to visit is the bathroom.

I go searching around the house and accidently find the dining room, patio, and the bedroom. This cottage is very nice! Although it's nice, I wish I could find the bathroom so I can leave, my feet are starting to hurt. Although this place is nice I still have an eerie feeling. Finally, I get to the back of the house where there's a closed door. Something tells me that this is the bathroom. I walk up to the door and stand outside of it for a minute. I can't shake this creepy feeling I have all over my body. I slowly ease the door open, afraid of what I might find. Again, I find everything in place except for the wet lavender petals on the ground right next to the bathtub. I'm definitely in the right place. I go to the petals and pick them up to examine them. They're still fresh; meaning they might have been brought this morning. This is very strange.

I stand up and look into the bathtub. There is a beautiful woman staring at me from underneath the water. I jump back and scream. She doesn't move. I regain my breathing and go back to the bathtub to really look at her face. She is lifelessly staring at me and I get a shiver down my spine. She's gorgeous. After looking at her for a couple of minutes I realize she reminds me of Ellie a bit. I get queasy at the thought. I run to the toilet and relieve myself of the breakfast I had with Jesus. I can't believe I'm staring at a dead woman. I wonder what happened to her. I know there's only one person who can give me that answer and that is Daniel, but I'm not going to confront him head on. I'm going to disarm his alliances first so that when he goes down he will not be able to get back up again. The first person I need to take down is Ms. Hannon, but how? She is really powerful. This isn't the time nor the place for me to think about that. I have to get out of this cottage.

I look at her again and feel sorry for her. She was so gorgeous, why would he do that to her? I reach in the tub and close her eyes. I will never forget the feeling of death on my fingertips and the smell of lavender. At least now she looks peaceful instead of creepy. It's the least I can do.

I leave the bathroom and close the door. I need to get to the police. As I'm leaving the room, I go back to the kitchen where there's a piece of paper lying on the counter. I read the information and gasp. She was pregnant! That's why Daniel killed her! He could not let this get back to the castle because of Ellie. It all makes sense now! I take the piece of paper and put it in my pocket. I turn around to leave and there is a strange man standing in the kitchen with me. I didn't even hear him come in. I'm too startled to scream. My eyes get big as saucers as he walks toward me.

"What are you doing here?"

He has authority in his voice.

I'm scared. There is nowhere to hide and nowhere to run. I have to face this man head on and hope that I can get out alive to start the downfall of Daniel. I regain my confidence,

I stand up high and address him with the same authority he has toward me.

"I should ask you the same thing!"

"My name is David and I'm Layla's best friend. Your turn."

"I am here because I saw something suspicious."

"The only person who's suspicious is you! Where is Layla?"

"I'll tell you in a minute. What you have to understand now is that you are dealing with something a lot bigger than you and, for your safety, I suggest you leave until the police get here."

"I'm not going anywhere. I need to know where Layla is!"

"I'll tell you where Layla is after I get some information! Whatever you can tell me about her might save both of our lives!"

He still has anger in his eyes but now he has stopped progressing toward me. I'm relieved at the sight of him standing still. I don't know if I could take him if I had to. He's way bigger than me.

"Layla is a sweet girl. She is very trusting and is quick to invite people to her house. I have told her before that she should not do this but she insists she's fine and nothing will happen to her. She just recently told me about someone she was dating. She said she could not give me his name just yet but they have been dating for about six months and she was pregnant. I was so happy for her and promised to come see her today to help her celebrate."

"Did she ever tell you anything about the man she was dating?"

"She didn't really give me that much information. She just told me he worked in the castle and he has two other children."

He just told me all the information I need to know, unbeknownst to him.

"Now, I gave you my information, now tell me where Layla is."

He has his teeth clenched as he gives me this demand.

The room is silent as I try to find a way to tell him the truth.

"TELL ME!"

I jump as he yells at me. Finally, in a whisper, I answer.

"She's dead; I think I might know who killed her."

The room goes silent. He looks at me as his eyes fill with tears.

"You are lying," he whispers.

"I'm a stranger in someone else's house caught red handed. What is the point of lying now? If you don't believe me then go look for yourself in the bathroom."

He looks me over and I get the feeling he's going through his options in his mind. I stay perfectly still, afraid that if I make a sudden move he'll kill me. He walks back toward the bathroom and opens the door. Suddenly, an animal like wail escapes from his mouth. All I can hear is him screaming Layla's name. Every time he emits another scream my heart wrenches a bit more. It seems like an eternity since he first went back there. I decide to leave and let him grieve privately. As I cross the living room to go outside, I get this weird feeling that I'm being watched. I turn around and he is right there standing in the hallway. His eyes are blood red and there's an angry scowl on his face. I'm scared for my life.

"You did this."

"No, I promise I didn't. I came in here because I saw someone leave who is evil and I wanted to make sure that everything was okay. If you'd let me leave I'm on my way right now to go get the police."

His face changes and now it has a creepy type of look to it.

"You're not going anywhere."

He starts to walk toward me and I become stiff.

"I told her that she should have left him alone and that he was not good for her, but she didn't listen."

He starts to walk around me in circles. I'm getting really nervous now.

"Now, she's dead. It's a good thing she's dead because now I don't have to do it. Why couldn't she love me? What's wrong with me? I knew her better than anyone and yet she still chose that other guy. Well, I'm glad that she's dead!"

With that sentence he stops right in front of me. He is so close to me that I can feel his breath on my face. He leans forward, smells me, and then whispers to me, "Because if I can't have her, nobody can."

A shiver runs down my body. He looks me up and down and starts to lick his lips.

"I need to go now."

"Like I said, you're not going anywhere. You're very pretty. Why are you not married?"

"What makes you think I'm not married?"

"You don't have a ring on your finger."

I blush.

"I don't feel as if that is any of your business, Sir."

"Oh, but I feel like it is part of my business."

He grabs me and licks me on the side of my face. I want to throw up. I feel like the only way I can get out of here alive is to run. He loosens his grip just a little bit, I push him as hard as I can and he stumbles backwards. I turn on my heel and try to run toward the door. He is up quickly and grabs me around my waist, picking me up. I scream as I pummel his body with punches. My punches don't seem to affect him in any way.

"Oh, you are feisty! I like that! You will be an excellent replacement to Layla."

He starts to carry me toward the back where the bedroom is. I'm starting to panic. I fight harder. I know this is the end. I'm tired now from all the struggling and the hitting. I stop fighting. It makes no sense. Nothing I do can overcome this beast. Inside I'm preparing for the worst.

Then, I hear a knock at the door. He stops. The knock comes a bit harder. He stops breathing and stands still. Suddenly I hear the sweetest sound I have heard in a while.

"Anastasia, come to the door!"

I hear the panic in Jesus voice.

"Baby, I'm in here! Help!"

He puts his hand over my mouth and now my screams are muffled.

"Shut up before I kill you right here!"

Tears are streaming down my face. How could this be happening to me? I thought I was doing a good deed and now I'm being held hostage by a grief-stricken, crazed best friend who wanted to be in a relationship with the girl that was killed. Hopelessness fills me as I stand here quietly crying. All goes quiet. Jesus has left. I'm distraught. He continues to go toward the back room and I come to terms with the fact that I'm about to die.

Suddenly, the door gives way and there stands Jesus. He looks murderous. David drops me on the floor and goes to meet Jesus. Jesus and David are about the same build except David is shorter. I try to get up to go to Jesus, but I can't move.

"Anastasia, stay there and cover your eyes. Don't uncover them until I tell you to."

Jesus' voice sounds scary. I can't look away from him.

"DO IT NOW!"

I lift my hands to cover my eyes as he tells me.

Suddenly, I hear a scuffle, punches being thrown, and grunts. Things are breaking as random curse words are being throw. I want to uncover my eyes so bad, but I know Jesus will be highly disappointed if I do. I hear more crashing, more things being broken, more profanities, and finally I hear a bone chilling crack as everything goes silent. I'm lifted up and carried somewhere, but I don't dare uncover my eyes.

"You can uncover your eyes now."

I uncover my eyes and the sun instantly burns.

"Why did I have to cover my eyes?"

"There are just some thing's that shouldn't be seen by a woman. That was one of them. You are not allowed to go back into that cabin. There's a real mess in there. He put up quite a fight."

I look at his face and see a cut right above his eye.

"Don't look so concerned, it's a scratch. Now, why did you go in there in the first place?"

"I saw Daniel running away from the cabin and I got a really bad feeling so decided I should check it out and offer help."

"Anastasia, although I admire your willingness to help, you have to realize we are already in enough trouble as is! You cannot go seeking danger! What if something would have happened to you! What would that have meant for me or for Ellie? I've already put myself in more danger by leaving the confines of my house! Do you know what this can do the mortal realm if Ms. Hannon has access to me? It's been my house keeping her away. I love you, but you have got to stop putting yourself and the ones you love in danger by trying to save people whom you don't even know!"

I have to take a second to think about what Jesus is saying, and he's right. I was just so concerned with bringing down Daniel that I had no regard for my personal safety. He sighs heavily when he sees the tears in my eyes and rubs his hands along his temple.

"It's fine. I know you meant well. Now, question is, what do we do about the bodies?"

"Can't you make them disappear with some sort of magic?"

"No, it will only transport them to another place."

"Well, I planned on alerting the authorities about Layla."

"Who is Layla?"

"Layla is the young woman I found in the bathtub, dead."

Jesus face goes white.

"Maybe we can spin the story so that you and I aren't involved?"

"That could work." There is a pause. "So you mean to tell me Daniel murdered a woman back there?"

"Yes, a woman pregnant with his child."

I hand him the paper and his face goes white. He hands the paper back to me as he puts his head in his hands.

"This isn't good. Things are progressing too fast. If there's any way to stop Daniel and bring an end to his tyranny it has to be done now."

"I agree, but how?"

"I never thought I would say this, but we may need to enlist the help of Ms. Hannon to take down her own son before we all die in the process."

After thirty minutes of slow trotting, I get back to the castle. Although I want to go faster, I realize that I have some very fragile things in the cart. If anything were to be brought to the castle broken I would be in deep trouble.

As I start to unload the items from the cart I realize my life is slowly starting to mimic the life I left behind with my mother and sister. I was always at their beck and call, never doing anything for myself, always putting their needs before my own. I'm tired of it! When can I be happy? When will I ever have my happily ever after? Is it not in the cards for me? Am I destined to walk upon this earth serving people unwillingly? I'm in a grumpy mood and I can't shake it. All I want is go back into town and cuddle in the bed with Jesus while eating more of his muffins. I can see me doing it for the rest of my life. That's where I want to be right now. I contemplate getting onto my horse and going to him when I'm stopped by Noelle. Again I'm struck with the feeling that I know her from somewhere.

"Anastasia, come quick, Ellie is sick!"

I hurry behind her and find a very sick Ellie in the bathroom.

"Ellie, what's wrong?"

I go to the closet, grab a wash cloth, dampen it, and start wiping the sweat off her face.

Ellie starts to cry.

I instruct Noelle to leave us and to go to the kitchen to get Ellie some tea and light biscuits in order to settle her stomach.

She leaves in a hurry to fulfill the request.

I help Ellie get off the floor and into bed. She looks terrible and I can't help but to feel sorry for her.

"Now, we got you all cleaned up and comfortable in bed. What's wrong?"

"Daniel keeps avoiding me. I've not seen nor spoken to him in three months. Why doesn't he love me? I have his children!"

I feel sick to my stomach. Hearing Ellie confirm and embrace this knowledge is sickening to me.

"Did you know, Anastasia? Did you know the kids are his?"

"Yes, I knew they were his kids when Jaylin was born. Does the Prince know?"

Ellie looks sad for a moment.

"No, he doesn't know, hence the reason why I'm sick now."

"What do you mean?"

"Since Daniel was ignoring me I found comfort in the arms of James."

She starts to cry uncontrollably.

I sit on the bed and comfort her the best way I know how. After a couple of minutes she regains her composure and looks at me with a look of sadness I've never seen in anyone before. She looks as if she's defeated and can't fight anymore. I hate seeing her like this. This is not the same Ellie I knew before. If it weren't for Daniel, everyone would be happy. At this moment I vow to kill him.

She just keeps looking at me and caressing my face like she used to do when we were kids and I allowed her in my room to do her hair. She looks as if she wants to say something.

"What's on your mind, Ellie?"

"I think I might be pregnant with James' baby."

I can't breathe.

"What if Daniel leaves me? What if he doesn't love me anymore? If he doesn't love me anymore I'll die, Anastasia, I'll just die!"

I feel like now is the time. If there is anything in the world that might wear this spell off and bring Ellie back to reality, it will be the knowledge that Daniel is a murderer.

"I have something to tell you, Ellie."

"What is it?"

"Daniel got another woman pregnant."

The color leaves her skin as her mind tries to wrap itself around what I just said. I take the paper out of my pocket and hand it to Ellie. She is stark white and looks as if she's going to be sick.

"That's not all."

"You mean there's something worse than him cheating on me with another woman and getting her pregnant?"

I want to tell her that she did the exact same thing but I decide to keep this comment to myself.

"Daniel killed her."

The color returns to her face and she looks at me with the most evil look.

"Daniel is a lot of things, but he's not a murderer."

"Ellie, I saw him."

"I don't want to hear your lies! Get out of my room before I throw you in prison for blasphemy!"

"Ellie, you have to listen to me. You and the babies are in danger! You have to listen to me if you want to live!"

"Maybe I don't want to live, Anastasia, have you thought of that? If I can't have Daniel and live my life how I want to then what is the point of living? I have to do what everyone else says and love who everyone else wants me to love. What about what *I* want? None of you care about me, you only care about the Prince and those damn kids!"

"Ellie, I care about you."

"You only care because I've not locked you up for killing your family! You never loved me. No one has ever loved me!"

"The Prince loves you."

"He only loves me because of my looks. He doesn't even know me. He doesn't know my favorite flower is a rose or that my favorite color is pink. He doesn't know anything about me! How can you love someone you don't know?"

I'm silent. She has a point. I've never seen them interact much, but at the same time when you're trying to save everyone's lives you tend to overlook the small details.

"I'm sure that's not true."

"It is true and you know it! Sam told me everything. And you want to know what? I'm glad he cast that damn spell because it gave me a reason to feel something real with someone else. I love him, Anastasia. I thought you would be the one person that would understand since you know all about forbidden love with Ms. Hannon but I see I was wrong."

"Ellie, you can trust me, but you have to believe me when I say that Daniel murdered that woman."
"Get out of my room, now!"

"Please, Ellie, don't do this."

"NOW!"

I leave the room defeated. There's nothing more I can do. I can't convince her that Daniel is evil because of that damn spell. She's not using common sense, but I know someone who will.

I go toward the library and, sure enough, the Prince is in there sitting in a chair staring out the window with a huge glass of amber colored liquor. The room reeks of booze. I gag just a little.

"Prince?"

"What do you want, Anastasia?" he replies to me without looking away from the window.

"I need to talk to you."

"Are you here to tell me that the children are Daniel's, not mine?"

The room goes silent. I don't know what to say. This is not at all the way I thought this was going to go.

"You don't have to say anything. I'm trying to find a way to prove that myself. Once I do, he's as good as dead. As well as all the other people who knew and thought they shouldn't tell me because I was too stupid to figure out what was going on!"

"What if I told you that you could kill him sooner? What if I told you I know something that you could hang him for?"

"Then I would spare your life for not telling me the truth about Ellie and Daniel."

I gulp.

"Now speak, you have my attention."

"Daniel murdered a woman in town. She was pregnant with his child. I was doing errands when I saw him leave the cottage in disarray. I went to investigate and found a man dead on the floor and a woman drowned in the bathtub surrounded by lavender petals."

I hand him the paper. He looks it over and a smile creeps over his face. Although I see the smile I can see the fire in his eyes. I'm scared.

"You did well, Anastasia."

"Can I also tell you something else?"

"Sure, I'm in a better spirit."

"You're the only one who has been in Ellie's presence for the past three months, correct?

"Yes, I made sure of it."

"Ellie is pregnant again."

His smile leaves his face.

"Are you sure?"

"Yes, I am. Congratulations."

I turn around to leave him to his thoughts and exit the room. I go down the stairs and across the big hall and out of the castle toward Ms. Hannon's cottage. Now I have to convince her to go against her son, and I have no idea how I'm going to do that.

I go into the cabin and Ms. Hannon isn't there, as usual. I look around the cabin and everything is spotless. It looks just the way I left it this morning. I'm starting to think she hasn't been in the house all day. I'm sad because I really needed to talk to her and I'm also sad because, if I had known she wasn't here, I could have stayed with Jesus longer. I'm just about to leave when I hear a whisper. I look around the room and don't see anything. I decide it was nothing more than the wind and decide to leave again. This time I hear the whisper, but it is a bit louder.

"Anastasia!"

I heard my name, I knew I did! I am not going crazy. I look around the room and my eyes rest on Ms. Hannon's spell book. It's slightly glowing which is weird because it never does that. I go toward the book and stand directly in front of it.

"*Abierto.*"

The book levitates, opens, and the guardian emerges.

"Thank you for listening, o ye pure of heart."

"You are very welcome, but why do you summon me?"

"To give you the information you seek, and to answer a question."

"Let's start with the question. How can you answer if I have not asked you a question?"

"Your question is in your heart. You want to know how

to break Ellie's spell. It is simple; you have to kill the son of Hannon, Anastasia."

"Why me?

"It's in the prophecy dear child, remember?

"Ignorant is as Ignorant does
Ellie is the one that has fallen in love
With a Prince but lo' and behold
She will suddenly swoon for a friend who is really a foe
A spell will be cast and will fall on two ears
A bond will be formed between the two that hears
It can only be broken with the death of one of the afflicted
One will die while the other will walk conflicted
With the death of one before a three day kiss
Will ensure that the other four parties will exist
But lo' if the kiss shall happen before the third moon
Then that kiss will be fatal and seal each life with doom
Two innocent lives will be forever changed
By this spell that will leave both parents slain
With nothing to lose and nothing to gain
The blood shall be shed by the one who was previously named"

The end of that prophecy mentions that you must kill the son of Hannon. What it doesn't say is why. If you kill the son of Hannon, then Ellie will be free of her curse. But, if someone else kills the son of Hannon, Ellie will die."

I feel sick to my stomach. I can't believe he just said that. I just gave the Prince a reason to kill Daniel. Now I have to save Daniel from the Prince in order to kill him myself? This is getting too complicated.

"Why are you helping me?"

"It is simple. I need your help too, o ye pure of heart."

"What can I do for you Guardian?"

"Help me escape. My name is not Guardian, my name is

Hernando, and I used to be a very powerful wizard twenty seven ago when I sold my soul to Hannon in order to save the love of my life only to find out that she killed her anyway. She was to let me raise my son until he was old enough to be safe on his own. She went back on her word when she tried to kill my son and so our deal was broken. Since she could not harvest my soul for herself she went to retrieve my soul from the spirit world and trapped me in her book. She made barter for my soul and now she has to make good on that trade. My power now resonates in this book and the only way I can be set free is if she is destroyed. I want to be free so that I may be with my son once more.

"Who is your son?"

"His name is Jesus De La Rosa."

My heart skips a beat. Could it be the same person?

"I know him."

"How do you know him?"

"He is my boyfriend."

He is silent for a minute.

"I knew there was a reason why I liked you. My son has great taste."

I blush.

"So, will you help me, Mija? Every day that I live in this book I grow more and more angry. I want revenge and you are the only person I know who can help me."

"How, Hernando? I don't know where the locket is!"

"I do. It's in the magical realm. I can give you directions to it. Go to back to my son, he can help you retrieve it and kill Hannon. Once you kill Hannon, all the spells she cast will cease and I will be free!"

"How do I get there?"

As I ask the question, a piece of paper comes out of the book and comes floating toward me.

"It's all there. Please, don't tell my son that I'm trapped here. If he finds out he will destroy the book trying to release me. If the book is destroyed, I will be destroyed. He can't know until I figure out the spell to return me to my physical state. Promise you will not tell him under any circumstance."

"I promise."

"Gracias, Mija. I knew I chose right. Please, help."

He disappears in the book and it returns to its dormant state. I put the piece of paper in my pocket and turn to leave. As I turn around Ms. Hannon is walking in the door. I'm petrified. So I do the only thing I know looks normal, I start to clean.

"Anastasia, when you are done can you come here, please?"

"I sure can, Ms. Hannon."

I straighten another pillow on the couch and follow her into the kitchen.

"Did you get everything I asked for?"

"Yes, it's outside by the cart, but there was an emergency with Ellie so I have not had time to put it up."

"Please see that you do immediately."

"Yes ma'am."

I turn to leave the room and I hear Ms. Hannon crying. I turn around and go to comfort her.

"Why don't you love me anymore, Anastasia?"

"I do love you, Ms. Hannon. I cook for you, I clean for you, and I am here every night in your bed. I love you."

"Then who is he? Who is this man that you've been seeing?"

I go quiet as I quickly think of something to say.

"I go to the Muffin Man every day to get fresh bread as you ask me to do."

"Then why are your trips getting longer and longer."

"Because your list keeps getting longer and longer, plus, I like to browse."

"Anastasia, don't lie to me! You've been seeing the Muffin Man haven't you! You've been intimate with him! Tell me the truth."

I don't know why, but I'm tired of this woman. I just want her to kick me out and be done with me. So I decide to be truthful.

"Yes. I have been intimate with him. Yes, I love him. Yes I want to be with him. I love you, Ms. Hannon, but now I love you more as a friend than a lover. You haven't touched me in months. You're not even here most of the time. He is always there! So, I'm leaving you and this job, and I'm going to go live with him!"

As I say this, a creepy smile forms on her face. She wipes away the tears and lifts up her hand.

"You're going nowhere."

I'm pinned to the wall and can't move. Ms. Hannon starts to cackle. My skin starts to crawl.

"Silly girl, you fell into my trap. I have been trying for years to get that man to come out of that house so that I may kill him, and now, I finally have the ammunition to do it. Will he choose his life or yours? "

"He has defeated you before, he can do it again!"

"Dear child, he defeated me because I was weak. Now, I have enough power to overthrow the whole magical Kingdom. The only thing standing between me and that crown is him!"

"You'll not get away with this."

"Oh, but I shall. He can't resist coming to me now that I have his future wife and his unborn child!"

"Excuse me?"

"Congratulations, you're having a boy. And just by the aura I'm getting from you he is going to be one powerful witch. Too bad he will never come to fruition."

I can't believe it. I'm pregnant. No wonder I've been feeling sick, craving muffins, and not fitting into my clothes. I should have stayed with Jesus, and now, I've put all our lives, including the one of my unborn son, in danger.

I look down at my stomach and mouth the words "I love you and I'm sorry" to the son I never thought I would have.

Right then and there I vow I will kill Daniel and Ms. Hannon so that Jesus, our child, and I will be happy. I first need to get out of this magical grip. I have no time to plan because a sharp pain engulfs my body and I black out with nothing but her cackling laughter echoing in my head.

CHAPTER TEN
And He Shall be Called King
Ellie

My life changed three months ago. The doctor came in, examined me, and told me I was in fact pregnant and I was three months along. This baby's different. I've hardly gained any weight and haven't gotten sick until the day I confessed to Anastasia. I didn't think I was so far along though. Now, I'm eight months pregnant and I'm miserable. I got really big during my seventh month. So big, in fact, I've been ordered to stay in bed for the remainder of my pregnancy because my petite body can't handle so much weight.

I miss Daniel and Anastasia. I've seen neither of them in a while. I haven't seen Daniel since three months after the twins were born and I haven't seen Anastasia for about four months, I think. I've since lost count. I keep going back to how I treated her when I last saw her. I feel bad for yelling at her and now I wish she was here so I would have someone to talk to. The only people I see are the nurses, my twins, who are getting so big, and James. James doesn't even sleep in the same bed as me anymore. I have no idea what's going on but every time he looks at me it's like he is disgusted. I know he doesn't know about the twins not being his, but something tells me he has a hunch. I'm lonely and at this moment I've burned all my bridges and I don't know who to call.

"Why the long face?"

I turn around and there is Sam, my mother, standing there with a sincere smile on her face. Just by seeing her I instantly break down in tears. Sam is by my side in an instant.

"I'm lonely; I don't have anyone to talk to. I don't know where Daniel is, I don't know where Anastasia is, and the Prince won't even look at me, let alone talk to me. I feel as if I've ruined everyone's lives and now I'm about to bring another life into the world and I'm not even happy."

She grabs me in her arms, strokes my head, and rocks me back and forth as I cry fitfully into her gown. Finally, I calm down. She lets me go and looks at me with a serious face. The face of a mother, the face I've longed for since I was young.

"I apologize for the way you feel, Ellie, but I can't be sorry that all this happened. I warned you what would happen if you kissed him and you did it anyway. I also told you what would happen if you had his children, yet you decided to still lie in the same bed with him. So don't place the blame on anyone else because it's nobody's fault but yours!"

I snatch away from Sam. My tears are now replaced with pure, unadulterated anger.

"I know what I've done; there's no need to remind me of that! How do I fix it?"

Sam starts playing with her hands and looks away not answering my question.

Slowly, I realize I'm in a bit deeper than I thought.

"There's no way to fix it is there, Sam?"

"I'm afraid not, at least not by you. The only person who can fix it is Anastasia and at this moment she can't be found."

"What do you mean she can't be found?"

"I have been trying to contact her for months. No answer. I've posed as a regular street commoner just to see if I can get any additional information. Apparently she hasn't been spotted. All of her regular errands have been done by Noelle."

My stomach drops, what happened to Anastasia? The only person who would have this information is Ms. Hannon and I plan on getting to the bottom of this.

"If you get any information on where she is or if you just need to talk to me you can reach me by rubbing on this."

She then reaches in her gown pocket and produces one of the most gorgeous necklaces I've ever seen with a big pink gem. My eyes start to water when I see it. It is literally the most gorgeous thing I've ever seen in my life, besides my children, of course. She places it around my neck and it's surprisingly light weight compared to what it looks like. Tears start to stream out of my eyes.

"Thank you Sam, it's beautiful."

"You're welcome, Ellie, and stop calling me Sam. I would prefer if you called me Mom."

"Thank you again, Mom, for all that you've done."

"No problem, just remember that everything I do for you is out of love, darling. I need to leave you now. Learn from your mistakes and take heed, child. True love's kiss in a time of desperation can break the strongest of spells."

With that, she steps out the window and disappears. I wonder why she told me that. It doesn't matter, spell or not, I'm in love with Daniel and there's nothing the Prince can do to make me change my mind. My stomach jumps. I have no idea what's going on but I'm getting a slight pain. Maybe I need to stop thinking about this and relax. As soon as I get comfortable the Prince walks in. So much for me being relaxed.

"Ellie, can we talk?"

"Sure, I was just sitting here getting comfortable and trying to relax but, I guess that doesn't matter. By all means, sit down."

"Enough with the sarcasm; I came to talk to you about something serious."

I sense the tension in the air and don't like where this conversation is going.

"What do you have to talk to me about?"

"Ellie, I know the twins aren't mine."

He's looking at me with an intense stare and I can't match it. I turn and look away.

"If it is not true, speak now."

I can't look at him. It was going to come out sooner or later. It might as well be now.

"Who told you?"

"No one told me. I figured it out on my own. It's because I love you that you're not dead right now and, for that reason I feel like a fool."

I swallow hard. I've only seen the Prince act this way once before, right before the twins were born.

"Why, Ellie? I gave you everything! How could you treat me this way?"

"James, I never meant to hurt you."

"How else is this supposed to make me feel?"

I jump as he hits the wall so hard one of the pictures falls and breaks.

"Am I supposed to be happy Daniel is sharing in my marital bliss without the work? I don't remember Daniel riding around the damn town trying to find you using only a shoe! I didn't see Daniel dealing with your step family and transitioning you to leave that house and come live with me! I didn't see Daniel fighting his parents saying that it was worth marrying you when I passed up many other brides who was more equipped to be a future queen than you! To put it bluntly, Daniel just rode my coattails and reaped the benefits after I put in all the work! Why did I do all this?"

He stops for a moment and starts breathing. He's trying to calm himself down. After a couple of minutes of silence he continues.

"I love you, Ellie, even though you don't deserve a man like me. You're worthless, and honestly, I have no need for you after you have my child."

My heart drops. I don't know why but I'm affected by his words and all I want to do is make it better.

"Don't say that, James."

"I just did, and I meant every word. I haven't seen Daniel or else I would kill him myself, but then I realized killing him with my bare hands will also kill my dreams of being King once my father steps down. So, with that being said, as much as I love you I'm going to let you go. You and the twins can leave my castle once the baby is born, but the newborn stays with me. If it is a boy I will raise him to be a good man and one day he shall be called King when I step down from my throne. If it is a girl I will teach her how to be a proper lady, nothing like her mother."

"What about Daniel?"

"It has been confirmed that Daniel was involved in a heinous crime in town. Based on that information and the blatant disrespect he has demonstrated toward me, he has been condemned to death. The next time he's spotted in my Kingdom, he is to be brought to me immediately and beheaded."

"You can't do that!"

"Why can't I, Ellie? Why can't I kill this man for taking another life and more importantly stealing my wife's heart from me?"

He starts to cry.

"I don't know what I did wrong. I've tried everything in my power to make this right but I can't fix something that is not seen as broken by the other person. Do you really think I gave you the key to my heart and my Kingdom only to have you give it to another man? Why don't you want me to kill him? Is it because you love him?"

I don't answer. I just look away. This makes him even more infuriated.

"You don't even have the decency to tell me how you feel to my face. How can I respect you as a woman if you can't even voice what you want? Well, since you're not brave enough to do it, I'll tell you how I feel. I love you, Ellie, but you are the most selfish person I've ever known and, honestly, I hope you die a slow, painful death so you can get a tiny glimpse of what I feel."

With that last sentence the room is silent. I can tell by his demeanor, stance, and tone that he means every word he said, and those words hurt me. Isn't this what I wanted? Didn't I want to escape with Daniel and leave this life of lies behind? Listening to James, I slowly start to realize there were no lies in the beginning. There is only one real truth I've overlooked, Daniel has never really been here for me. It has always been the Prince. It has been James that held me when I felt insecure. It was James who held me when I gave birth to the twins. It was James who gave meaning to my life, not Daniel. How could I be a fool?

James turns to walk out of the room and I feel if he walks out of the room he may very well walk out of my life for good. My heart hurts right now. I know that it's wrong of me, but I want James more than I want Daniel. Everything he said to me is true. I know loving James is the right thing to do. All I want to do is kiss him repetitively and apologize for being so naïve.

"James!"

He stops dead in his tracks but does not turn around to look at me as I start to cry.

"James, I'm sorry. I love you too. I don't want to be with anyone else but you. I know I haven't been the ideal wife but I want to fix it. Daniel was someone whom I could talk to when things were not going right. I mistook a great friend for something more. Being with Daniel made me realize how much I was missing out on with you. I'm so sorry, Baby. Please forgive me and let's start all over again. I can't live without you. Please!"

With every word I speak I feel more and more weak. It is like my heart and my mind are fighting. My mind wants me to stay with Daniel, but my heart is crying out for James. I feel like I'm fighting for my life. All I know right now is I am desperate for him. I want him to come to me and kiss me and tell me he loves me and that we can work this out as a family, but he just stands there. He doesn't move. I cry harder. Why won't he turn around? I see his fist clenching and unclenching. I don't know what's going on in his head, but I so badly want to get out of this bed and go to him but I can't. I'm trapped, confined to this bed, and it's killing me.

"James, please, I need you. If you can't see it in your heart to forgive me I understand and I will leave as soon as I regain my strength from the baby. You can leave now."

I'm begging him to turn around, begging for him to love me. He's still not turning around and I see now I've lost him for good. I cover my face and sob heavily into my hands.

Suddenly, he is by my side, taking my hands away from my eyes. His eyes are red and puffy from crying as well. He leans down and he kisses me hard. It's one of the fiercest kisses I've ever had in my life. There is so much that is said in his kiss. Love me. I forgive you. Don't ever leave me again. My kiss gives him all the answer he needs. I will love you. I'm sorry and I won't ever leave again. As I kiss him my body is filled with a painful bliss I can't explain. My mind is exploding with excruciating pain, but my heart is allowing me to remain conscious. The kiss gets deeper, he feels on my face, then my breasts, and finally down in between my legs. He stops, pulls away from the kiss, and looks at his hand. It's covered in blood. The pain takes over and I pass out.

I come to and try to get up, but I'm in a lot of pain. My lips are dry and I desperately want some water. I look around and don't see anyone in the room. The only thing I remember is there being a lot of blood, bad pain, and passing out. I put my hands on my stomach and the baby bump is gone. I start to panic. *Where is my baby?* I try to scream but my throat is so dry it comes out as a whisper. My eyes move frantically around the room. I'm in my bedroom. I attempt to get up again when a god awful feeling rips through my stomach. A scream emerges and hurts me even more. *What is going on?* I collapse back on the bed hoping and praying someone will come to my rescue. I reach around my neck and feel the gem. Even though every cell in my body hurts I use the remaining bit of my energy to summon the one person I know can help, my Mother.

She appears instantly. She comes to the bed and stands over me. She touches my skin with her fingertips and instantly pulls away as if she touched something hot.

"You have a lot of pain there."

"Please. Help me."

"Sure, now I'm going to have you drink something. I always carry around a vial for myself but I feel like you need it more than I do. I must warn you, it will be one of the best things that you have ever tasted in your life but the pain that follows is going to be excruciating. Worse than what you are experiencing now. It will only last for a minute. Once the pain subsides you will be healed. Do you want me to give you the drink?"

I slowly nod my head. I can't imagine a pain worse than this. She pulls this small vial out of her pocket, puts it to my mouth, and pours the liquid in. Once the liquid touches my lips it is the sweetest taste I've ever experienced in my life. All the words in the dictionary could not describe the type of taste that's swimming around my taste buds. I feel my body slowly becoming functional when, suddenly, I see a white light. It feels as if every bone in my body has been cracked, every vein has been popped, and every cell has burst. The pain is so unbearable I can't do anything but grip the sheets and emit silent screams. Just when I think I'm about to die from the pain, it ends abruptly. I'm still clenching the sheets, fearing the pain will suddenly come back. I slowly open my eyes and there is Sam, looking at me with a concerned look.

"Are you okay?"

"Yes, I'm okay. Thank you."

"You're welcome."

We share a moment. Suddenly, the Prince walks in holding a blue blanket in his arms. He walks over and kisses me on the forehead, oblivious to the fact that I'm awake and Sam is here. He just has his face in this blanket with a weird, goofy, look on his face.

"What happened?"

He jumps at the sound of my voice. He slowly looks up from the blanket and realizes I'm awake and Sam is still standing there.

"Who are you?"

"Hello, James. I'm Sam. I'm Ellie's Fairy Godmother and also her birth mother."

He looks back and forth between me and Sam. His jaw slowly drops.

"Why have I never seen you before?"

"It was too dangerous. It still is dangerous but I needed to be here for my daughter."

"I see, well, nice to finally meet you."

"You as well. I wish it were under better circumstances."

I love the fact that my mother and my husband are getting along, but I still need to know what happened.

"What happened, James?"

"When you passed out I called the doctor. You went into labor and were unresponsive and there was a complication with the baby. They didn't think you or the baby was going to survive if they didn't do something quickly. The only way they could preserve both of your lives was to do an emergency C-section. Afterwards, your vitals were so low the doctor decided to put you in an induced coma so your body could heal. We didn't think you were going to make it."

He pauses and looks sad for a moment. I can see a tear escaping his eye and I'm truly touched at the amount of love this man has for me.

"I'm glad you're awake, Baby. I have come in here every day for two weeks with the baby, hoping you would wake up. Here is baby James Alexander Charming the second, but I just call him Alexander. I took the liberty of naming him."

He puts the baby in my arms and he looks just like James. I never thought that there would be more room to love in my heart after the twins, but this baby just proved me wrong. I love him more than life itself. I look over at Sam, she's smiling. Slowly, her smile starts to fade. I get a bit uneasy watching the transition.

"Do you want to hold the baby?" I ask her, trying to ease the tension in the room.

"No. Not right now." She looks towards James. "James, go get the twins and bring them in here now! Do not grab anything but the children, you do not have time for anything else. Do you understand me?"

James looks panicked as he nods his head and runs out of the room. He returns a couple of minutes later holding Jaylin in one arm and Jayson in the other.

"Good, now get on the bed with Ellie."

He does as he's told without asking any questions. Sam then starts to speak a language I don't understand as she waves her hands and her wand around us. Slowly there is a barely visible force field that surrounds all five of us. As soon as she completes the spell she turns and mouths the words, "I love you" and looks toward the door. I don't know what is going on, but I have never seen my mother act this way. She has always been so calm. So, to see that she is frazzled and a bit panicked makes me uneasy.

Shortly after, Ms. Hannon bursts through the doors. Her hair is floating around her, electricity is shooting from her fingertips, and she has a wicked smile plastered on her face. Even though I can't hear what is being said, I can feel the tension.

Ms. Hannon points at us and tries to shoot something from her fingertips. It repels off the force field. My mother gets in front of us and blocks Ms. Hannon from hitting us with more of that electricity. Ms. Hannon is taken aback by this and tries to hit us again as another wave of electricity emits from her fingertips. It hits my mother, and she falls, unmoving, to the ground. I scream. Suddenly, a big Hispanic man bursts through the door and calls out Ms. Hannon's name. Her smile widens as she turns to face him. They exchange words as my mother slowly gets up off of the ground. While Ms. Hannon is turned around, she takes a moment to regain her strength as she stands on shaky legs. She then tackles Ms. Hannon from behind and pins her to the floor. The Hispanic guy points both hands toward us and is mouthing something. I can't read his lips because they're moving so fast. Ms. Hannon struggles to get free of my mother's grip, slowly inching toward the Hispanic man. Finally Hannon breaks free and is going towards Jesus.

I put my hand on the force field as I cry out for the mother I barely know.

She turns toward me with tears in her eyes and mouths the words, "Be strong, I love you."

After she mouths those words she turns around and attacks Hannon from behind. I'm now beating on the force field. I need her to stop fighting and get on the bed with me. I need her with me. I need her to be my mother. They are on the floor fighting, the Hispanic man returns his gaze to the force field, points his hands towards us and we disappear and reappear in a place that is foreign to us. The force field drops and we are able to explore.

Sitting on the table right in front of me is a note with my name. I open it up and read:

Dear Ellie,

You do not know me, but I know all about you. My name is Jesus, and I am a good friend of your mother's. Welcome to my home. It is surrounded by magic so you will be safe. I transported you here because I knew this would be the safest place for you and your family. You are not to leave this house until either I, or your mother, have given you the ok. There is everything that you, the Prince, and your children could possibly want and need in this cottage.

As you may know by now, Ms. Hannon is evil and I, for one, plan on destroying her with or without your mother's help. It is believed that Anastasia has been held captive in her cottage to try to draw me to her and it worked.

If neither I, nor your, mother survives and Ms. Hannon wins, may God have mercy on your soul.

Yours Truly
Jesus, the Muffin Man

I fold the paper and look at James as I start to cry. I may have just lost my mother for the second time in my life, but this time, it may be forever. Now, I really have no family to turn to. With the thought of me being without my mother and Anastasia, I start to sob harder as I grab my children and hug them like there is no tomorrow because, at this moment, tomorrow is not promised.

CHAPTER ELEVEN
There Can be Only One Muffin Man
(Twenty-seven years ago)

"Again!"

I struggle to control the object in front of me as my father yells at me from the sidelines. I'm sweating and all I want to do is go play with my friends. Why do I have to learn this stupid magic stuff anyway?

"I said again, Jesus. We are going to keep doing it until you get it right!"

I start to pout. I really just want to go play. Why must he be so hard on me all the time? I start to sweat harder as I concentrate on the stuffed animal a couple of feet away from me, trying to make it float. Finally, after hours of trying, it lifts off the ground just a couple of feet, then plops down to the ground. Although this training has taken a good amount of my day, I start to smile.

My father starts to smile, and for a moment things are good.

He runs toward me, picks me up, and swings me in the air.

"Great job, Mijo!"

"Thank you, Papa! Why do I need to learn this stupid magic stuff anyway?"

His face turns dark and I get a bit scared.

"Mijo, this is not just stupid magic stuff, this is the thing that is going to save your life one day. One day, I'm not going to be here and it's going to be up to you to keep the legacy alive. You don't understand, but what I'm teaching you is important. What I'm teaching you will help you when you are a grown man."

"Why can't I learn it when I'm grown?" I whine.

"Things like this need to be perfected! You can't just do it one day and master it the next! Do you see how long it took you to get that stuffed animal off the ground?"

I lower my head in shame. I don't like to disappoint Papa and I tried hard, I really did. He looks at me and softens up a bit.

"You may go and play with your friends for an hour. There are cookies on the counter, take some to your friends. When you come back, we need to start prepping the bread to bake tomorrow and continue training."

I smile really big and hug his leg as I go to the front of the bakery, grab the cookies, and run out the door to meet my friends.

My father is the best baker in the whole magical realm. People come from faraway places just to eat his bread. He used to be a very powerful wizard, but gave it up once my mother died. I don't know how she died, Papa will not tell me, but I know it was bad because when he talks about her he gets really sad and mad at the same time. I miss her every day.

"Hey, Jesus," my friend Hector is waving frantically as I run toward him.

"Hey, Hector!"

"What do you have there?"

He points to the bag and I smile big.

"Mi Papa's galletas!"

"You brought some of your father's cookies?"

I give him one as I start to eat the other one.

"Where's Jaime?"

"His family moved."

I'm shocked by this. Jamie, Hector, and I were known in our town as the tres amigos. With him gone, I feel like I've lost an arm.

"Why did they move?"

"His mother said something about the big, mean lady called Hannon getting closer."

"Who is Hannon?"

"I don't know, but all the grown-ups are pretty scared of her."

Hector stuffs the rest of his cookie in his mouth and wipes crumbs off his face onto his shirt.

"I'm not afraid of nothing 'cause I can do this!"

I lift my hands and I concentrate hard on the crumbs on Hector's shirt. I concentrate for a couple of minutes while Hector looks at me confused.

"Is something supposed to happen?"

"Shhh, be quiet. I almost got it."

I concentrate harder. I think of my father being proud of me and it makes me really happy inside. I feel myself getting calmer as I think about making him proud. Suddenly there is a yell and I realize Hector is floating high in the air.

"Jesus, put me down!"

"I don't know how!"

I hold my hands up as I try to control where he goes. I move my hands to the right and he goes to the right. I move my hands left and he goes to the left. Pretty soon, Hector is doing loops in the air and is having the time of his life. I did it! I really learned how to do it!

"Great job, Mijo."

I turn around and my father is standing behind me.

"Don't lose concentration. If you lose focus you'll drop him. Bring him down slowly."

I slowly bring my hands down and place Hector back on the ground, landing perfectly on his feet.

"That was awesome! How did you learn to do that?"

Hector is now breathless and smiling goofily.

"Mi Papa."

I turn around and he's smiling big.

"I'm going to go home and help get the bread ready for tomorrow. I'll see you later!"

I turn away from a happy Hector and run toward the house, eager to learn more.

I get to the house first and start bouncing up and down as I wait for Papa to catch up. He finally walks in the door and I'm ready.

"What are we going to learn next, Papa?"

He looks at me as if he is thinking.

"How did you learn to levitate so fast?"

"Le-vi-tate?"

"It means to make something float. How did you make Hector float in the air like that?"

"I concentrated really hard like you told me to. I was trying to make the crumbs float but it didn't work. Then I thought about making you proud and I started feeling all warm inside and Hector started to float. Every time I thought about being happy he floated higher."

He looks at me with a very surprised look.

"I never thought I would see it in this lifetime."

"What is that Papa?"

"El poder del corazón ardiente."

"What is the 'power of the warm heart'?"

"It's a special kind of power we wizards have heard about, but have never seen. It's a power that is fueled by strong emotion. If you are angry, sad, happy, or annoyed, your power is swayed by emotions. The power of a warm heart uses the strongest of these emotions, happiness and love. Your power, if used right, can bring down even the most powerful of wizards or witches and could make you the most powerful wizard known in history. Have you ever had weird stuff happen when you get emotional?"

Come to think of it, weird stuff always happens to me. Like rocks turning to candy in my hands or bugs following me or, weirdest of all, the sparks from my fingertips. I never knew what this meant and now that he is explaining it to me, I get excited. I always wanted to be a wizard. My friends are all jealous of me because Papa is teaching me magic while their parents won't teach them anything until they are older.

"Yes. Weird stuff happens to me all the time. So what does this mean, Papa?"

"It means we might have a special, secret weapon to defeat Hannon."

"Who is Hannon?"

"She is a very powerful witch that is trying to rule the world. She is a very bad lady. She…" He starts to choke up and can't finish the sentence. Tears start to well up in his eyes.

"She did what? Tell me, Papa. I'm a big, strong boy. I can handle anything."

He looks at me and smiles with sadness in his eyes.

"Your mother would have adored you. You have her heart and her eyes."

He stops and takes a breath to collect himself as he continues, "Hannon is the reason why your mother isn't here."

It takes a minute to understand what he said. She is the reason why my mother is not here? She is the reason why I don't get the bedtime stories, the kisses on my cheek, and the extra cookies when Papa isn't looking? Never in my life have a felt so much anger. This woman took mi Mama away from me! Tears start to well up in my eyes. I close my eyes because I don't want mi Papa to see that I'm crying. I'm a big strong boy and big strong boys don't cry. As much as I'm trying, I can't contain my emotion. I want to kill her myself. What kind of person takes someone's Mama?

As I think more and more of how angry I feel, I feel this weird sensation going through my arms. This sensation builds and builds until I can't hold it in any longer and I scream. I scream long and hard as everything comes crashing down around me, but I don't dare open my eyes. I cry and I scream and I curse the name of Hannon for taking something that meant so much to me.

Finally, the sensation is starting to die down and I feel myself calming down. I open my eyes and my father is looking at me with a very surprised and scared expression on his face. Around him, the whole bakery is in shambles. Glass is everywhere, wood is split, equipment is broken, and bread is everywhere. I look at my hands and I see sparks. They were very vibrant at first but now it has gone down to nothing more than a couple of sparks here and there. I look up at my father and hold up my hands to him.

"El poder del corazón ardiente?"

"El poder del corazón ardiente. Now that I have seen this power firsthand I know that you are capable of learning this very difficult spell that can only be done by someone with your power.

"Sure, what is it called?"

"It's called the "Love/Hate spell."

These are the two most powerful emotions on the planet. These two emotions can dictate a person's future because each emotion is based on impulse. When you hate someone, you immediately want to hurt them and when you love someone, you want to protect them. These two emotions are very contradicting and can destroy a person if both exist in the body at the same time. That is where you come in. You have the power to draw from both and to create such a force that it will ultimately destroy anyone or anything it touches."

"Do you really think I can do it, Papa?"

"Yes, Mijo, from what you just did when I told you what Hannon did to your mother just confirms what I already know. Now, we are going to start training tonight after we get through prepping the bread. I want you to understand this going to be one of the hardest and most draining things you have ever had to do. Are you ready, and willing, to learn?"

"Yes, Papa, if it will end the reign of Hannon, I'm ready to do anything."

I stand there with my chest poked out and my chin held high. I look at my father and he is grinning from ear to ear.

"I was hoping you would say that. Let's start prepping the bread so we can get started on this spell."

"But, Papa, the kitchen is a mess."

"I know."

He waves his hand over the kitchen and everything returns back to the way it was. I'm amazed.

"How did you do that?"

"Years of practice."

"If you can do it that way, why do we prep the bread every day?"

"Magic can only take you so far in life, Mijo. It's through hard work, dedication, and persistence that you will make it far in life.

"What is persistence?"

"It means that you keep trying and never give up."

I'm in awe. I've never seen someone so smart in my life. I make a vow that when I grow up I want to be just like him.

"Ok, Papa, let's start prepping the bread. I want to learn everything you have to teach me no matter how long it takes."

It has been a month and I think I finally have the "Love/Hate" spell down. Of course, I haven't had anyone to test it out on, but I think I can use it if I need to. The thing I keep struggling with is having a little bit too much love or too much hate. Papa has explained if I have too much of one it will destroy a person temporarily, but not permanently. It is one of those spells where, if it's done right, it can destroy every cell of a witch or wizard so they can't come back to life. I can't wait for the day I get to use it against Hannon.

During this time he has also taught me how to prepare bread and run the kitchen. I'm running the kitchen by myself while Papa runs errands. In between running the kitchen, learning the "Love/Hate" spell, and other little spells here and there, I haven't seen Hector in a month and I wouldn't have it any other way.

One day, while I'm cleaning the bakery and getting ready to close for the night, Papa calls me into the living room. I quickly get through with my chores and set everything up for tomorrow. I'm anxious and wonder if he's going to teach me something new tonight. I try to rush through my chores, but I do them right. I don't want to be woken up in the middle of the night to redo them. I only made that mistake once and I will not make it again. I get finished with my chores and go into the living room.

He is sitting in front of a big, old, book that has pages sticking out of it from all sides. It looks worn and looks like it should have been thrown in the trash a long time ago. I wonder what he is going to do with this book. I take a seat opposite him and look him square in his eyes.

"Mijo, what I have here is our family spell book. It has been passed down from generation to generation. Normally, it is given to a young man when he reaches the age of twelve, not yet a teen, but not a child. Son, I hate to tell you this, but I don't think I'll have the opportunity to give it to you then. So, I have decided to give it to you now."

He scoots the book toward me and I pick it up and hug it to my chest. The book is heavy but I don't want him to see me struggle. As I hold onto the book I can't help but feel sad and I don't know why.

"Papa, what do you mean you won't be here when I'm twelve? You are supposed to be here forever."

Tears start streaming down his face.

"Mijo, there are things happening that you don't quite understand. The woman Hannon is after me. I promised her something years ago and now she is coming to collect it. If she takes it away from me then I will not be here with you in the physical world."

"What does that mean? What does she want from you?"

"My soul."

I get angry. First, she takes mi Mama, and now she wants mi Papa as well! I feel the electricity surging through my fingertips.

"Calm down, Mijo. Save it for when she comes here. She is coming a lot sooner than expected. I don't know what she is going to do but if she tries to hurt you, use the spell I taught you."

"What about you? Why can't I save you?"

I start to cry. I can't imagine my life without mi Papa.

"A man only has one thing in this world and that is his word. If I have taught you nothing else, know that you need to always be a man of your word. Whatever you say you are going to do, you must be man enough to do it. I knew what I was doing when I offered my soul to Hannon. I was protecting you. I need you to live so that the De La Rosa name can continue. Do you understand me, son?"

I nod my head. I'm still too hurt to talk.

"I know this doesn't make sense to you now, but when you're older, you'll understand. I promise."

I nod my head slowly. Suddenly there's a knock on the door. Without taking his eyes off mine and showing no fear, he tells me to go upstairs and study my book.

Inside I'm shaking. What if this is the last time I see him. I get halfway up the stairs as the stranger knocks on the door again. I run back downstairs and give mi Papa a hug. He hugs me back. I then run upstairs and go into my room, waiting for the worse.

I'm in my room for what seems to be an eternity. Finally, I decide if mi Papa is in danger I'm going to help. That's what big boys do! I place the book on my bed and sneak halfway down the stairs. I look through the railings, careful not to make a sound, and I see mi Papa and another woman kissing. I instantly feel sick. This woman looks a lot like mi Mama. She is very beautiful with dark skin, long dark hair, and beautiful eyes. She is very slender and looks like a child in my father's arms. Why is he kissing another woman? Doesn't he miss Mama? I watch curiously from the stairs, waiting to see what happens.

"No, Hernando, we can't do this!"

The beautiful woman pushes herself out of my father's arms and goes across the room and crosses her arms.

"Sam, you love me and I love you. Why can't you leave that mortal and come be with me?"

"Hernando, I love him and I love my child."

"If you love them why are you here?"

The room is silent for a moment.

"You know why I'm here, Hernando."

She says it so quietly I can barely hear her.

"That's not enough for me, Sam! You know, by your staying in the mortal realm, it's putting everything you love in danger. You and I are the only ones who can defeat Hannon. Leave him and come with me. You, Jesus, and I can be a powerful trio."

"You are asking me to leave my husband and child to help you try to defeat a woman that we might not be able to defeat!"

"I'm asking you to leave your silly thoughts of safety in the mortal realm and join reality. We don't know if we can defeat her if we don't try. You can't devote yourself to protecting the people you know and love by going back and forth between the mortal realm and the magical realm. You have to choose."

"Hernando, I love you, but I love him more."

The room is silent.

"You don't mean that."

"I do, I'm not doing this anymore. That's why I came here. I came here to tell you we are done. I love my husband and I can't keep sneaking around with you."

"Please, don't leave me, Sam. I lost my wife, please, don't leave me too."

"As it is spoken…"

The beautiful lady called Sam is cut off as the front door comes crashing in. There stands a woman about the same color as Sam. Her hair is long and floating around her as if she is standing in wind. Her eyes are hazel and are really bright, but her features are hard. She looks really pretty but really mean at the same time. All I know is she must be very strong to be able to knock the door down. The beautiful lady named Sam looks scared but mi Papa does not.

"Well, well, well. What do we have here? Star crossed lovers?"

"This doesn't concern you, Hannon."

"Do you think I care about your meaningless love? I have come to collect what I've been promised!"

"No, you can't take his soul. I love him."

"This doesn't concern you woman!"

The woman named Hannon lifts her hand and Sam goes flying across the room. She's knocked out cold in an instant. My father gets angry and approaches the woman.

"She has nothing to do with this. You leave her out of it!"

"You know I can't do that. I can't leave any witnesses, including your son, who is sitting on the stairs."

As soon as she says that I know I'm in trouble. I slowly stand up and walk downstairs with a bravery I've seen mi papa use a lot. I stand right by mi Papa.

"He is so adorable too bad I have to kill him."

"You'll do no such thing! You have to go through me to kill him. You know what happens if I die without willingly offering you my soul. You'll not be able to harvest it for yourself."

When mi Papa finishes saying this she looked a little taken back.

"Without your soul I can't become immortal."

"Then choose. You leave Sam and my son alone or I'll not willingly give you anything."

She thinks about this for a while and gives a sneaky smile.

"I'll leave both of them alone, for now."

"If you can't guarantee their safety after I've passed then I'll not give you anything."

I grab onto his leg. I don't want him to go. I start to cry.

"Shut up you little brat! I don't want to hear your sniffling!"

"Don't talk to my son that way."

"I'll talk to whomever I want, however I want, Hernando. Now, let's stop with the pleasantries and give me what I came here for."

Mi Papa looks the woman called Hannon in her eyes for a moment, then bends down and talks to me.

"Mijo, this is the time where I must leave you. Remember, I told you a man is only as good as his word. I promised

Hannon something and now I have to go through with it. Be brave for me, son. You must promise to not hate Hannon but only love her for she is only doing what she must."

He then gives me a wink and walks toward Hannon. I know what I must do.

Mi Papa and Hannon exchange more words but I can't hear them. I can't hear much of anything right now. I'm concentrating. I first think about the love my mother gave to me up until she died. I think about the love my father shows me every day and the love everyone shows me around town. My heart swells and I feel my feet leave the ground. I then think about the hate I feel toward Hannon. How she wants to take mi Papa and has already taken mi Mama. I think about the hurt and the pain she has given to people and I feel myself slowly start to spin. I place my hands in front of me in a circle and a small sphere of light starts to form in my hands. I'm doing it! I turn around faster and faster as I feel the love and the hate swelling up inside of me. I try to not lose concentration but mi Papa and Hannon are fighting. She is pointing her fingers at me. I keep spinning. Light shoots out of her fingers and Papa jumps in front of the light. It hits him and he crumples to the floor. The love/hate spell is not ready but I feel myself let it go as I call out mi Papa's name. It hits Hannon and she flies out of the door. I feel my feet hit the ground and I run to mi Papa. I call out his name. I hit his face. I shake him as hard as I can. He doesn't wake. I start to cry.

"Papa! Papa! Please wake up. Ayudame! Help me!"

The beautiful lady stirs. She sits up and rubs her head. She looks at me, then at my father, and back at me again. Her eyes well up with tears. She crawls over to mi Papa and starts crying loudly.

"Hernando! Hernando! Wake up! I didn't mean it! I love you."

She leans over my father and starts to sob. I look out the

door and I see Hannon slowly start to get up. She is badly wounded but she has a look of determination in her eyes. She starts slowly inching her way back into the house and I'm scared. I don't have enough time to complete the love/hate spell. I leave my father and run upstairs and grab the book I left in my room. I then go back down to my father's body and I shake Sam back to her senses.

"Mi Papa is dead! We have to leave, now! If we don't leave she will kill us."

"What about Hernando?"

"Mi Papa can't help us now. I'm sad too, but if we stay, he will have died for nothing."

She looks at me really hard. I can't tell what she's thinking.

"You have your father's spirit and wisdom paired with your mother's eyes and heart; a deadly combination. Grab onto my hand."

I grab onto her hand and she starts speaking a spell in another language. Suddenly my father's body, Sam, and I are transported to another place.

We were transported to a little cottage. I explore every room to make sure we're safe. I like this place. It reminds me of home. I go outside and see a little brook right next to the house and a little town. I close the door and go back to the beautiful woman they call Sam. She is cradling my father's head in her lap. I feel very sad for her and my father, but if I plan on defeating Hannon, for both mi Mama and mi Papa, I have to be strong.

"Your name is Sam, right?"

She looks up at me with red eyes and slowly nods.

"Sam, we have to stick together. Hannon will be after both of us and your family. If you don't want them to suffer the way mi Papa did, I think you better come up with a plan. Mi Papa was strong and taught me a lot and what he didn't teach me is in this book. He wouldn't want me to waste time crying over him. We bury him at dawn."

I then go into the living room and kiss mi Papa on the cheek as a tear rolls down my face. I tell him I'm going to be strong and learn everything I can. I grab the book and go to the nearest room. I get underneath the covers, clutch the book to my chest, and wail as I vow to kill Hannon one day. Now, I'm truly alone.

I awaken at 3 am. I know its 3 am because this is what time I get up every day to make bread and set up the bakery. I'm now up for a different reason. I get up, take a shower, and put on the same clothes I had on the previous day. It is then that I realize I don't have a lot of things. I wonder when it will be safe to go back to my house. After thinking about it, I realize I could never return to my father's house and bakery. I'll really miss seeing Hector, but in order to defeat Hannon, I have to stay out of sight.

I go into the living room and see Sam and my father lying on the floor. I go up to Sam and see the slow rise and fall of her chest. Her tear stained face has a peaceful look. I can see why my father loved her. She looks like my mother, but she's not my mother, and for this I resent her. Even though I dislike her, I'm somewhat elated to see she is alive. I couldn't handle two bodies by myself. As I watch her, I realize she is now family. I have to protect her just like my father would. I don't know if I'm ready for this responsibility, but at this time, I don't have a choice. I shake her slightly. She stirs, but doesn't let go of my father.

"It's time."

"Can I just have a couple more minutes?"

"No, people will be up soon so they can start their day. We don't need to draw more attention to ourselves than is needed."

She just nods.

"I'm going outside and dig a grave. Can you please get him ready?"

She nods again.

I leave her to do her work. I go behind the cottage and see there is a tiny shed. I look in and see a lot of gardening tools, one of which is a shovel. I grab the shovel and go down by the creek. The dirt is nice, cool, and soft. This will be the perfect place to bury him. I start to dig and it's surprisingly easy. As I dig, I think about how I could have done this with magic. I guess I wanted to feel something besides numbness. My arms are starting to hurt. As I get deeper into the ground, I get deeper into my feelings. Suddenly, I start to cry. It's really happening.

My life has changed a lot in the last couple of months. My life was simplistic a couple of months ago. I smile thinking about my daily routine back then. Right now, I would be getting up kneading dough preparing to put it in the oven. Hours later, I would bring fresh bread to Hector's family and then watch cartoons. I wonder where they are. I wonder what they have been doing for bread. It seems like I've grown up in a matter of days. I barely recognize myself, but that's what happens when everything you love is taken away from you. What did I do to deserve this? The hole is really deep and I have to climb out of it. It's difficult at first because of the soft earth, but I eventually get out.

I go back into the cottage and my father is wrapped in a gold blanket. It's a gorgeous blanket. I don't know where it came from and I choose to not ask any questions.

Sam is quiet; moving slow as if she has no life.

"Are you done?"

She nods her head. She goes to lift her hand and I stop her.

"It is mi Papa, let me do it."

I concentrate just like he taught me. I think about how happy he made me feel. I extend my hand out to his body and slowly lift it in the air. His body follows my hand. I motion for Sam to open the door. When she opens the door, I slowly walk outside with a sad Sam following behind me. She begins to hum as we walk toward his grave. Her voice is so beautiful, I have to concentrate harder so I don't start crying and drop his body.

Finally, we get to the grave and I slowly place his body at the bottom. I then close my hand in a fist and turn toward the pile of dirt. I extend my fingers again and take control of the dirt and place it on top of his body. Sam and I sit there for a couple of minutes looking at the mound of dirt, silent. Tears stream down our faces as we are temporarily connected by our pain and our mutual love for mi Papa.

Sometime later, we make it back into the house and I make us homemade bread as she makes breakfast of eggs, bacon, and oatmeal. The bread takes a while to cook but the eggs, bacon, and oatmeal are ready in no time. She sets the table and motions for me to wash my hands and sit down to eat. I do as I'm told and sit across the table from her. She motions for me to dig in. Neither of us moves.

"Where have you taken us, Sam?"

"I brought us to the mortal realm. This cottage is where my parents used to go on vacation. It is so peaceful here and the people here are so kind."

"Sam, don't you know that is only going to put the people here in danger?"

"I wasn't thinking! Hannon is not going to come after us now anyway. She needs her strength. In the meantime, we can build up a force field around here so she won't be able to find us. If she can't find us, she'll have no reason to come looking for us here."

I nod my head. What she's saying makes perfect sense.

"What about your family?"

"I have to forget them and leave them behind in order for them to be safe."

I see a hint of sadness in her eyes.

"Tell me about them."

There's a silence in the room and then she begins.

"There's John. I met John one year when I was vacationing here with my parents. It was love at first sight. He's a gorgeous man with skin the color of milk and hair the color of wheat. His eyes are as blue as the ocean and he has a voice that melts my heart."

"If he's that great, why did you come back to mi Papa?"

"You never forget your first love, Jesus. Although John is a great man, we just don't have enough of a connection. I waited for your father, but he married your mother, so I moved on. After being with John for three years I finally had a child. Her name is Ellie. She is the most gorgeous little girl I've ever seen. Her eyes are just as blue as her fathers with a mix of my skin tone and his. She's a perfect caramel color. Her hair is just as long, black, and thick as it wants to be. I love that little girl with all my heart."

"What do you plan to do?"

"In order to have her live, I have to die. That's where you come in."

"What can I do?"

"I need you to deliver a letter for me, while we are still safe."

"What does the letter say?"

"To sum it up, it says I died."

"Does John know what you are?"

"Yes."

I look at the tears welling up in her eyes.

"Are you going to be ok?"

She nods her head, hands me a piece of paper with instructions, and leaves the room.

I go to the bathroom and wash up and make sure I look ok. I don't want them to think I'm just some homeless kid delivering a letter. When I think I look okay, I leave the cottage. It takes about twenty minutes on foot to reach the address she wrote for me. That's after I got lost for about ten of those minutes and finally stopped for help.

The house is very plain on the outside and looks like a typical residence. Nothing spectacular, nothing of importance, but I know different. Inside holds the two things Sam holds nearest and dearest to her heart. I stare at the house for a minute before I gather the courage to go to the door. I slowly approach the house, lift my hand, and knock. A couple of seconds later the door is opened by a man with skin the color of milk. He looks exactly the way she described.

"Are you John?"

"Why, yes I am, young man."

I extend the letter to him and he looks at me strangely. He opens the letter and reads the contents. His big blue eyes fill with tears.

"Do you know anything about what is in this letter?"

He sounds angry and I'm taken aback by how much power lies behind his voice.

"No, sir, I was only told to deliver the letter. I don't know what it says."

I'm telling him the truth. She didn't tell me what the letter said word for word but she did tell me it mentioned she died. I watch the man break down in front of me. Tears are rapidly falling from his eyes as he calls out to a god I have no knowledge about.

Suddenly, a little girl appears by his side.

"Daddy, what's wrong? "

"Go back in the house, Ellie."

The man can't even look at his daughter now. She turns toward me, hands on her hips, and attitude in her voice. She is gorgeous. Her blue eyes make me want to protect her. She's going to grow up one day and demand the Kingdom just with her looks alone.

"What did you do to my Daddy?"

I try not to smile, but her little four-year old attitude is adorable. I wonder if I had the same attitude. I don't know how Sam could keep anything from this little girl because she makes you want to tell her the truth.

"I didn't do anything!"

"Why is he crying?"

"He'll talk to you. I have to go."

"Don't come back, meanie head!"

She closes the door and I can hear her talking to her Daddy. My heart hurts right now. If only they knew Sam was a ten minute walk away. If only they knew she was doing this in order to protect them. If only they knew Sam was depressed and longed to be with them, I wouldn't be a "meanie head".

If only they knew.

(Five years later)

It's been five years since my father was murdered by Hannon. Five years since everything was taken from me and I had to go on the run with a woman I barely knew. Five years since I had to deliver a message that would change the lives of so many people.

Five. Long. Years.

Things have been really quiet. Sam has been getting information from the magical realm. According to her sources Hannon has been laying low. There's also a rumor that she had a child, a son. For her sake I hope that is just a rumor. If she has a child I plan on killing the child first so she can get a glimpse of what I felt when she took mi Mama and Papa away from me. Then, I will kill her slowly.

Everything has been silent. There has been no threat and Hannon hasn't tried to seek us out at all, but that has not stopped our training. I'm now twelve and I've learned everything in the book my father gave me, which is unheard of. Normally, when a child hits twelve that is when the family's magical book is given to him. I was given this book at seven, and five years later, I know everything there is to know in this book.

Sam has also been teaching me everything she knows and I've been teaching her everything I know as well. So, both she and I have a mixture of dark and light magic. Also, Sam has been researching information about people with "warm heart" magic. To date, there have only been three other wizards and one witch with this power. Each of them great, each of them deadly, and each of them were evil.

I'm determined to not let this power turn me into something dark. I want to fight for the powers of good. I know mi Papa would be really proud of me.

In addition to learning magic, I've also been going to mortal school. I'm now in what they call Middle School and will be going to High School next year. Schooling in the mortal realm is a lot different than in the magical realm, but, I need to go to school or I wouldn't blend in. I'm very tall for my age and get a lot of attention from girls. I see Ellie all the time. She's now nine and is in Elementary School. She's gorgeous but, by the way she carries herself, you would think she doesn't know it. She always has on tattered clothing and shoes that aren't her size. I want to take her away from the pain she feels and take her to her mother, but I know I can't. So, I do the next best thing, I report everything I see and hear about Ellie to Sam. She now has two step sisters as well; Drusilla, who is eight, and Anastasia, who is seven. I've seen both of them and neither of them are as beautiful as Ellie, but they are always nicely dressed. I don't know why, but the youngest one, Anastasia, keeps my attention. There's something about her that calls me to her. I don't know what this means but, maybe one day, I'll figure this out. I don't know why, but Sam keeps a close tab on her husband. Maybe it's a way for her cope with the idea she can't be close to him. Every time she sees him and his new wife she gets angry and every day I remind her this is the life she chose.

One day, as I'm walking through the door, I'm greeted with a very worried Sam sitting on the couch looking very distant. I've only seen Sam like this one other time and I'm scared.

"What's wrong, Sam?"

"Hannon knows that I'm in the mortal realm."

My heart starts to beat rapidly.

"How does she know?"

"She tortured one of my friends until she told her about John."

Her eyes suddenly turn dark.

"That friend is dead now."

"What about Ellie, does she know about her?"

"No. That information makes me happy."

"What do you plan to do?"

"What can I do? If I put a protective spell around his house it's only going to draw her attention because of the amount of power the house will give off. So, the only thing I can do is watch from a distance and wait. If that woman touches my husband or my child I'll kill her myself."

"Sam, you're not strong enough."

"How do you know? I could kill her if I wanted to. I used to be one of the most powerful witches in the magical realm."

"You used to be, there's a lot of updated magic now. There are a lot of things we don't know about. Sam, it's been five years. Face it, we're outdated."

"I'll figure out how to get some updated magic books. In the meantime, I need you to watch Ellie a little closer. I need you to tell me when she's not in school, if she looks like someone has hit her, or if her clothes are more tattered than usual.

"Yes, Sam."

I start to head to my room, then remember I have to give her something. I reach in my backpack and give her a note.

"What is this?"

"My teacher wants to talk to you."

"Why do they want to talk to me?"

"You are my guardian. I don't know what they want to talk to you about, but they want you to come in tomorrow."

"How can I do that without Ellie seeing me? The Elementary School is right next to the Middle School. She is bound to recognize me."

"Put on a disguise. You'll figure it out. You wanted me to go to mortal school so now you have to deal with everything that comes along with it."

I walk away from Sam and go to my room. I throw my bag on the floor and lay on my bed facing the ceiling. I'm tired of hiding and I want to go back to the magical realm. I want to be a normal teenager and I want to know if Hector and Jaime are doing okay. I haven't seen Jaime since they moved away when I used to live with mi Papa. I still think about him from time to time. I want to be worry-free, but it seems like this will never happen and it makes me sad. I decide, tonight, I'm going to do what I want and what I want to do is go to sleep. I roll over, turn off the lamp next to my bed, and cuddle up in my covers. I'll worry about school, homework, and the impending doom that lurks tomorrow but for tonight, I sleep.

I awaken the next morning to screams from the kitchen. I hop out of bed and run downstairs to unleash the deadliest of magic and all I see is Sam holding the newspaper screaming.

"I'm going to kill her!"

"Kill who? What is going on?"

She hands me the newspaper, plops down in a chair, puts her head on the table, and sobs.

I read the front page.

LOCAL MAN BRUTALLY KILLED IN HIS HOME WHILE WIFE AND CHILDREN SOUND ASLEEP UPSTAIRS

I look at the picture of the man and see John's face. He's smiling really big and looks so happy. Then I see a picture of the crime scene. There's blood smeared everywhere. Written in blood on the wall are three words. They are in another language and I don't know what it means.

"Sam, what does that mean?"

I point to the words on the wall.

"You are next. It is written in Latin."

"Do you think this is Hannon?"

"I know it's her. She's trying to draw me out and it's working. Why would she kill him? He has nothing to do with this! I left him five years ago just so this wouldn't happen."

"How did she know you left him? She just now got information that you were married in the mortal realm, do you really think she was going to know that you left him?"

"You have a point. I want revenge!"

"How do you think I feel? She took both my mother and my father and for what? Immortality? Why would you want to live forever if no one loves you now?"

She nods her head in agreement.

"What are you thinking, Sam?"

"I'm thinking it is time for us to put an end to this. I think it's time for her to die."

"I agree, but how? We cannot do it where humans can see. We would never be able to return and you'll never be able to see Ellie again."

"I know. That's why I'm going to lead her back to the

magical realm and you, my warm hearted wizard, are going to destroy her once and for all."

I smile big and wide. This is a day I've been waiting five long years for.

"Tell me what I need to do."

"First, we need to call your school. You're not going to be in attendance today."

We arrive back in the magical realm a short time after the call. We go directly to the last town we were in before we fled. We have one destination in mind, my father's bakery. We arrive there about twenty minutes later and it still looks the same as it did before we fled. I stop outside of the door and I'm overcome with emotions. My fingers start to tingle as the magic fights to escape. I calm down. I look over at Sam and she has tears coming out of her eyes as well. This place holds emotional value.

I open the door and the smell of sour yeast assaults my nose. It's so strong I can't stop coughing. I quickly lift my hands toward the mop and bucket and other cleaning supplies. In no time, the room is clean, everything is back in order, and the trash is taken out. I go to the cabinets and everything is expired. I really have a craving for some homemade bread and mi Papa's galletas. I decide I'm going to the store. The idea is to be visible, right?

I start cleaning the house and getting everything organized. When I'm finally done it's almost dark. Sam has decided to find something in the house to eat for dinner while I go to the store. I go a couple of blocks over to Mr. Williams' corner store. Surprisingly, it's still there. I go in, grab a basket, and get flour, sugar, eggs, and other ingredients I'm going to need. I get to the counter and Mr. Williams is looking at a newspaper and doesn't see me. I politely clear my throat.

He puts down the newspaper, annoyed, until he notices who I am.

"Oh my goodness, Jesus, is that you?"

"Yes sir."

"Everybody thought you were dead! I heard what happened to your father. I'm so sorry."

"It's fine."

He starts to ring up the things in my basket and starts to smile.

"You're about to bake, aren't you?"

"Yes sir."

"Well, bring me some of whatever you bake. If you can bake anything like your father I know it's going to be delicious."

"I will."

I give him the money. He tries to give me change but I don't take it. I take my bags off the counter and walk back to the house. It's dark but I'm not afraid. As I get closer to the house I get a weird feeling I'm being watched. I decide I'm going to go the kitchen from the back entry way. I go into the house and instantly see smoke. I put the bags down and rush to the oven. I take out the pan of burnt chicken and vegetables and place it onto the top of the stove. An alarm goes off in my head. Sam isn't the best cook but she's never burned food, ever. The room is smoky and I can't see a thing but I'm on guard. Something isn't right. I slowly make my way toward the living room with electricity surging through my fingertips. I'm ready to attack the first person I see. I'm walking forward and everything looks normal. I hear a sound from behind me. I immediately turn and fire. Nothing stirs. I turn around and bump right into Sam. We both raise our hands at the same time but lower them quickly.

"Do you feel like someone's watching you?"

Sam looks all around her as she asks me this question.

"Yes. That's why I took the back entrance. Is that why you burned the chicken?"

"Yes, I left in order to inspect the house, but I found nothing."

We sit there for a moment trying to figure out what to do next.

"I'm going upstairs to check again. I'll be right back."

Sam nods as I ascend the stairs. I check my room, the bathroom, the guest room, and then pause outside of my father's room. My hand shakes as I open the door. As the door opens I'm hit by a wave of good smelling cologne. His bed is still made, his clothes are still there, and his shoes are still lined up perfectly. I go to the dresser and see his watch lying there. It was his favorite watch. The watch was handed down from his father to him and now, by default, to me. I put it on and it's still a bit big around my wrist. I decide to put it in my pocket. I can grow into it, but for now, it makes me feel closer to him.

Suddenly I hear a scream and a crash downstairs and I know that Sam has found something or someone.

I rush out of the room and stand at the top of the stairs. I see Hannon standing there looking calm and collected as if she and Sam are old time buddies. I start to conjure the love/hate spell at the top of the stairs. This time, I don't intend to mess this up.

"Well, well, well, Sam, I thought I would never find you."

"Do you really think I would let you get away with murdering my husband?"

Hannon shrugs.

"You didn't have a choice."

Sam's fingers sizzle as she tries to hit Hannon with a bit of magic. She just flings it away as if it were child's play.

"Silly girl, you're not the only one who's been studying."

Sam tries a couple of more spells as Hannon just flings them away, laughing hysterically.

She then extends her arms toward Sam. Sam immediately puts her hands to her throat as if someone is choking her. Hannon slowly lifts her hand and holds Sam in the air as she struggles to breathe.

I'm concentrating on the spell and I'm nearly done.

"I told you; no survivors. You took away my chance at immortality. He died before I could properly harvest his soul for my own selfish endeavors. If you and that little boy would have just left, I would be invincible right now. For you being so meddlesome I now have to take your life."

She starts to squeeze her hand just little bit more and Sam is starting to turn blue. The spell is finished. I run down the stairs and hit Hannon with the spell. She drops Sam and crumples to the floor. Sam tries to catch her breath as I walk over to Hannon and stand over her.

She has blood coming out of her mouth and her hair is everywhere but she is laughing.

I stand over her with a magical ball formulating in my hand.

"You are the son of De La Rosa. All is not lost for me. I can still be all the way immortal once I gather your soul."

"How do you expect to gather anything after I kill you?"

"My dear boy, study up on your magic. Even though you may defeat me this time I will be back. I transferred a piece of my soul into an object that can only be destroyed with the mention of my first name. I will always return until you discover my name. Just know, when I come back, I will come after you until I get the soul of a De La Rosa and merge it with my own. When I do, I will be invincible."

She starts to laugh and I get angry with every cackle that escapes her mouth. I aim and fire a huge ball of hateful magic right into her mouth. She stops cackling immediately as she bursts into flames. I'm angry. If we wouldn't have waited so long I could have destroyed her before she discovered that magic. Now, I have to live in constant fear until I figure out what her first name is. I didn't sign up for this, but I know now I have no choice. I have to keep fighting because, if I give up, it will be the end of both the magical and mortal world.

(22 years later — present day)

I've been hiding behind the safety of these magical walls surrounding my house but no more.

Sam has since left. We talk off and on but I have not seen her for 22 years. After she left I didn't want to deal with the magical world. I've lost too many people near and dear to me whenever I even think about that place. So, I kept everyone of magic out and lead a simple life. I can no longer hide in the shadows. Today is the day that I face Hannon. She has made her presence known and it's time to end her reign in the mortal realm. I don't have anything to lose. Anastasia left me and she was the only person that kept me breathing. How else can I explain not seeing her for a couple of months? I've been waiting for her to grace my doorstep with her presence. Every day that she doesn't show up my heart breaks a little more. I thought we had something special. I've never loved another like I've loved her. Her not being next to me is the worst kind of death. So, if I can't have her, I don't want to live. Today, if I die, I will die with valor. I will die protecting the people of both the magical and mortal realm. Today, I sacrifice myself so others may live. Today, if I die, it will be a sweet relief from the pain I feel without having Anastasia.

I prepare myself for battle. I put on some light clothing so that I'm able to move swiftly. I brush up on a couple of new spells I just learned, and spend some time relaxing my mind. Finally, after a couple of hours, I'm ready for war.

I leave everything behind except for the shoes on my feet and the clothes on my back. There's no need to take anything with me. As I walk out the door I take a look back into the cottage that has kept me safe for so many years. I can't help but get emotional as I think I may never return to this place again. I wipe away the tear that has escaped my eyes and turn to walk out the door. As I close the door I can't help but feel I'm closing one chapter and beginning a new one.

I make the slow journey toward the castle. As I get closer to the castle I start to get an uneasy feeling. I don't know what it is, but I feel myself being drawn away from the castle and toward a small, quaint, cottage on the outskirts of the castle grounds. Although my body wants me to go investigate, I can't falter from my main goal. If I make it through this I'll go explore the cottage further, but right now, I have a job to do.

I walk up to the castle's main door and find it odd the door is slightly ajar. Aren't castle doors supposed to be closed and locked so no one can walk in unannounced like I just did? I can't focus on that now, I have to find Hannon. I walk along the big corridor and hear the echo of every footstep I make. Where are all the servants? The castle is very empty and it's kind of eerie. I wonder if I am in the right place.

Suddenly, there's a crash from upstairs and people screaming. I create a magic ball and place it in my palm as I run up the stairs to investigate. I get to the top of the stairs and have to stop to catch my breath. They really should have another way to get up these stairs. After a couple of moments I straighten up, magic ball still in hand, and go toward the source of the screams.

I turn right and run down the hall. Suddenly, I'm in front of a big door. All is quiet and I'm concerned. Where did the screams go? Did I turn the right way? Suddenly another scream comes from behind the door and I'm certain this where I need to go and where one of us is to meet our doom.

I burst through the door to see Ms. Hannon standing over Sam with a magic ball aimed at Sam's head. I also see a very grown Ellie, the Prince, and three children all crowded on the bed with a protective spell around them. Ellie is crying. Things don't look good.

"Hannon!"

When she hears her name she loses concentration and looks back at me with an eerie smile.

"Son of De La Rosa, or is it the Muffin Man now? I don't know what to call you anymore. It took me some years, but I finally figured out who you were. I see you got my invitation. It's so nice of you to join us!"

"You leave Sam alone!"

Hannon steps away from Sam as she walks toward me, looking squarely into my eyes.

"Or what?"

"I will destroy you."

"If you destroy me, dear little Jesus, you will never know where your precious Anastasia is!"

My heart jumps in my chest.

"What have you done with Anastasia?"

"Don't worry, she and her child are safe."

"Child?"

"Yes, a boy."

I feel weak when Hannon mentions that Anastasia is pregnant. Why didn't she tell me herself? Now I'm even more infuriated. Just by what Hannon is telling me it lets me know she had something to do with her disappearance. The fight in me returns. I feel myself getting angrier than I've ever been before. My hands are exploding with power as I think of all the tortuous things she could have done to Anastasia while she is carrying my child.

"Oh, are you getting angry, Jesus?"

I feel a power surge. I can't contain my anger my longer. I raise my hands toward Hannon. Today she dies.

"I will only ask you one more time, where is Anastasia?"

"I am not...,"

Before Hannon could finish her sentence Sam attacks her from behind. She and Hannon wrestle to the floor. They're moving so much that I can't focus to hit Hannon so instead I focus on the five people on the bed. I start speaking the transportation incantation. Ellie looks afraid, the children are crying, and the Prince looks confused. I hope that things work out and that one day all of this can be explained. I finish the incantation and they are successfully sent to my cottage. I take my hand, write words in the air, and then blow on them. A piece of paper materializes and sends itself to my cottage.

Hannon breaks free of Sam and screams, "You fool! Do you realize what you've done?"

She runs toward the bed and starts to feel around.

"No, but I realize what I'm about to do."

I feel all my anger return as I aim my fingers at Hannon.

"You have taken everything from me and now it is time for you to die."

"Jesus, it doesn't have to be this way. You and I can join forces. Together we can rule the magical and mortal realm. You can be King and I can be Queen."

"My Queen is Anastasia! You'll never compare to her!"

"You can't blame a girl for trying."

My anger increases. I've never handled this much power before and I'm kind of scared, but I can't not turn back. My anger has consumed every part of me and all I see is red.

As my power increases, Hannon visibly becomes more afraid.

"I've never seen anyone with so much power before."

"You have now. Hannon, this is where your story ends!"

Hannon starts to run toward the door. I take aim and

fire in her direction. A mixture of red and gold magic emits from my fingertips. Hannon runs harder. As she's running she trips on the carpet in the room and the magic ball misses her and hits Sam. Time goes slowly. Sam is lifted into the air and then falls out onto the ground. Red and gold sparks jump from her skin. She's not moving. I scream. It's a scream of pain mixed with anger. This woman has taken everything from me.

I go to where Hannon has fallen and pick her up by her neck. I start to choke her. I want to feel the life go out of her. I want to look into her eyes and know that she is dead, at least for now. I know she will find a way to return until I find that object and she knows this. She starts to struggle and scratch my arm. I tighten my grasp. I let the emotions I feel flow through my fingertips and she starts to convulse. After what seems like an eternity, she finally gives up. Her arms fall limp and her legs have stopped thrashing. She looks at me with pain and bewilderment in her eyes but her lips curl up into a smile as she closes her eyes and takes her last breath. I then snap her neck and throw her on the floor as if she was garbage. A second later a black mist expels from her body, the whole room is filled with black mist. Once the mist clears, her body is gone.

I run over to Sam and she is barely breathing. Sparks are still jumping off of her skin. I kneel next to her and grab her hand. She smiles at me and places a hand on my cheek. I start to cry. Sam has always been there for me since my father died. I can't lose her now.

"Hold on, Sam, I'm going to try to save you."

For a moment I mentally run through all of the spells that could possibly save her.

Only one comes to mind, the "Soul Splitter."

This spell is really tricky. I need at least five minutes to cut my soul in half and have it transfer to her. I have to be really still, with no distractions. The slightest distraction can cause me to kill myself because I would have damaged my soul. I realize that Sam, next to Anastasia, is one of the most important people in my life and I feel as if she needs to live so we can fight another day. I'm hoping that she can hold on at least five more minutes.

I sit cross legged on the right side of her. I close my eyes, put my hands on my knees, and focus on my soul. I go deep inside myself. I go past all the memories, the heart breaks, and the rejection to find my soul buried under years of emotional neglect. I mentally grab hold of my soul and rip it in half. I feel a searing pain rip through my body. I want to scream but I know if I scream I will lose all concentration. I leave one half there and slowly start to mentally bring the other piece out. Suddenly, I feel something in my mouth. I lean over Sam and put my lips on her lips as the transfer starts. As I feel my soul leaving my mouth and going into hers I see her smile start to fade as her eyes start to roll in the back of her head. I want to scream for her to stay with me. I want to scream that she can make it. Just give me one more minute, please! Her eyes slowly shut as the soul leaves my mouth. My soul is now in her mouth as she takes her last breath. It's too late.

Sam has died.

I scream and grab her into my arms. I tell her I never meant to hurt her and that she is the best thing to ever happen to me, besides Anastasia. If it wasn't for her I would be dead. In a way, Sam is my mother and I've now lost her forever and it is nobody's fault but mine. I wave my hands in a circle and a beautiful locket appears. It has a picture of Sam inside of it. I lay Sam down on the floor and get on my knees beside her. I wave my hands slowly across Sam's body and she turns to mist. The mist floats up into the air and slowly starts to go into the locket. I put it around my neck. This way she will be with me forever in spirit even though her body is no longer here in the physical. I sit in the middle of the room and cry harder than I ever have before.

It is the worst feeling in the world to be a motherless and fatherless child. I don't know how to handle this new realization.

※

The task is finished. I can now breathe a bit easier. I at least have some time to try to find the object Hannon has put a bit of her soul in so I can destroy her once and for all. I walk downstairs and out of the castle and I pass the cottage again. For some reason, the cottage is calling out to me again. Although I'm emotionally drained and tired I go toward the cottage.

I stand outside of the door and hear the oddest sound. It's the sound of lost souls wailing. I have no idea what's going on, but I want to be prepared. I think of the times Sam, my father, and Anastasia made me happy and I conjure a spirit sword. The best way to defeat evil spirits is with happiness. I don't know if they're evil or not but, by the sounds I'm hearing, I don't doubt it. I take a deep breath and kick down the door.

Spirits swarm around me. There are so many the air around me has become black. I swing my sword and each time I do, another spirit bursts into flames. They keep coming from everywhere, attacking me, scratching me, wailing loudly. I press on. I fight against the beast trying to push my way inside the cottage. I can't fail. I need to get into the cottage. It calls out to me.

I'm badly beaten and bruised. One of the cuts is bleeding profusely and with each swing I grow more and more tired. I want to turn back and quit. I want to run but my heart wills me on. I keep fighting until I get one foot into the cottage. As I step into the cottage, all the spirits disappear.

I'm exhausted and I need to rest for a minute, but there is no time for rest. I can rest when I'm done, or dead, whichever comes first.

Now that I'm in the cottage, I have no idea what I'm looking for or why I'm even here. I look toward the living room and see a book on the mantel. It glows and I feel compelled to take it. As I walk closer to it the glow gets brighter. Suddenly, a ray of light shines out of the book and points me in the direction of a room. It's like this book is the one that called out to me and is leading me where I need to go. I need to take this book with me, but for now I need to deal with what is in that room.

I walk toward the room and open the door. I see Anastasia crumpled up on the floor in the corner. I go toward her and see that she has been badly beaten and has bruises all over her body. I look down at her belly and it's slightly protruded. I hold her in my arms as I cry and rock her back and forth.

"Jesus."

It's the sweetest sound I've heard in my life. I move her head from my shoulder and look down at my beautiful Anastasia. Her golden hair is a mess and her blue eyes are almost swollen shut; but she has never looked more beautiful.

"Yes, mi amour, it is me."

"I thought I was going to die."

"Don't speak of such things. I'm here now."

I lift her up in my arms and carry her out of the room. As I'm leaving I see a knapsack hanging on the wall. I grab it and go back into the living room. Putting Anastasia down, I go to the book and lift it off the mantle. It glows in my hands. I feel a warm sensation as I hold it close to my chest. I put the book in the knapsack and sling it over my shoulder. I pick up Anastasia and leave the cottage.

It seems like forever, but we make it to my cottage. It's now dark. I know in the morning I'm going to have to deal with questions from Ellie and the Prince, but for now, my focus is on my love. I lay her down on the bed and she smiles at me as she drifts off to sleep. For now, I let her rest. I start to take the tattered clothing off her when a piece of paper falls out of her dress pocket. I look at the information on the paper and gasp. On the paper it lists all the information I need in order to find the thing that Hannon put her soul in and how to destroy it. Apparently, it's a locket. I'm elated. In my moment of joy I look down at the paper and my smile turns into a puzzled look. Upon further examination I realize the instructions are written in my father's handwriting.

CHAPTER TWELVE
Three's a Crowd
Prince James

It's been a couple of weeks since the incident at the castle and I'm still confused. I have more questions than answers and it doesn't look as if that is going to change soon. Ms. Hannon was a witch? Sam and Ms. Hannon hated each other? And where is Daniel? Jesus, or the Muffin Man, or whatever he's called has been helping us as much as he possibly can. Jesus told me he got word that Daniel is hiding in the magical realm with someone that followed the ruling of Hannon. I didn't even know the magical realm existed. Nonetheless, I'm assuming Daniel is going to come back soon to avenge his mother's death and when he steps back into to this realm I'll be waiting for him with death by my side.

We've now returned to the castle. I had to hire a new employee manager and life at the castle has returned to normalcy, everything but Ellie. Ellie heard the news about her mother and has emotionally shut down. She has not really spoken to anyone. All she does is stay in the kid's room all day. It seems like the kids are the only thing that can pull her out of her bad mood. For now, I'm not going to press the issue. I'm just going to let her work through her mother's death and whatever else is ailing her in her own way.

Every day I go back to Jesus' cottage looking for word that Daniel has left the magical realm. Every day I'm disappointed. I'll never truly be happy until Daniel's head is mounted. He has taken everything from me; the joy of having my first child with Ellie and the trust I once had for my wife. Finally, he took the most important thing from me, Ellie's heart.

"What does he have that I don't? It's clear that his absence is a part of the reason why Ellie is not herself."

Jesus and I have become the best of friends. He understands my frustration and tries to give me advice on things he is knowledgeable about, but today he has no answers for me.

"I understand amigo. I would be devastated too if the one I love suddenly had no interest in me. I think you should talk to Anastasia. She might be able to say something to reverse this mood you're in."

I take a second to think about it. Anastasia was close to Ms. Hannon and Ellie. She might be able to shed some light on my questions.

"How does she look? Is everything better?"

"Yes, everything's fine. She's still a little bruised, but she will otherwise be okay. She'll not tell me what Hannon did to her though and it's driving me crazy."

"Don't dwell on things you can't change. She's gone."

"Don't be so sure. Anastasia is in the room in the back."

I wonder what he meant by that. Is the reign of Ms. Hannon not over? Just thinking about that woman coming back from death sends shivers down my spine. I walk toward the back and lightly knock on the door.

"Come in."

I walk into the room and Anastasia is sitting up in the bed with a book in her hand sporting a huge belly. I kiss her on the cheek. She still has some of the bruises from when Hannon kept her captive but she acts as if they aren't there. I commend her for that.

"How are you doing, Anastasia?"

"I'm fine, but what about you? How are you really doing?"

"I could be doing better."

"I can see that. You and I have never really been close so something must be troubling you for you to come to me."

"You caught me. I'm confused, I'm hurt, and I'm angry. I don't know what to do about Ellie and Jesus thought it would be a good thing to come talk to you."

"That's my fiancé for you. I have a question."

"Sure. Ask me anything."

"Do you really think Ellie's actions were by her own doing?"

I stop and think for a second. I never had that question run across my mind.

"Honestly. Yes. When I married her she was so young and naïve, I can see how someone like Daniel could tempt her, but at the same time she's mature enough to make her own decisions."

"Then you, sir, are mistaken. It wasn't Daniel that did it, but magic."

"Magic? What do you mean?"

"If you have some time I'd like to explain it to you."

Explain she did. We talked for three hours. She explained everything to me from the spell, to the kids, and everything in between. After it was all explained to me it made total sense. My love for Ellie became deeper. It wasn't her that deceived me, but my treacherous, so-called friend Daniel. The only thing Ellie was guilty of was being too beautiful and desirable. That isn't something she could help. After she's done with her explanation I have tears in my eyes. I never realized all this was going on, I just knew about Daniel and Ellie. I'm glad I didn't jump to anger and have both of them executed.

I thank Anastasia for the information she gave me and promise I'll come and visit her and Jesus in a couple of days. I leave the room with a smile on my face and a burden lifted from my shoulders. I walk past the kitchen where Jesus is baking and wave goodbye as I walk out the door. I make my way back toward the castle, greeting each commoner as I pass them. I want to go home, I want to kiss all my kids, and I want to apologize to Ellie so we can truly have our happily ever after. I start to whistle a song of happiness as I get closer to the castle. Today is the day our relationship will change for the better. Today, nothing can go wrong.

I get back to the castle and open the front doors. As soon as I open the door I see all of my servants congregated in the main hall. I walk in and everyone turns toward me and goes silent at the same time. I'm confused and the silence is eerie. Nina, my newest cook, comes up to me with tears in her eyes.

"I'm so sorry for your loss, Monsieur."

"What are you talking about?"

She goes silent.

Then Robert, the gardener, comes up and starts to talk in place of Nina.

"You don't know?"

"Don't know what? I've been gone all day. Someone better tell me what's going on, better yet, tell me where my wife is and I will get the answers from her."

Everyone goes quiet again. Then, in a very silent and emotional tone Nina tells me she is upstairs in the garden and immediately starts crying. I thank her and run upstairs, turning left, then going to the end of the corridor where the big iron door lies that leads to the upstairs garden. I get to the door and its wide open. I have the weirdest feeling I shouldn't go up there, but I need to see my wife. I need to tell her I know about everything and I forgive her. I have to tell her I love her.

After staring at the door for a couple of minutes I finally get the courage to walk up the stairs. I get to the top of the stairs and admire the beautiful garden. That is one thing I can give credit to Daniel for. He has created a really beautiful and tranquil place. I call out to Ellie and I get no response. I go to a big pink rose bush and see a piece of paper attached to one of the roses.

James,

Please forgive me. I could not take it anymore so I came to the last place where I was truly happy. I love you to the moon and back and it is for that reason I have relieved you of your burden of me. I couldn't bear to see you hurting anymore nor could I bear to feel the constant internal turmoil. Please remember the good times.

Love Ellie

I read the note and get a bad feeling in the pit of my stomach. I turn to my right and see Ellie hanging from the arch in the middle of the garden. Her beautiful body is swinging back and forth while she is surrounded by beautiful roses. I drop to my knees and start to howl. *I was coming to make things right! I was coming to offer my apology! I wanted us to be a family!* If I would have gotten here just a couple of minutes sooner this would have not happened.

I go up to her body and she's still warm. I look at her beautiful face and see the tear stains streaking her cheeks. Even in death she looks beautiful. I reach up and take the rope from around her neck, take her down and cradle her in my arms. I sit on the ground and rock back and forth, crying out for a do over. I want to rewind time so I can tell her how I feel. I whisper, "I love you," in her ear and kiss her now cold lips. I hope she can hear me, wherever she is. I wrap my arms around her, hoping the heat from my body and my tears will somehow revive her. I hug her with all my might hoping that she will wake and tell me this is a joke, but I know, deep in my heart, she's never coming back.

I spared no expense for her funeral. Everyone came out to pay their respects. Her body was drawn to her burial site by a white carriage and two horses. I remember her leaving me before in a white carriage pulled by horses but she returned to me. This time, I know she's not coming back.

My closest friends and family are the only ones allowed at the burial site. As the priest pays his last respects before we place her in the ground, I look up and see Daniel in the distance looking toward the burial site crying. I'm instantly enraged. Who gave him the right to be here? We lock eyes and share a menacing look. We both know after this funeral we will meet again and when we do, one of us is not going to make it out alive. He wipes his eyes, stands up straight, and gives me a smile and a nod, and then turns and walks away. I want to chase him down and kill him where he stands, but for the sake of Ellie I stay put. I'm looking forward to the end of this service because then I can have my revenge. I want it so badly I can taste it, and it tastes sweet.

I'm exhausted after the long burial service and the even longer reception to honor the memory of Ellie. I finally make my way back to the castle, riding my horse. I pass by Ms. Hannon's old cottage and I see lights are on. I slow my horse to a slow trot. I proceed to look in the windows of the cottage as I'm riding by. I see Daniel with his hands on his head, looking both petrified and confused. He's looking at the mantle as if something is supposed to be there. I stop the horse. I realize if I go up the stable to put the horse away I'm not going to return to the cottage to confront Daniel. I decide to tie the horse to a tree. I reach in the knapsack on the side of the horse and give her an apple. I pet her mane and tell her I'll be right back, I have something to handle.

I walk up to the door and kick it in. Daniel is startled for a moment, then looks at me and returns his gaze back to the mantle and scratches his head. He doesn't even look at me as he addresses me.

"State your business, James. I have more pressing matters."

"You know what I'm here for."

"Actually, I don't."

He turns toward me and gives me a smile.

All I want to do is wipe that smile off of his face.

"I came to pay my respects to my best friend's wife and collect something that was promised to me by my mother."

My blood starts to boil.

"Why did you do it?"

"Do what?"

I calmly walk over to him and punch him square in the face. He lands on the ground and grabs his jaw. A look of death flashes across his eyes.

"Don't play innocent with me, Daniel. We're both too smart for you to be playing dumb. Now, I'll ask you again, why did you do it?"

He looks at me with a cold look in his eyes.

"Why do I need a reason? You always get the best of everything. This time, I couldn't stand by and let you have her. She was too perfect for you. You didn't deserve her."

I hit him again. He wipes the blood that trickles out of his mouth. He smiles at me.

"I understand that you're angry. I'll let you get away with the first two hits. If you hit me again we will have a serious problem."

I hit him again. He lifts his hand and pins me against the wall. I can't breathe.

"James, do you really think that the son of a powerful witch is not going to learn a trick or two?"

"If you are a man fight me as such. Don't fight me as the cowardly little magician that you are!"

After I say those words Daniel looks at me struggling against the wall and finally put his hand down. I feel the hold on me release and I fall to the ground. I catch my breath and then stand up.

He's smiling.

I charge toward him and start throwing punches. A good amount of them land on his body. He cringes. Suddenly, he uppercuts me and I go flying across the room and land on my back.

He then jumps on me.

I roll over and he hits the ground hard. I sit on top of him and start pummeling his face with punches. He gathers his strength and rolls me over so that he's on top and starts to hit me with punches. He hits me in my throat and I can't breathe. He continues to hit me but I can't defend myself because I can't breathe. Every time he hits me I feel as if I'm going to pass out. I keep telling myself that I will make it. I have to defeat him. I have to restore honor to my name.

Daniel starts to mutter something as his hand hovers above my face with his fingers outstretched. There is a little ball of light that starts to form right above my head. I have only seen that light one other time and that's the light Sam was hit with. I'm scared, but I'll not die without valor. I look him straight in his eyes. I want my gaze to be forever imprinted on his brain. I want him to remember my face every time he goes to bed. My face will haunt him.

Suddenly, he stops mumbling and his eyes go wide. His head slowly starts to fall from his body, hits the floor and rolls across the room. His mouth is in an "O" shape and his eyes are wide with fear. I look at his body, still sitting on me headless. I push it off and scurry across the room. With my back against the wall I look up and see a very pregnant Anastasia holding a sword. The sword is dripping with blood. The blade moved so fast and precise I didn't even see it slide through his neck. She has a wild look in her eyes and is breathing heavy.

"I thought you might need some help."

"You came just in time."

"I know, I saw him at the burial site when you did. Against Jesus' wishes I'm here. He wouldn't let me come unless he came too. He's outside with both our horses."

"How can I ever repay you?"

"You can replay me by not mentioning it again."

She turns and waddles out of the cottage. The next thing I see is Jesus riding past with Anastasia being pulled behind him in a wagon. I look at Daniel's body on one side of the room and his head on the other side. There is no way that I can keep this from getting out. After sitting there for a minute I know what I must do. I go searching in the house and find matches and kerosene. I drench everything in the house. I then go outside and pour the kerosene around the house. I strike a match and throw it on the cottage. The cottage is quickly engulfed in flames. I watch it burn for a couple of minutes before I turn away, and walk toward my horse. I mount it and ride toward the stables. I feel a sense of relief as I ride away from the thing that has been ailing me for so long. I feel free because I finally got my revenge, even though I wasn't the person who swung the sword.

CHAPTER THIRTEEN
The First Noelle
Noelle

Finally, everything is falling into place just as mother said. She told me to be patient and that my time would come, and that time is now. Now that Ellie is dead and gone and my idiot brother Daniel has played his part, I can now move on to the next phase. My mother wants to rule both the magical and the mortal realms and that can be achieved with my help.

It took a couple of months, but I found the locket and the other things that are required to bring my mother back from the land of the dead. The locket is safe around my neck until she returns. I need to be very careful because this locket has the potential to kill my mother if it ends up in the wrong hands. It will take a long time for her to fully come back but, in the meantime, I have some things to do.

Ellie has been dead for a year and I'm now in charge of the children. I despise these children with all of my being, but I know in order for me to get close to the Prince I have to first get close to the children. It's not like I don't already have experience with children. I've been taking care of Daniel's son Symon for the last five years. He has been passed off as my child, which is fine by me. I don't want to have children, but in order for this plan to work, I need to have just one child and that child needs to be fathered by the Prince.

Nobody would have thought I was a Hannon. I don't look anything like my mother or my brother. They were dark skinned, I'm light skinned. They have hazel eyes and my eyes are green. Their hair is thick and my hair is fine. With me looking so different it was easy to have me live with another family as an adopted child. Nobody pays attention to a discarded baby. So for years I've been playing my role in the background and now it's time for me to be brought to the forefront.

After I put the children down to sleep I go up the study to talk to the Prince. I get to the big oak doors and knock lightly as I walk in. The Prince is sitting at his desk, going over paperwork, and is really engulfed in the decrees that have been set before him to sign. He doesn't notice that I'm in the room. I take a second to look at him. The Prince is really such a handsome man and I'm genuinely happy when I'm around him, but it hurts me that he's only being used to serve a purpose. I can't think of this now, I have a job to do. Today is the day I plan to consummate this secret relationship.

I walk over to him, go behind the chair, and start to give him a massage. His tension lessens. I pull the chair back slightly, walk around the chair and sit in his lap. I start to kiss him passionately as he wraps his muscular arms around my slender body. The kiss deepens as moans escape out of his and my mouth. God, he is such a good kisser. He trails kisses from my lips to my neck and then to my chest and everywhere in between. He then picks me up with one arm and sweeps the papers off of his desk with the other. He lays me down on top of the desk. I look him in his eyes as I seductively start to take off my clothing. His eyes never leave mine. He has a look of hunger as he devours every inch of my body visually. He starts to take off his clothes, parts my legs, and inserts himself into the deepest part of my love. This is the start of a very long night that ends with him giving me the greatest gift of all, his seed.

After we're done, we lay on the floor panting heavily, and looking at each other with awe.

"We can't do this again."

As the words leave his mouth I became instantly disappointed.

"Why?"

"I'm just not ready for this."

"Why, James? She's not coming back. It's time to move on. Your kids need a mother, you need a lover, and I can be both. Just give me a chance."

"This was a mistake."

There is an air of awkwardness. Neither one of us knows what to say to the other. I'm deeply hurt by his words. Although gaining his love and trust is just a part of an intricate plot, I'm finding myself falling deeper in love with him as the days go by.

"Why?"

"It's a mistake because the last woman I loved hurt me beyond repair. Although it wasn't by her doing, it still hurt me deeply. I don't know if I'm ready to profess my love and start a new life with someone else."

"I understand, but at least I know you love me."

"I didn't say that."

"Yes, you did. If it's not the truth, speak now and correct me."

He's silent.

"That's all I needed to know. At least I know these past

nine months we have spent with each other have not been in vain. I have your heart and the next thing I have to gain is your trust."

I kiss him sweetly on the lips.

"By the way, I love you too."

I get up, put my clothes back on, and leave the study.

The next day, I put in a leave of absence from the castle for two weeks. There are some other things I have to do. Symon is now attending school so I have to go shopping for him, plus I'm starting to teach him magic as well. I also have to follow up with some of the Hannon supporters to make sure that everything is going according to plan.

I keep getting telegrams from the Prince asking me to come back to the castle and that he is sorry. I send each one of them back with no response. After a couple of days of telegrams, my house is bombarded with gifts. Expensive jewelry, beautiful clothes, and exotic fragrances come in different sized boxes every day for a week straight. Each time I received a gift I returned it to the Prince without a response. The last day of my leave I get another knock on the door. Symon is lying down in the back, taking a nap so I decide I can entertain for a moment. I go to the door, open it, and there stands the Prince.

"I can't stop thinking about you."

"I know. What's your point?"

"Noelle, I was wrong to compare you to Ellie. I want you, please come back to me."

"I don't think I want to. This was a mistake."

I look at him coolly. His face drops into a disappointed pout.

"I'm sorry for that, Noelle. The truth is I love you. You were there to help me pick up the pieces. I need you in my life."

He then gets down on one knee and pulls a small black box out of his pocket. He opens the box and there is the most amazing diamond ring I have ever seen in my life. My mouth drools a little.

"Noelle Giselle Han, will you be my wife?"

I'm speechless, I didn't think he would ask me this quickly. I look him in his handsome face and smile sweetly and grab his face in my hands.

"No."

I then step back into my cottage and close the door gently, going back to what I was doing. I start to laugh. I have him where I want him now. It's only a matter of time, Mama. It's only a matter of time.

I start working back at the castle the next day. All the children missed me. They can't say so because they still can't talk, but the amount of enthusiasm on their faces says everything. I still despise these children but, once again, I pretend as if I missed them as well. I'm laying the children down for a nap when one of the other employees mentions that the Prince wants to see me. I tell them I'll be there in a minute. After I lay the twins down, I look at them for a minute. My mother said one is evil and one is good. She told me to keep an eye out for the evil one because that is the one that will eventually need to be killed or else he or she will be the downfall to our plan. I've spent every day with these children for a year and I still can't tell which is which. Only time will tell.

I leave the nursery and go back to the study. Every time I pass that study I get tingles in places I shouldn't when I think back to that night. It was the most passion filled night I've had in my life. To be honest, I can't get that night of my head. I knock lightly on the door and walk into the study. James is sitting at his desk looking directly at me. He motions for me to take a seat in front of the desk.

"Thank you for joining me today."

"Please cut the pleasantries. Why was I called into your office?"

"I wanted to discuss your future employment here at the castle."

This makes me nervous.

"What do you mean?"

"Having you here is a conflict of interest for me. I can't possibly see the person I love working for me for minimum wage. So, with that being said, I'm afraid I'm going to have to terminate your services."

I panic a little inside. I can't lose this job. My mother is counting on me to get close to the Prince and get inside information. If I fail she'll kill me. I prepare to beg when I think about something really important.

"Why didn't the person who manages all of the staff give me my termination?"

Things get quiet.

"Is that the real reason you called me in here?"

"That's only part of the reason."

"What's the other part?"

He rounds the desk and stands in front of me, offering me his hand. I take it. He then puts his hand on my cheek and looks me in my eyes. He pulls my face close to his and gives me a very passionate kiss that has so much meaning. When he pulls away I'm breathless. I didn't know passion like that existed. He goes to grab me again, but I dodge him and turn to walk out of the room.

"I'll send for my things."

The next thing I know he grabs my hand, turns me back around, and kisses me again, this time grabbing a handful of my hair in the process. My knees get weak. He picks me up and I wrap my legs around him. He smothers me with kisses as I softly moan. I try to fight it, but he has a hold on me. My slender body has nothing on his muscular frame. He sets me on the edge of his desk and begins to undress me slowly, teasing me along the way. His dark chocolate hands compliment my butterscotch skin. After I'm undressed he undresses in front of me. I drink up every inch of his body. He slowly walks back toward me and picks me up again, taking me to the window. He puts me down and presses my face against the window as he slowly presses his way inside my walls. I moan loudly. He shushes me. He goes slowly at first and then the motions become faster and more animalistic. He grabs my hair and bites my neck as his hands explore every inch of my body. My mind explodes with the most pleasurable sensations.

"All of this can be yours. Look out the window; this could be your kingdom."

He presses into me again, I squeal.

"All you have to do is say yes."

He grabs my hips and goes deeper, I moan louder.

"Just say one, simple, word. Say yes."

I shake my head.

He pulls out.

I try to direct him back to me.

He pulls away further.

My mind is going crazy. I can't do this.

He comes back and presses into me again and holds it.

"Say yes."

"Yes!"

With that he brings me to an ecstasy that people only dream about. Afterwards we talk about everything from my childhood to having more children and everything in between. When night falls, we already have our wedding, and our lives, all planned out. In my mind I'm all smiles. I never thought I could make him fall so quickly. Now, the fun can truly begin. Mother would be so proud. And to think, none of this would be possible if I hadn't killed Ellie. I start to laugh to myself. If only he knew the type of problems that are about to happen, he would think twice about marrying me.

After he falls asleep on the floor, I get dressed and leave the castle to return to my own house. The baby sitter is asleep on the couch and Symon is asleep in his room. I quietly go into my room and go to the closet. I open the door and go to the alter I built for speaking directly to my mother in the underworld. I light the candles and kneel in front of it.

I have been doing this ritual every night since I got the locket. I have been trying to call out to her to let her know that her transformation can begin and that it is safe to return. Tonight, I start the ritual as normal, updating her about my life with the Prince and then ending it by begging and pleading for her to give me any indication of when she is to return. Suddenly, my chest grows warm. I open my eyes to see that my locket is now glowing green. A slow smile starts to creep upon my face. She has heard my cries and has finally answered me. My mother is now ready to come back. Now the fun can begin.

CHAPTER FOURTEEN
Light at the End of the Tunnel
Anastasia

It has been two years and Jesus is now my husband. We eloped a little after I healed. I never wanted a big fancy wedding anyway. *Who would I invite?* Not too long after we eloped we had our son, Juan Antonio De La Rosa. Juan seems to get smarter each and every day, and the love Jesus shows me every day deepens. I never knew a man could love a woman this deeply. I have everything I could ask for, I have a nice cottage, a child, and a loving husband. Also, Jesus is now rich due to re-opening the bakery in the magical realm as well as maintaining the bakery here in the mortal realm. Anything I want I get. So, why am I so unhappy?

Jesus constantly reminds me that Hannon is coming back and that danger is still looming over our heads. He has tried for years to find the object that is needed to destroy Hannon and keeps coming up empty. It's like finding that locket has become an obsession. Ever since I was held captive by Hannon my feelings for her have changed.

I have constant flashbacks of what she did to me while I was in her captivity. She abused me mentally, sexually, and most of all spiritually. Every time I had a will in me to fight, she would counter it with a reason why I should quit and give up the soul of my child. Every day I would refuse. Every day after I refused we would have some of the best, mind blowing, escapades followed by the most brutal of whippings. Each day I looked forward to the escapades but dreaded what came after. It's like my body craved her but my mind resented her.

She pounded the thought in my head that she loved me first and that no one will be able to love me like she has. She told me we will be forever connected by spirit, and I am starting to believe her. My body longs for Hannon and I feel like my cravings for her are diminishing the spirit to fight for the family I have. I want to feel her touch, her embrace, her kiss. I don't want to break Jesus' heart, but every day I question if being with him is the right thing. Every now and then the thought crosses my mind and each day I rebuke it as I go on living my life with my husband and child who love me for me and not my physical attributes. I don't know why I feel this way, but I don't dare tell Jesus for fear of him leaving. If it's of magic influence, I will find a way to defeat it. I just wish Sam was here. She could help me sort this out. In the meantime, I have Noelle.

I still get the feeling there is something familiar about Noelle. She and I have become really close friends. We came in together when I first came into the castle as a lady in waiting to Ellie. I moved up in the ranks and she just became everyone's errand girl. She went from babysitting the Prince's children to getting a ring. I'm really happy the Prince found someone to love. I was getting worried about him, but Noelle was somehow able to pull him out of his funk. Now, two of my most cherished friends are husband and wife. It doesn't get any better than this.

Thursday's are the days all the children get together and play. It gives me a chance to visit my niece and nephews and at the same time catch up on castle gossip and air some of my dirty laundry I can't share with anyone else. The children have all grown so fast. Symon, Noelle's son, is 7, the twins Jaylin and Jayson are 4, and James is 3. They are all the perfect playmates and good influences little Juan needs right now.

I pack little Juan, his things, and a pie Jesus baked the other day into the wagon. I make sure Juan is secure and the wagon is attached securely to the horse before I get on the horse to make my way to the castle. In no time, I'm there and Noelle greets me with all four of the kids at the door with two nannies standing right beside her.

"I thought you would never make it!"

Noelle comes up to me with her arms outstretched and engulfs me in a hug.

"I had to wait for Jesus to leave. For some reason he doesn't like me coming to the castle to you."

A look of anger sweeps over her face but it's quickly replaced with a smile.

I take note of that.

"Where is he now?"

She's making her way toward the wagon and picks up Juan.

"He's working. Today is delivery day."

"So, that means I have you for the majority of the day!"

She turns toward one of the nannies and hands her Juan. She then signals for me to follow her. I grab the pie out of the wagon, put the knapsack across my shoulders, and follow Noelle into the castle.

It's been a long time since I've been in this castle. Just walking in the doors has a bittersweet feeling for me. This is the first time I have been in the castle since before I was captured and enslaved by Ms. Hannon for those long three months. Every time Noelle and I meet it's at the local park. I wonder why she wanted me to meet her here today.

We get to the kitchen and she takes the pie, places it on the counter, and gets out plates and silverware. She cuts two pieces of pie and puts them on the two plates. She places a fork on each plate and puts one in front of me and one in front of herself. She takes a bite and rolls her eyes as she savors the flavor. I make myself comfortable as I take off my knapsack and put it on the table. I grab the plate and take a bite of the pie. It is delicious, my husband never disappoints.

"Your husband makes some of the best pastries I have ever tasted in my life. Where did he learn how to bake like this?"

"He learned from his father."

"Oh that's nice. I bet Juan loves playing with his grandfather."

"Jesus' father is dead."

I get a knot in my stomach as I try to digest the lie I just told. I know about Jesus' father in the book but I have yet to tell Jesus. That book has been the cause of so much evil and I don't think if it is Jesus' father he will be the same good man he was. Being surrounded by evil things tends to change a person for the worse. If anyone knows how true that statement is, it's me.

"Oh, I'm sorry to hear that," her speaking her condolences snaps me back to reality.

"It's fine. His father died when he was young so he has learned to deal with it."

"That's good. Anyway, Anastasia, there's a reason why I called you to the castle today. Wait here while I go get something."

As she turns to leave the room I start to slowly eat some more of my pie. With each bite I take, I feel even more horrible not telling Jesus about his dad. I make up my mind when

I go home I'm going to tell him. Hopefully we can figure a way to get him out of the book.

Noelle returns a short while later holding a small, leather bound book.

"I found this amongst the rubble where that one woman, Ms. Hannon's cottage used to be."

She starts to hand me the book and, sure enough, it has her last name embellished on the front of the book. I open it up and the first page has the tell-tale signs of her handwriting.

I look up at Noelle.

"Why are you giving me this?"

"I read a little bit of it and found out it's a diary she used to keep. After reading a couple of pages it mentioned your name a lot. I figured since you guys were friends, you may want to hold onto this book."

I hold the book close to me and feel a tingling sensation in my nether regions. Suddenly, the intensity of the moment hits me. I'm back in the same kitchen where she and I used to prepare meals together. I'm not that far from where her cottage used to stand. It's all so surreal. I hand the book back to Noelle.

"I thank you for the thought, but I can't accept it."

"Why not?"

"My husband didn't like Ms. Hannon that much."

"Why?"

"I don't know, something about an old feud or something similar."

A look passes across her face that I can't read, but I decide to leave it alone.

"Well, how do you feel?"

"I don't know."

"Do you still love her?"

"I don't know."

The room grows quiet and uncomfortable.

"I need to leave. You can have the remainder of the pie. Tell the Prince I said hello."

I grab my knapsack and run out of the room, tears threatening to escape from my eyes. I go down the back of the castle and all of the kids are there playing. I grab Juan, load him up in the cart, and quickly get away from the castle. I need to breathe.

I get home and Jesus isn't there. I'm ecstatic. I put Juan down for a nap and go back to the living room to unload my bag. As I'm going through my bag I feel the smooth texture of leather. I pull out the object and gasp. In my hand I hold Ms. Hannon's diary.

I have decided to read her diary. I feel myself getting sucked into her life as I slowly turn the pages. Suddenly, I'm startled as I feel a set of lips on my forehead. My husband has returned and I was so into the book I didn't even hear him come into the house.

"Hey honey, how was your day?" I ask as I continue to read my book as he fumbles around trying to put things away.

"It was fine," he calls out from the kitchen. "A lot of deliveries as usual but that is to be expected."

"Why don't we hire a delivery boy?"

"We had this discussion. I feel like it's good customer service to see the customers. What did you do today?

"I went to see Noelle."

The room gets quiet. He has stopped moving in the kitchen. He comes out of the kitchen and comes into the living room with me.

"I don't like Noelle."

"Why?"

"I don't trust her. Something tells me that she is off."

"Don't you trust me?"

He gets quiet.

No answer.

I put down the book and look at him. He has a cold look on his face.

"Don't you trust me?"

Again, there is no answer.

He reaches in his pocket and pulls out the paper that has the information about the locket written in his father's handwriting.

I thought I lost that paper. I become speechless.

"Were you ever going to tell me? I've not been able to sleep trying to find this stupid object to destroy Hannon as well as looking for my father. For two long years I have searched and for two long years I've come up empty. I thought I could handle it on my own. I didn't want to bother you with this knowing you have been trying to keep the business together and raise our son, but now, it's time for answers. Why didn't you tell me about the paper?"

"I don't even know what is in your hand. What is it?"

I play stupid, but he doesn't buy it. I don't know how long I can keep my promise to Hernando. Jesus is smart and I fear he will find a way to get the information out of me. He punches a hole in the wall. I jump.

"Where did you get this?"

I don't say a word. "

Answer me!"

"When were you going to tell me that you don't trust me?"

"Don't answer my question with a question!"

"If you don't trust me what makes you think you are going to believe me when I tell you where I got that paper."

He goes quiet.

"Where did you get the paper?"

"What have I done to ever have you question my loyalty and trust toward you?"

"Damn it, woman, answer the question!"

"Not until you answer mine! Ms. Hannon would have never doubted me!"

I cover my mouth. The words came out before I thought about it.

"What did you just say?"

I just shake my head.

"What are you reading?"

I hide the book.

He comes over to me and tries to take the book from me.

I slap him.

"Don't take this away from me."

He tries to grab it again.

I slap him harder.

He grabs me in his huge muscular arms in one hand and grabs my hair in the other.

I can barely hold onto the book. Jesus is scaring me.

"Escuchame. I'm trying to save your life. The book you have in your hand is emitting some very powerful dark magic. If you value your life, you'll never put your hands on me again, and you'll get rid of that book. I've given you nothing but the utmost respect. I don't care if you are my wife and the mother of my child, no one hits me. Do you understand?"

I nod. I look down at the locket around Jesus' neck and it is glowing green.

"Jesus, the locket, it's glowing! What does that mean?"

He lets me go, puts me on the ground, and holds the locket in his hand. He looks bewildered and doesn't speak for a moment. Finally, he answers me in a hushed tone.

"I never thought this day would come. I never thought this would happen. By the locket glowing green that can only mean one thing, Sam is alive and is ready to come out."

NEXT IN THE SERIES:

happily NEVER after
SYMON SAYS

TL Jones

Early on, TL Jones discovered a love for creativity with songwriting and poetry. Aside from creative writing, TL also enjoys acting and singing. Following a dream of becoming a songwriter, that creativity was soon channeled into a novel. An entertainer at heart, TL soon gave audiences what they demanded as they were pulled into a story full of romance and magic. With a Midwestern zest for life, TL appreciates all ranges of music as well as fashion.

TL's next book in the Happily Never After series, Symon Says, will be released in 2016.

Connect with TL Jones...
Twitter: @author_tljones
Facebook: www.facebook.com/tl.jones.77

ACKNOWLEDGEMENTS

I first want to thank God for giving me the ability to be able to imagine and write this type of story.

To my mother and family, is there really a need for an explanation?

To my sister and my grandmother, may you rest well in heaven.

To the people who were my fans before I even got through with the book, I want to thank you. You helped me more than you'll ever know. Although I did not mention you by name (because there are just way to many) you helped me by reading this book, dealing with pestering questions and encouraging me to continue even though there were times that I wanted to give up. I love each and every one of you.

To Stacy; I thank you for being my impromptu editor, my confidant, my cheerleader and most importantly my friend. This would not have been possible without you.

To Damara (Ninja), Monique and Courtney (my BFF) thank you for listening to my pipe dreams, holding my hand when I cried and for just being you.

To Avigail (Avi), Betty, Sharon, Amanda W and Melissa I thank you for taking up with my foolishness at work. Whenever I was in a writing slump I could talk to you guys and get out of it quick. Some of the best ideas for this book came from you five. I love you guys to pieces (even though I hired and fired Avi every other day).

Last but not least, I want to thank Will. If you had not broken my heart and made me believe that Happily Ever After's didn't exist I wouldn't have worked so hard to prove that it does. Now, because of you, I am an author. Enjoy your life, no hard feelings.

happily NEVER after
SYMON SAYS

T.L. JONES

CHAPTER ONE
Once Upon a Time
Jaylin
(Six years later)

Once upon a time there were two children. One named Jaylin and one name Jayson. Their mother's name was Ellie and she was the fairest of them all. Love became too much of a burden so she decided to leave and go to heaven.

"I don't like how you wrote this story Jaylin." Jayson pouted.

"That's because I'm not finished."

"When are you going to talk about Noelle treating us like dirt and making us clean everything and how we can never see any of our friends?"

"I'm getting to that Jayson!"

"Well, your story sucks. I'm not going to stay up and listen to you give this awful story. I'm going to go to sleep so

I won't be tired tomorrow so I can finish all my chores. You better do the same or else Noelle is going to get you."

After he says that he rolls over in his bed, pulls the cover over his head and buries his face in the pillow. Jayson is right, my story does suck. Our mother died when we were really young and all I can remember of her is that she was really beautiful. Most people say I look like her and I think that's the reason why Noelle treats me and Jayson so badly. We have a younger brother and his name is James Alexander the second, but we call him Alex. We also have an older step brother, his name is Symon. Both of them are treated well. They share the big room, they get to eat at the table, lie around all day and do nothing and they get to go wherever they please whenever they please while Jayson and I are stuck cleaning. Alex is a brat. He purposely taunts us and makes messes so that we have to clean it up. He also tells Noelle every little thing we do so that we can get in trouble. Sometimes he does things so we can be blamed for them. Symon is different. He's loving, caring and kind. He tries to help us out whenever we really need it and he talks to Noelle whenever we have a request. Even with his constant pleading our daily ritual has not changed.

Every day it's the same thing. We wake up before the sun and feed all of the animals. Then, we go around and collect all the laundry and get that started. Then Jayson goes and tend the animals while I go to the kitchen to help the cook prepare breakfast. After breakfast we all go to school. After school we decline playing with our friends to rush home. Once we get home we clean the whole castle from top to bottom. Once we are done with that we are too exhausted to do anything else but eat our supper, take our baths and go to bed.

If things are not up to Noelle's standards we have to get up out of our sleep and clean everything again including the mess she made in order to make a point. Or worse, she will take us to the back and beat us within an inch of our lives, pour water on our wounds and then make us clean the whole house again while she watches.

We tried to tell father what was going on once. After we finished telling him what was going on he looked at us with a sad expression and told us that it's just a misunderstanding. He promised he would talk to Noelle and then sent us on our way. He talked to her, she then came to us afterwards and punished us harder than she had before because we told. So we learned to keep our mouths shut. We've told no one of our predicament. I escape by writing in my journal but Jayson grows more and more angry every day and I fear one day that anger might get us in big trouble, or worse, get us hurt. It makes me sad that I have to walk past Father every day and pretend that everything is fine. I just hope Noelle comes to her senses before it is too late and he finds out what is really going on.

Tomorrow is our tenth birthday and we are hoping that Noelle will be nice enough to let us have a party at the castle so we are getting up extra early to clean and cook so we can get on Noelle's good side. If I plan on getting up early, I need to go to bed now. I close my journal promising myself to write more of my story tomorrow; I snuggle down into bed and go to sleep.

We wake up two hours earlier than usual to make sure the house is spotless before Noelle wakes up. I also go into the kitchen and make her favorite coffee and breakfast. Jayson is outside trying to pick flowers and find things to make her breakfast tray look pretty. It takes about an hour but we finally get everything set up and ready to present to Noelle.

We tip toe slowly upstairs and go to the room that Father and Noelle share. Father is gone on business so we do not have to worry about disturbing him when we go and give Noelle her food. We open the door quietly. I stand there with the tray as Jayson goes to softly shake her to awaken her. He shakes her; she rolls over and lets out a loud snore followed by gas. I giggle silently. I regain my composure really quick so that I don't drop the tray. Jayson tries again and this time she slowly starts to stir. She sits up in bed and removes her sleeping mask and looks directly at me. I give her my most beautiful smile.

"Good morning Noelle!"

She stretches her arms up to the sky and opens her mouth really big omitting a loud yawn.

"What do you have there girl?"

"I have breakfast for you. Eggs, bacon, pancakes, fresh squeezed orange juice and a hot cup of coffee."

"Don't just stand there, give it to me. I'm starving!"

I carefully go towards her and place the tray on her lap. She doesn't even wait for me to take my hand off of the tray before attacks the food. She keeps moaning and saying the food is delicious. Me and Jayson just smile.

"Noelle, we wanted to ask you something."

"Hurry up girl; don't you see that I'm eating?"

"Well, our birthday is today and we were wondering if we can have some friends over to the house?"

"You have friends?"

She looks at both of us and starts laughing really hard. She laughs so hard that she starts to choke on her food. I look at her with a plain look on my face but on the inside I secretly hope she would die.

"I didn't know that children wanted to be friends with urchins."

My blood is boiling. I want to jump across the bed and choke her until I see no life in her eyes. I shake my head trying to shake those thoughts out. I've never felt so strongly before. I will have to remember to write that down in my diary.

"So is that why you made me this breakfast?"

We both slowly nod our heads.

"I don't appreciate you guys making me this breakfast so that you could feed me lies. I know neither one of you have friends besides a boom and a mop. So the answer is no. Now, clean up my tray and get ready for school."

I turn to leave the room with tears in my eyes as Jason grabs the tray from Noelle. *How can someone be so cruel? We have done nothing to her for her to treat us this way. Why is life so unfair?* All I want to do is crawl back into bed and sleep the day away. *How am I going to go to school and face all my friends?* I bragged about having a nice party and that I was going to have cake and ice-cream. Now I have to go to school and cancel. I'm so upset that I could scream. I stomp off to our room and start to throw things around. The more I scream the better I feel. I start to tear up things in our room knowing that I'm going to have to clean it up later but I don't care. All I want to do right now is destroy things. All I want to do is cause someone harm. All I want to do right now is kill Noelle, but I can't. I dive into my bed and bury my face in my pillow. *What did I do to deserve such treatment?* I kick and scream and hit the pillow thinking it is going to ease some of my anger. I get up and the anger is pulsing through my veins. The angrier I get the more it seems as if things are floating through the air. That can't be. This has never happened before. It scares and excites me at the same time. I scream and I feel something in mouth. I can't swallow whatever it is. I feel like I have to throw up. I dry heave for a couple of minutes and I feel the need to tilt my head backwards instead of forward. I look towards the ceiling and a half circle comes out of my mouth. It's black with a white circle in the middle and hovers above me.

Jayson bursts into the room. His mouth is moving but I can't hear him. He looks up and sees the half circle above me and looks at me with a panicked look. He mouths the words *'what do I do'* and all I can do is outstretch my hands to him.

He grabs my hand and tries to move me. I can't move from this spot.

This half black circle is the most beautiful thing I've ever seen and my body doesn't want to move. Instead of pulling me away from the half circle he is sucked into its beauty. As he looks at the half black circle his eyes begin roll in the back of his head. He tilts his head backwards and then a white half circle with a black dot in the middle comes out of his mouth.

What is happening? I'm panicking on the inside but on the outside I can't move. I watch in horror as his half circle combines with mine to form the yin-yang sign. Once the two half circles combine together the now completed big circle starts spinning and spinning and spinning and eventually creates a hole in the wall. The power is so great that it starts dragging us towards it.

The hold that was placed on us is lifted and I can move. Jayson collapses on the floor and is now lying lifeless on the floor. I try to pull him to safety but he instantly sucked into the hole. I scream out his name but it can't be heard over the deafening wails of the wind coming out of that hole. I try to fight it. I try to crawl away but I find myself losing the battle. I do something I thought I would never do, I call out for Noelle, but it's too late. I'm sucked into the hole and all I see is darkness.

I wake up with a set of green eyes staring at me. I panic and sit up fast and our heads collide.

"Ouch nina!"

I focus and realize that voice came from Mr. De La Rosa, Juan's dad. My eyes start to focus and I realize that I'm in Juan's living room. I start to breathe rapidly as I frantically search the room for Jayson. I finally see him laying a couple of feet away from me, I breathe easier. Mr. De La Rosa studies my face and my actions. A confused look is plastered on this face. "What happened?" he asks.

"I was in my room and I was angry. I was screaming and throwing things because Noelle wouldn't give me a birthday party with Jayson even though we did what we were supposed to do."

"What were you supposed to do?"

I hesitate. No one can know how Noelle really treats us. It would mean that we would be punished and I will not put me and my brother through that again.

"Clean our rooms."

He nods his head.

I breathe a sigh of relief because he accepted my answer. I continue. "When I was throwing things I got so angry that I became sick and had the feeling that I needed to throw up. I tilted my head back and out came this black half circle with a white dot in it. After it came out I couldn't do anything but just stand there. Jayson came in and saw the half circle and tried to save me but when he touched me he threw up another half circle that was white with a black circle. The two half circles combined and started spinning and from there it created this black hole. It sucked us in and now I'm waking up in your house talking to you."

"Ay Dios Mios!"

"What does that mean?"

"It means that we are in trouble. Follow me."

"What about Jayson?"

"He will wake up in a minute. I need you to follow me, now!"

I am a bit taken back. I have never seen him so serious. He has always been so playful. He is the reason why I know how to make homemade bread and cookies. He takes me into the back room and at this point I don't know what to expect.

"Sit down por favor."

I take a seat on this very comfortable green couch. I watch

as Mr. De Las Rosa goes from book to book, flipping pages and making grunting sounds. Finally, after searching through several books he stops at one big black book that is on a mantle. On the outside it reads *El libro de la famila De La Rosa*. I wonder what the means. He slowly flips through the pages. His brow furrows as he concentrates on the words on the page. Finally, he stops flipping. His gaze turns cold and stony as he stares at this page in the book. I get a shiver up my spine.

"This is not good."

"What is it Mr. De La Rosa?"

"Please just call me Jesus."

"Ok, sure. What is it Mr. Jesus?"

He lets out a sigh.

"We will address that later but, for now, I have a serious question for you. Do you know what a Dualist is?"

"No, I don't know what that is"

"Ok, do you know anything about magic?"

"You mean when someone pulls a rabbit out of a hat?"

Mr. Jesus puts his head in his hands.

"No. That is not what I'm talking about at all. How about this, have you ever had anything weird happen around you before?"

"Like what?"

"Things floating in the air, weather changing depending on your mood or things happening when you are very emotional?"

I sit and think for a while.

"Yes, actually all the time."

Mr. Jesus nodes his head.

"Do you know who your father is?"

"Yes! My daddy is Prince James the first."

"Lo siento I hate to tell you this but that is not true. Your father was the son of a very powerful witch. This woman was very evil and tried to take over the mortal and magical realm.

I believe that you and your brother both have magical abilities that you need to start practicing really quickly."

I'm in shock. The person whom I've known as my father is not my father? Then who is he and why am I with him? I feel tears streaming down my face. Why do people feel the need to not tell Jayson and me anything? We are not babies and we can handle whatever is told to us. I wipe away the tears. There is no time for crying. Right now, I need to know what to do next.

"How long have you known?"

I dread hearing the answer, but I feel as if this is something that needs to be known.

"Since you were born."

After Mr. Jesus gave me his answer I feel my whole word crash around me.

"Why didn't you tell us?" I ask Mr. Jesus as tears start streaming out of my eyes.

"We thought that Prince James told you."

"It's fine. I will deal with that information later." I compose myself and wipe my eyes. "What do those symbols mean?"

"Well, there is a prophecy that states that there will be a set of twins that will be very unique. One will have dark magic and one will have light magic. When these twins are born and display the yin-yang sign the dualist has been named and will reign over the land."

"What is a dualist?"

"I have to find the book because I'm a little shady on some areas. Honestly, I never thought I would live to see the day that it would actually happen. We all thought it was a myth. It is a story that has been passed along for hundreds of years."

"Are we in danger?"

"It depends on which side the dualist chooses."

"Do you know who it is?"

"No."

That is not the answer that I wanted to hear. Right now,

my head is swimming. I don't know what to think anymore. *What is a dualist? Why are Jayson and I important? What does that mean for us? If I have magic when can I use it?* There are so many questions going through my head but there is just one that keeps bugging me; one question that I need the answer to right now.

"Mr. Jesus, since I had the black half circle with the white dot in it, what does that mean?"

"It means that you have the dark magic."

COMING 2016!

Printed in Great Britain
by Amazon.co.uk, Ltd.,
Marston Gate.